I0819889

JUSTIN PETTYJOHN

A House Hungry for Blood

First published by JW Pettyjohn Books LLC 2026

First edition

ISBN: 979-8-9946832-0-0

Cover art by Alam Twaha

This book was professionally typeset on Reedsy.
Find out more at reedsy.com

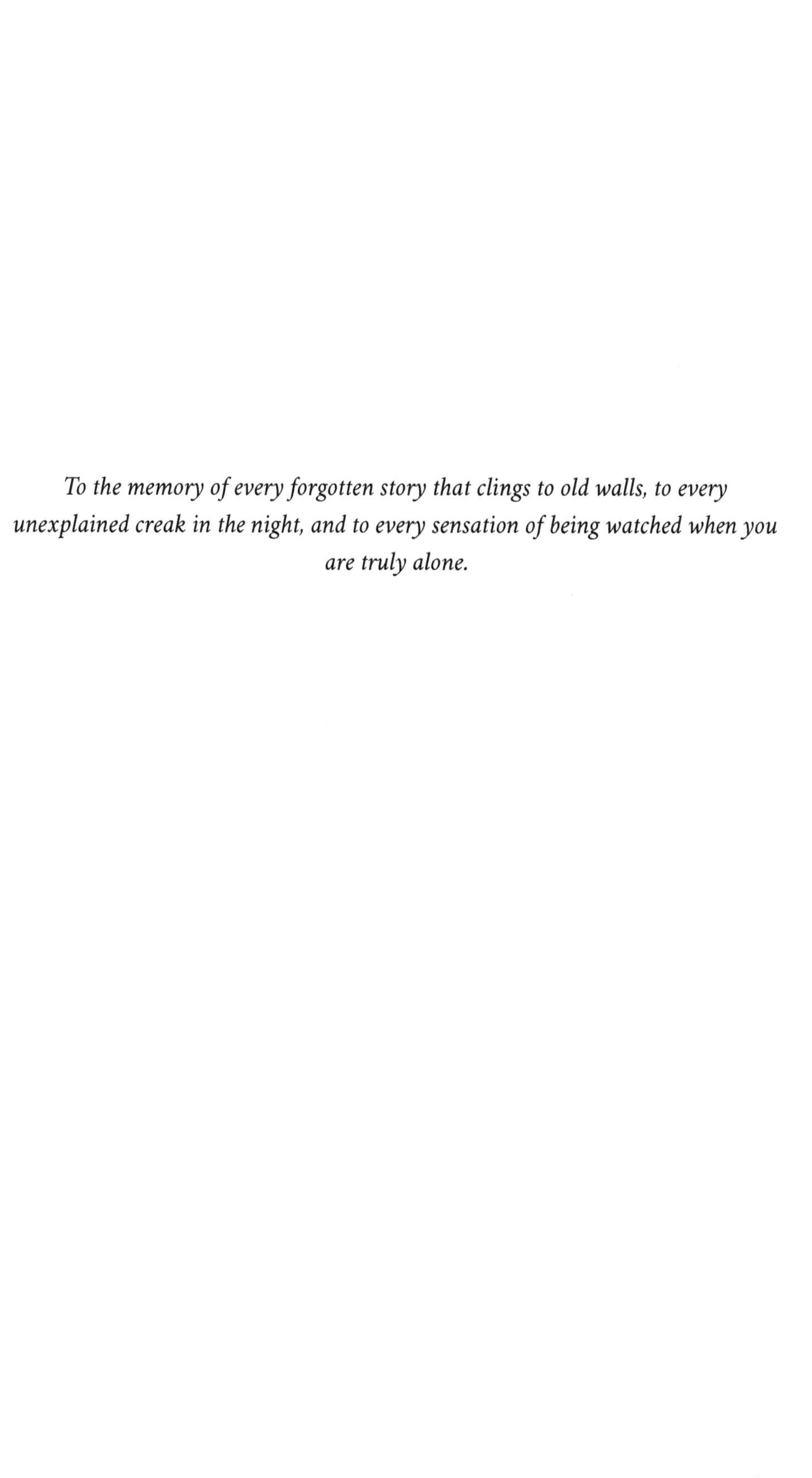

To the memory of every forgotten story that clings to old walls, to every unexplained creak in the night, and to every sensation of being watched when you are truly alone.

Contents

Acknowledgments

To the brave souls who have stared into the abyss and returned, scarred but not broken, this story is for you. To my partner, who endured my late-night ramblings and provided a light in my own personal darkness. To the editors and readers who offered their keen eyes and even keener insights, for without your guidance, the shadows would have remained too deep. And to the authors whose words have haunted my dreams and inspired my own creative nightmares, thank you for paving the way.

Chapter 1: The Victorian Dream

A Facade of Perfection

The city, a huge beast of concrete and noise that never stops, was starting to feel like a cage. The tight grip of the thing had become too much for Eleanor and Thomas. It hurt deep in their bones. They longed for a different rhythm, a life with softer colors, far away from the busy faces and the never-ending rush. It was this shared desire, a quiet need for peace, that brought them to Blackwood Manor.

The house had an undeniable pull from the moment they first saw it through the wrought-iron gates, which were half-hidden by a riot of wild plants. It stood on a gentle rise, a monument to a time long gone. Its Victorian shape stood out against the sky, which was always bruised with the colors of twilight. Gargoyles leered from the eaves, their stone faces worn smooth by centuries of wind and rain. Ivy, thick as a shroud, clung to the stone, making the edges of its imposing architecture less clear. The air around it was still, and the smell of wet earth and flowers that couldn't be seen was strong. This was very different from the city's bad smells. It wasn't just a house; it was a promise, a quiet call to a life that wasn't so ordinary, and a safe place to escape the constant stress of modern life.

Eleanor, an artist whose heart resonated with the sad beauty of things that had been forgotten and broken, saw poetry in its worn-out face. She thought about the sound of silk gowns rustling in its echoing halls, the smell of woodsmoke curling from its chimneys, and the quiet thinking that must have happened there. It was a blank canvas that was waiting for her to touch it. It was a place where she could finally find the space to breathe, create, and just be. The overgrown gardens, which showed how strong nature is, made her think of wild beauty and secrets waiting to be found. She thought they would tame it not by getting rid of its past, but by adding their own lives to its rich tapestry.

Thomas was an architect who liked structure and form. He saw potential where others might have seen ruin. But he was also drawn to the design's sheer ambition, which was practical. The detailed gingerbread trim, the high gables, and the big bay windows all showed that the house was made with care and that beauty was not a luxury but a necessity in the past. He pictured spending his weekends sanding down fancy woodwork, fixing plaster, and bringing back the beauty that had been hidden under years of neglect. It would be their project, something they worked on together, a sign of how much they cared about each other, and a way to get away from the boring things in life. He didn't see it as a fixer-upper; he saw it as a challenge, a work of art that needed to be brought back to life.

Mr. Abernathy, the estate agent, was their guide through this new dream. He was a man whose smile never quite reached his eyes. They had a strange, almost glassy emptiness, as if they were reflecting a world that was very different from the real world. He spoke in a smooth, practiced way that included words like "character," "original features," and "a touch of TLC." He pointed with his long, thin fingers at the dusty parlors and the big, dark staircase, painting a picture of a house that needed work and was waiting to be polished. He talked about its "storied past" in a way that suggested there was more to it than just history.

Abernathy had said in a voice that sounded like dry leaves skittering across pavement, "A house of this age always comes with its own unique story." Blackwood Manor is no different. It has seen and done a lot. But think about the possibilities. The pure, untainted potential."

He conveniently left out any mention of its more unusual past, like the quiet rumors that clung to the estate like ivy. The sudden departures of past families, the whispered stories of strange events, and the fact that it had changed hands so many times in less-than-ideal conditions were all too messy for the clean brochure of their new beginning. He pitched it as a romantic fixer-upper, a place where a young couple could build their future, far away from the worries of living in the city.

Eleanor felt a strange thrill as she stood on the overgrown driveway in the late afternoon sun, which cast long, skeletal shadows over the lawn. It was a mix of fear and excitement. The house seemed to let out a breath of cool air that smelled like secrets and time. This beauty, this promise of happiness at home that came from its dark windows, was like a siren song. It called to them, its huge size a stark contrast to their simple lives in the city. It offered an escape that was so deep and complete that it felt almost intoxicating. They told themselves that this was it. Their perfect start. The noise of the city would soon fade away, replaced by the peace and shared purpose they longed for so much at Blackwood Manor. But the dream was already starting to cast its evil spell, a subtle enchantment that hid the darkness that lay beneath the surface of Victorian charm.

Whispers of the Past

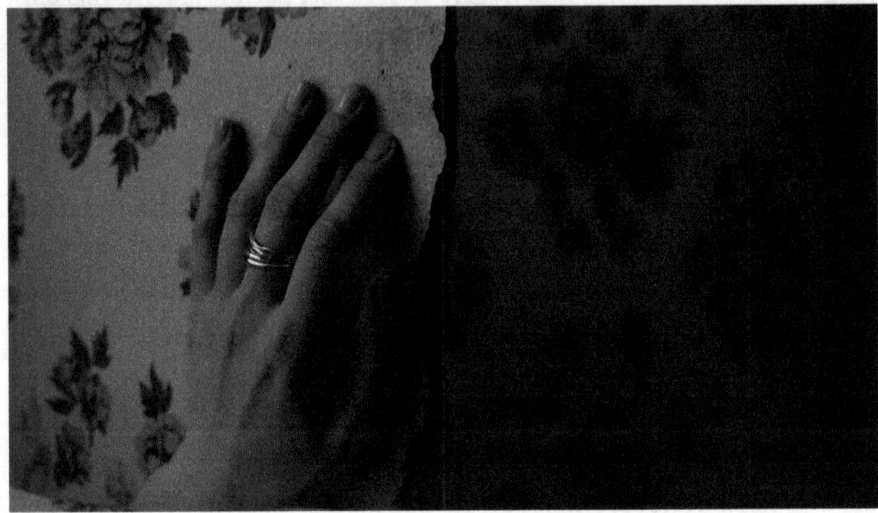

The sheer number of boxes threatened to fill up the grand entrance hall. Each box was a physical piece of their old life that was now being thrown into the huge mouth of Blackwood Manor. Dust motes danced in the weak sunlight that came through the dirty leaded windows. The light made the work ahead look very clear and not romantic. Eleanor's fingers were already dirty when she started going through the smaller crates. Her artist's instinct drew her to the textures and colors of the packing paper, which was a subtle way of showing that the house was falling apart. Thomas, always practical, started to plan how to unpack. He could already see the blueprints for their new life in his mind, a mental clearing of the clutter.

It was in these first few moments of being displaced, when their things were all over the place, that the first small differences started to show. A strange, faint smell that wasn't too bad but was definitely out of place started to fill the air. It smelled like damp earth after a long drought, the deep, loamy smell of a freshly dug grave, and there was a faint, almost sweet scent of something rotting, like flowers that had been forgotten. Eleanor stopped and took a deep breath. It wasn't the smell of dust or old wood, which is common in a house this old. It was something more basic, as if the very foundations of the manor were breathing the breath of the earth itself. She tried to figure out where it was coming from by moving from one corner to another, but it seemed to come from the walls themselves, a thick fog that hung in the air and wouldn't go away.

"Do you smell that, Thomas?" she asked, her voice full of curiosity that was quickly turning into a feeling of unease.

Thomas grunted as he struggled with a cardboard box that wouldn't budge. "Smell what?" Dust? Wet? Eleanor, sweetheart, this place is a piece of Victorian history. It will definitely have its "smell oddities." He grunted in victory as he forced the box open, revealing a pile of old books. "We have bigger things to worry about than smelling the decorations."

Eleanor shook her head and frowned. It was more than just dirt or wetness. It was a deeper, more unsettling smell, one that hinted at things that were buried and wouldn't stay put. She went into the drawing room, which is the biggest of the reception rooms on the first floor. The thick velvet curtains made it hard for the sun to get in. The smell here seemed stronger and more focused. She always noticed the small details in pictures, and this time she noticed the intricate floral wallpaper. It was a deep, rich red with a pattern of trailing roses and ivy on it. But as she looked more closely, her artist's eye catching small differences, her unease turned into a quiet certainty.

"Thomas," she yelled again, this time with a firmer voice. "Come here." "Check out this wallpaper."

He came out of the hall and wiped his hands on his pants. "What's up with it? It's a bit dramatic, but I think it has a certain charm from that time. He walked up to her and looked over the wall.

"No, not the charm," Eleanor said firmly, her finger following an invisible line along the pattern. "Look here." This part. The roses are a little different. The leaves of the ivy are a different color here. It's like... like some parts have been repapered. But they have tried to match it. "Badly."

Thomas leaned in and squinted. Eleanor was correct. There were small, almost unnoticeable changes in the pattern, like when the color saturation dropped and the brushstrokes of the design seemed to stop and start again with a jarring lack of continuity. It looked like someone had tried to fix a flaw, like a wound in the room's fabric, with a clumsy, rushed hand.

"Hmm," he thought, his architect's mind taking note of the strange thing. "You're right. It's not great. Most likely done by the people who lived there before. Maybe a water stain or some damage they wanted to hide before selling. Don't worry about it. They probably couldn't find an exact match, so they made do. Eleanor, this house is old. "Flaws are a part of its story." He squeezed her arm to let her know everything would be okay. "Don't let it bother you." It can be stressful to move. You're probably just a little on edge.

Eleanor nodded, but the explanation didn't seem enough. The repair was so bad that it seemed like they were trying to hide something, not just hide it. And the smell of decay, which was strong in these places where the wallpaper didn't match, seemed to be the strongest. She couldn't help but want to peel back the layers and see what was underneath the hastily put up façade.

As the days turned into weeks and the initial chaos of unpacking gave way to a sense of order in the home, the house kept telling its secrets. It was never a loud threat or a direct threat, but a series of sneaky, creeping suggestions that got into their heads. Eleanor, who spent more time in her makeshift studio in the old library, was always drawn to how the light and shadow played in the room. The fancy bookshelves that went all the way up to the ceiling and were full of books that seemed to absorb rather than reflect the light made the room always seem like it was twilight. She started to feel like someone was watching her here, in the quiet stillness. It wasn't the friendly look of a neighbor who was curious or the watchful eye of a pet. It was something colder and more distant, a prickling on the back of her neck that made her skin crawl. She would turn around, sure that someone was right behind her, but there was nothing there, the shadows were still, and the silence was complete.

Thomas also had these scary times. He would often stop working in his study, which was always cool because it was on the north side of the house, and his pen would hover over his notepad. That corner of the room always had air that was a few degrees colder than the rest of the house. It was a pocket of unnatural chill that no amount of heating could get rid of. He would have called it a draft or a quirk of the old building's ventilation system, but the feeling didn't go away. It wasn't the air that was cold; it was something inside him that made him feel cold. It was a presence that seemed to brush against him and leave him with a lingering sense of unease.

One night, while they were sitting by the small fire in the drawing room, the wind outside sounded like a lost soul. Eleanor shivered and pulled her shawl tighter. "Did you feel that?" she asked in a low voice, her eyes wide.

Thomas put down his newspaper. "Feel what?"

"A cold spot." Right here. She patted the armchair next to her. "It felt like someone walked right through me."

Thomas reached out, his hand hovering over the spot. "Just the wind, my love." This old house has more drafts than a church organ. He tried to sound calm, but there was a brief flash of something—maybe shared worry—between them. He was becoming more and more sure that Eleanor's sensitivities weren't just because of the stress of moving.

The house, with its quietness, seemed to keep its past like a miser keeps gold. It was a past that would not stay buried; it was a collection of ghostly echoes that hung in the air and in the walls themselves. Eleanor would sometimes smell lavender, as if a lady who had been gone for a long time had left a faint scent behind. Sometimes, a ghostly smell of cigar smoke would waft through the hallways, bringing back memories of a time long gone. These weren't separate memories; they were impressions, bits of sensory information that suggested lives lived and moments that may have been too strong to completely fade away.

The feeling of being watched grew stronger. The house was full of this feeling, like there was an audience watching their every move without them knowing. Eleanor looked over her shoulder more often, her artistic eye now scanning the edges for movement that wasn't there. She would be drawing and then suddenly feel like someone was standing in the doorway, staring at her. There was only the empty space when she looked, and the shadows were deep and still. But the feeling stayed, a light pressure that made her feel heavy.

Thomas also had trouble focusing more and more. He was carefully measuring a wall for a new bookshelf when he noticed that his attention was wandering. He kept looking at a dark corner of the room, as if he were expecting to see a figure come out of the darkness. He would feel a clear presence, a small change in the air that told him he wasn't alone. He would shake his head and say it was because he was tired from the mental work of fixing up such a big and complicated property. But the reasons for doing it seemed less and less convincing, like excuses that had been used up.

The house seemed to be vibrating with the energy that was left over from the people who used to live there. There was no violent energy, just a lingering resonance, a quiet insistence that their stories were not over yet. Eleanor found a child's rocking horse in the dusty attic. The paint was chipped, and the eyes that used to be bright were now dull and empty. When she reached out to touch it, a sudden, inexplicable wave of sadness hit her so hard that she had to lean against a trunk for support. It was like a memory that wasn't hers, a ghostly sadness that had attached itself to the object and, by extension, to her. She ran away from the attic then, unable to handle the heavy weight of unspoken sadness.

Thomas felt a sudden, jarring chill on a perfectly still afternoon while he was looking at the stonework on the outside. He looked up, expecting to see a cloud blocking the sun, but the sky was a bright blue with no clouds. The cold seemed to come from the stone itself, creating a small area of icy stillness that felt very strange. He ran his hand over the rough surface, as if he thought he might find a hidden vent that was causing the problem. But there was nothing there, just old, solid stone that seemed to hum with a strange, unsettling energy.

At first, they talked about it slowly, but then they got more and more urgent. The "feelings" they had were too strong and too common to be just figments of their imagination. The cold spots, the brief feelings of being watched, and the ghostly smells were all parts of a puzzle that was slowly coming together, a mosaic of unease that Blackwood Manor seemed determined to show.

Eleanor told Thomas one night, in a voice so low that it was like she was afraid the house would hear her, "It's like they never left." "The people who used to live here. It's like their presence is... ingrained. "Like a picture developing on photographic paper, but in the air."

Thomas, who is usually very logical and reasonable, nodded, and a knot of unease grew in his stomach. He had always been proud of how well he could analyze and break things down. But Blackwood Manor didn't fit into such a logical breakdown. It worked on a different frequency, one that hummed with the things that weren't said or seen. He started to pay more attention to the creaks and groans of the old house. Instead of just ignoring them as normal sounds of settling wood, he thought of them as possible words, whispers from the past.

Eleanor couldn't stop thinking about how the wallpaper didn't match up. She started to draw the patterns, carefully writing down the differences, the small changes in color and design. It felt like a rebellious act, a way to bring order to the house's natural disorder. She was drawn to these patched areas, and her fingers often traced the lines where the old paper met the new, as if she were looking for a hidden seam, a way to get to what was underneath. The smell of wet dirt and decay seemed to come together in these places, creating a low-level hum of unease that made her think that something important had been hidden on purpose.

One afternoon, for no clear reason, Eleanor found herself in the upstairs hallway, standing in front of a section of wall where the floral pattern seemed to be especially out of place. The roses were a little too pale, the leaves were a little too green, and the whole thing looked very amateurish. She ran her hand over the paper and felt a slight bumpiness under the surface. She noticed a loose edge and pulled on it gently. A small piece of the wallpaper started to come off, showing not plaster but a darker, older material underneath. A faint, almost imperceptible breath of air came out of the gap, carrying with it a strong whiff of that unsettling, earthy smell. Her heart started to race. This repair was not normal. This was a cover-up. She knew that the whispers of the past were getting louder.

The Contract of Silence

The last strokes of the pen didn't feel like a signature; they felt more like the snap of a chain in the sky. Eleanor saw Thomas's hand move across the paper, and each loop and flourish was like a tiny hammer blow sealing their fate. The room, which was clean and impersonal in the middle of the city, seemed to close in on them. The air was thick with the smell of old paper and a faint, sour smell of ink. The lawyer, whose smile never quite reached his eyes, gave a quick nod and stared at the check Eleanor had just given him. It was a lot of money, a sign of their savings and their hopeful leap into the unknown that was Blackwood Manor.

"All in order," the lawyer droned on, his voice as dry and brittle as the parchment in front of them. "Of course, there are a few old clauses." Normal for homes of this age. He waved his hand in the direction of the long, dense paragraphs of legal text, sounding dismissive. "The rules about... cyclical regeneration and the residency tithe. Just formalities from the past. The previous custodians made sure that the chain of ownership was never broken, in case there ever came a time when a claim needed to be made again. "Don't worry about anything."

Eleanor's eyes were fixed on the offending clauses. Her artist's eye was drawn to the strange phrasing that seemed to writhe on the page like dark tendrils.

"Unique cyclical regeneration." The words brought to mind an unsettling image, not of a garden blooming again, but of something much more basic, something that ate and changed. What about the "residency tithe"? It sounded like a sacrifice, a debt that had to be paid not in money, but with time, presence, and... life. Her fingers, still wet from the ink, suddenly felt very cold, as if she had touched something much older and more alive than just paper.

"A reassertion of claim?" she repeated in a voice that was barely a whisper. The solicitor's casual dismissal did nothing to calm the fear that was creeping up her spine. There was a shadow over the sunlit promise of Blackwood Manor, as if its bright colors had faded a little bit.

The lawyer laughed, but it was a short, sharp sound that didn't sound real. "A very strange word, indeed." This just means that families have owned the property for hundreds of years and have passed it on to others. If an owner were to, say, leave it alone for a long time, a distant relative or the original patrons of the estate might, in theory, have a reason to... get it back. But this is very rare these days. Especially since there is such a strong market for old houses. He put the signed papers into a leather-bound folder, and the sound of the thud echoed in the sudden silence. "Think of it as a piece of history, Mrs. Davies." Just a historical curiosity, nothing more.

But Thomas was already mentally moving on, and the practicalities of their new life made any doubts he had go away. He smiled broadly and confidently as he clapped the lawyer on the shoulder. "Great! Thanks for your help. We can't wait to start fixing up Blackwood Manor and making it our own. He looked at Eleanor with a look of happy expectation. "Come on, sweetheart. The sooner we get things settled, the sooner we can really start. "Think of all the things that could happen!"

But Eleanor couldn't shake the feeling that an invisible hand was pushing down on her, a silent duty that had just been written into the very fabric of their lives. She thought it was a deal not only with the lawyers and real estate agents, but also with something much older, something that lived in the stones of Blackwood Manor. The cyclical regeneration and the residency tithe were not just things that happened in the past. They were a contract, a silent agreement that had been passed down through the years. They had just signed their names to it without knowing it. The weight of it settled on her shoulders like a ghostly cloak made of threads of duty and a chilling, dawning premonition.

The busy London street felt strange as they walked out of the lawyer's office. The noise of horse-drawn carriages and shouting vendors, which used to be a familiar part of city life, now sounded like a jangle that didn't fit in with the quiet dread that had settled in her. Thomas, who had no idea what was going on inside her, chattered excitedly about paint colors and garden designs. His excitement was the exact opposite of the knot of fear that was tightening in her chest. He thought of Blackwood Manor as a big painting that needed to be done with energy and intelligence. Eleanor, on the other hand, saw it as something much more complicated: a living thing with its own ancient rhythms and needs.

The trip to Blackwood Manor was a blur of ticking clocks and changing scenery. The well-kept fields of the home counties gave way to rougher, wilder land. The air got cooler and smelled like pine and wet ground, the same earthy smell that had bothered Eleanor so much on their first visit. It was a smell that made you think of things buried and secrets that the soil kept close. The lawyer's legalese in the contract, which she ignored, kept coming back to her mind: unique cyclical regeneration... residency tax...

As the carriage rolled up the long, winding drive, Blackwood Manor came into view, a dark shape against the bruised sky at dusk. The Gothic architecture was sharper and more unforgiving than she remembered, and the windows looked like empty eyes looking out from a weathered face. There was a real stillness around the estate, a silence that wasn't empty but full of unspoken history. It felt like the air was buzzing with an ancient, hidden energy.

Mrs. Gable, the housekeeper, met them at the big oak doors. She had a stern look on her face and a tightly pulled bun, which made Eleanor think that she lived a very organized life. Eleanor also thought that Mrs. Gable knew more about the house than she was willing to tell. She greeted them politely but coolly, and her eyes missed nothing as she took in their luggage and hopeful faces.

"Welcome to Blackwood Manor, Mr. and Mrs. Davies," she said in a calm, low voice. "I hope your trip was… uneventful." The stress on the last word was very light, almost hard to notice, but Eleanor noticed it. It made the housekeeper's calm demeanor seem a little uneasy.

The air inside the manor was different from the air outside when they walked in. It was cooler and heavier, and it had a faint, almost sickening smell of dried flowers and something else… something old and musky, like the smell of old velvet. In the dim light coming through the stained-glass windows, dust motes swirled around, making a ghostly dance in the big entrance hall. The grand staircase, with its intricately carved balustrade, seemed to rise into the dark, promising a world of secrets above.

Eleanor felt it again, that invisible pressure that was stronger and more persistent this time. It was like the house itself was breathing them in, like a huge, sleeping thing that had been awakened by their presence. The contract, which had seemed so strange and far away in the lawyer's office, now felt like a part of the air itself, a force that had brought them all here, no matter what they wanted.

Thomas, always the practical one, was already telling the porters what to do, and his voice had a new authority. "The library will be my study, Eleanor." I think the drawing room in the west wing will be yours. There is a lot of light for your painting. He walked with purpose, wanting to impose his will on the old manor and make his own space within its ancient walls.

But Eleanor stayed in the hall, with her hand on the cool marble of a pedestal nearby. She shut her eyes and tried to figure out what the feeling was that was all around her. It wasn't just the heavy weight of the house or the uneasy feeling left over from the contract. They felt a deep sense of duty, as if they had taken on a role in a play that had been rehearsing for hundreds of years. The "residency tithe" wasn't a request for rent; it was a requirement for them to be there, living within these walls, at certain times, maybe even set times.

She remembered a part of an old book of folklore she had read years ago. It was about spirits that were tied to their ancestors' land and whose power grew and shrank with the presence of the living. Were they just new tenants, or were they somehow meant to be the channels for this "cyclical regeneration"? The thought made her shiver, a cold fear that had nothing to do with the drafts in the manor.

Mrs. Gable walked up to Eleanor quietly, noticing that she was still. "Is something wrong, madam?" She asked, her voice lacking warmth but full of professional interest.

Eleanor opened her eyes and looked at the housekeeper. "No, Mrs. Gable," she said, forcing a smile. "Just taking it all in." Isn't it pretty great?

A flicker, so small that it was almost unnoticeable, crossed the housekeeper's face. "It has a... long memory, madam," she said, looking over the darkened portraits that lined the stairs. "And it doesn't forget easily."

The words hung in the air, a polite warning that was hard to see. Eleanor suddenly had an overwhelming need to go over the purchase papers again and look for more hidden meanings in every line of old text. But the moment was lost when Thomas came back, carrying a box of art supplies in his arms.

"Come, Eleanor!" I found the best place for your easel in the drawing room. "The light is just divine!" He gently pulled her away, and his excitement was like a rock in the sea of her worry.

The painted eyes of the portraits on the wall seemed to follow them as they climbed the grand staircase. Their stern, unsmiling faces were those of men and women from a different time. Their expressions hinted at lives lived within these walls, lives that may have been affected by the same unseen forces that brought Eleanor and Thomas here. Every portrait seemed to ask a silent question, a challenge: Are you ready?

The days that came after were full of things to do. They unpacked boxes, moved furniture around, and the empty Blackwood Manor started to fill with the sounds of their lives. Thomas, who had a lot of energy and was very organized, started planning the renovations. He laid out his blueprints on the library table like a map of their future. He was determined to give the old house a new look and feel, to make it more modern and unique, and to make it truly theirs.

But Eleanor became more and more interested in the manor's natural character and the stories it told about the past. She spent hours looking around its nooks and crannies, her artist's curiosity piqued by the faded grandeur and the feeling of lives lived there. She found secret alcoves, old fireplaces, and rooms that seemed to be holding their breath, waiting for someone to find them again. She found a bunch of old dolls in the empty nursery. Their porcelain faces were cracked, and their button eyes were staring blankly ahead. She felt an overwhelming sadness wash over her as she gently picked one up. It was so strong that it made her cry. It was a sadness that wasn't hers, a ghostly echo of a long-lost pain.

The "cyclical regeneration" and the "residency tithe" were always on my mind. She read the contract again late at night, when the words were hard to read in the light of the lamp. The lawyer's dismissive tone now seemed like a deliberate lie, a carefully crafted cover-up to hide a much bigger truth. What did it mean to "regenerate"? What was the real meaning of this "tithe"? Did they have to live here, or did they have to do more than that?

Eleanor went to see Mrs. Gable one night while Thomas was reading his architectural journals. She hoped to get some insight or indirect confirmation of her fears. She saw the housekeeper in the dark kitchen, carefully polishing a set of silverware.

Eleanor started, "Mrs. Gable," her voice shaky. "About the... deal. The parts about where you live. Has this ever happened before in history? Has it ever... come into effect before?

Mrs. Gable stopped polishing and her face was unreadable. Her dark eyes seemed to see right through Eleanor. "Madam, Blackwood Manor has seen many families. And a lot of seasons. Her voice was neutral, but the words had a weight that made it seem like more than just the passage of time. "The house," she said, her voice dropping to a near whisper, "has its own ways of making sure it stays the same."

"Continuity?" Eleanor asked, her heart racing. "What do you mean?"

The housekeeper started polishing again, moving her hands carefully and on purpose. "Some people say the house needs what it's owed." That the land itself needs a certain... balance. The old families knew this. They kept their word.

"Deal?" Eleanor's voice was strained. "What deal?"

Finally, Mrs. Gable looked Eleanor in the eye again. There was a tiredness in her eyes and a sense of giving up that said she had been carrying too many burdens for too long. "The pact of silence, madam," she said in a low voice. "Knowing that some things shouldn't be questioned." That you have to pay some debts without complaining. The house remembers. And it gathers.

The simple, scary statement fell over Eleanor like a shroud. An agreement to stay quiet. A debt has been paid. It confirmed her worst fears: they hadn't just bought a house; they had made an ancient deal with unseen forces that required a price. The unique cyclical regeneration wasn't a passive renewal; it was an active process, and the residents didn't want to be a part of it. The tithe was not money, but life. The only thing that kept them safe was the silence. It was the only way they could figure out the hidden demands of Blackwood Manor. Eleanor heard Mrs. Gable's words echoing in the quiet kitchen, and she knew for sure that their dream of a new life had turned into a waking nightmare. They were stuck in a contract they had signed too quickly and were now forced to keep quiet about. The shadows in the manor seemed to get darker, and the weight of that unseen duty felt heavier than it ever had before.

First Night in the Labyrinth

The first night at Blackwood Manor was a symphony of strange things. Sleep, which Eleanor had desperately wanted, turned out to be a fragile thing that the house's sneaky intrusions could easily break. It started out as a faint noise in the back of her mind, like dry leaves moving across a stone floor. After that, the creaks began. Not the random, settling groans of an old building, but a steady, planned rhythm. The floorboards in the hallway outside their bedroom sighed and groaned, not with the sudden, sharp snap of settling wood, but with a slow, drawn-out protest, as if something heavy were being moved around. Thump, creak, drag, thump, creak, drag. It sounded like furniture being moved, like wardrobes being pushed an inch closer to the wall, and like chairs being dragged across floors that they hadn't yet explored.

Eleanor's eyes flew open. The room was very dark, and the only light came from the faint, ghostly glow of the moonlight coming through the thick velvet curtains. Thomas breathed deeply next to her, and he slept soundly. This was very different from the feeling of unease that crawled across her skin. She lay still, straining her ears to understand the strange music. The noises were too planned and too... intentional to be just figments of an overactive mind or the natural settling of an old house. They were unnervingly smart, and there was a whisper that someone or something was moving around their new home on purpose.

She reached for the lamp on the nightstand, which had a cool brass base. She wanted to make a small pool of light so she could be sure that the shadows only held furniture and things she knew. But her fingers touched nothing. The lamp, which she clearly remembered putting to her left, was gone. She felt a cold, sharp fear take hold of her. She felt a ghostly weight in her hand, like the shape of the lamp she knew so well. She was confused and fumbled around in the dark, her heart pounding against her ribs. Her hand finally touched cool metal, but it was on the other side of the bed, right where Thomas was sleeping. He moved a little and let out a low murmur, but he didn't move otherwise. There was a change in the lamp. It had been moved, a quiet and unsettling change in the middle of the night. How? She had locked the door to her bedroom herself, making sure that no one could get in. But it was right there, on Thomas's side.

She felt a tremor go through her. It wasn't just the light. The whole room felt different. The air was colder, and when the creaking stopped, the silence was heavy and full of expectation. It seemed like the house was holding its breath and watching her, waiting. She tried to make sense of it. Maybe she moved it while she was sleeping, which was something she had never done before. But the rhythmic thuds coming from the hallway and the feeling of purposeful movement all pointed to something more.

Eleanor sat up and wrapped the heavy quilt around her shoulders. The grand staircase in the entrance hall looked even bigger in the dark. You could see it from the top of the landing, where their bedroom door was. The shadows that clung to its carved balustrade and the spaces beneath its flights seemed to have gotten darker, forming something more real than just a lack of light. It looked less like a useful staircase and more like a gaping mouth, leading down into the manor's darker, deeper heart. The wood, which had been used for hundreds of years and polished over time, seemed to soak up the moonlight, giving it a watchful presence. She thought she saw eyes peeking out from the dark wood grain and the carved figures that decorated its structure, all of them silently watching their new owners.

Thomas finally woke up and rolled over with a soft groan. "Eleanor? "What is it?" he mumbled, his voice heavy with sleep.

"The lamp," she said in a tight voice. "It was on my side, but now it's on your side."

He grunted and fumbled for the lamp. His hand found its new place with an ease that made Eleanor's blood run cold. He mumbled, "I must have knocked it over in my sleep," and then turned it off again with a familiar click. The sudden darkness made things feel even worse. "Sweetheart, go back to sleep. It's late.

But sleep was a faraway place. She lay next to him, her mind racing as she thought about what the lawyer had said: unique cyclical regeneration... residency tithe... Did they sign up for a never-ending haunting? Was this the "reassertion of claim" that he had so easily ignored? The idea itself seemed crazy, like a gothic fantasy brought on by the manor's oppressive atmosphere and the lingering unease from the contract. But what her senses told her was very different. It was all too real: the lamp, the creaking floorboards, and the feeling that someone was always watching.

The distant thuds kept going, but now they were only every now and then, which was still scary. They seemed to be coming from the west wing, which Mrs. Gable had politely but firmly told them to stay away from during their first tour because the floors were unstable and repairs were still going on. Eleanor had thought at first that the housekeeper's silence was just a matter of professional discretion, but now it seemed like she was trying to hide something. Could the repairs have just been a cover-up, a way to keep them away from... whatever was going on in those hidden rooms? It was silly to think that furniture could be moved in an empty wing, but the sounds kept happening.

Eleanor's eyes moved to the thick oak door of their bedroom. She remembered Thomas locking it and the loud sound the bolt made when it slid into place. He was very careful, almost to the point of being obsessive, about safety. But she couldn't shake the feeling, a nagging doubt, that she had heard it move. There was no creak, just a soft, almost unnoticeable click, followed by a faint scraping sound. A door that is open. She had been thinking about it but didn't want to say it out loud because she was afraid of what it might mean. But now that the lamp had been moved and there were strange noises coming from the hallway, it seemed very likely. Was it open the whole time? Or was it opened on purpose, without anyone noticing? The thought made her feel cold all over again. It meant that whatever was moving through the house wasn't just in the hallways; it could also get into their safe place.

She started to write down every sound and feeling. There was a faint smell of dried flowers and something musky, almost earthy, in the air in their room. When the moonlight did get through the thick curtains, it made shadows that looked like they were alive and twisted and stretched. The heavy silence that would fall between the strange noises, a silence that felt more threatening than the noises themselves, as if the house were getting ready for its next show.

Thomas finally woke up from a restless sleep and stretched and yawned. "Are you still awake?" he asked in a hoarse voice.

Eleanor thought for a moment. It felt like betraying their shared dream to say what she was afraid of, like giving up before they had even really started. But the worry was so strong that it felt like a weight in her chest that made it hard to breathe. "I heard… things," she said quietly. "Floorboards creaking, and it sounded like furniture was being moved." The lamp was on my side, and now it's on yours.

Thomas sat up, and for a moment, his eyes showed concern. Then he frowned in a practical way. "Sweetheart, this house is old. They make sounds. You must have moved the lamp. "You were restless." He reached for her, and his touch was warm and comforting. "All the doors are locked." I looked at them myself. Eleanor, we're safe. "That's just the house settling."

He spoke with such conviction and such a natural belief in logical explanations that for a moment, she almost believed him. He was a logical and orderly man who saw Blackwood Manor as a project that needed to be understood and mastered. But Eleanor, who was an artist, could feel the house's subtle, all-encompassing consciousness. It wasn't just settling down; it was acting.

"But the thuds, Thomas," she said again, her voice barely above a whisper. "From the west wing." And the door… I think I heard the door to the bedroom open.

He ran his hand through his hair and frowned. "Don't forget that the west wing is being fixed?" It's probably people who work. What about the door? Old houses have drafts that can make doors creak open. "Don't worry about it." He kissed her forehead, and his lips were cool against her skin. "Please try to sleep, Eleanor. We have a lot to get done tomorrow. We need to begin making plans for the renovations. "Think about what could happen!"

He lay back down, his breathing evened out, and soon he was asleep again. Eleanor, on the other hand, stayed awake, her senses sharp and her mind open to every creak and groan. She looked at the stairs again. In the moonlight, they looked dark and scary, like a guard in the hall. It seemed to call to her, to pull her deeper into its depths, promising secrets that were beyond what she already knew. The wood grain swirled in hypnotic patterns, and for a brief, terrifying moment, she thought the figures carved into the balustrade were moving, their sculpted eyes blinking slowly in the dark.

She couldn't stop thinking about how the lawyer had thrown out the old clauses. Just formalities from the past. But what if they weren't? What if the "cyclical regeneration" was an ongoing process that was important to the manor and the "residency tithe" was their required participation? Could the house itself have been a living thing, with its needs being met by the people who lived there? The thought sent shivers down my spine, like I was going into a kind of primitive, basic horror.

Eleanor finally fell into a shallow, uneasy sleep as the first hint of pre-dawn gray began to lighten the sky. Her dreams were filled with shifting landscapes, whispering shadows, and the ever-present, looming presence of the grand staircase. The night had been a prologue, a subtle introduction to the manor's hidden life. This life was already making itself known, not through dramatic hauntings, but through a much more insidious form of unease: the quiet certainty that they were not alone and that Blackwood Manor was very much awake and aware. The sounds of the night had been its voice, and they had said a lot. The lamp's movement, the floorboards' deliberate groans, and the imagined movement in the west wing were all whispers from the house, hints of a deeper, darker reality that was woven into the very fabric of Blackwood Manor. Eleanor knew that this first night was just the beginning of a long and scary stay as the pale light of morning started to come through the curtains. The house had welcomed them, not with open arms, but with a series of unsettling overtures, a symphony of disquiet designed to lull them into a false sense of security before the true performance began. The shadows in the hall seemed to fade away with the dawn, but their memory stayed with them, showing that Blackwood Manor was a maze of stone and shadow and that they had only just crossed its threshold. The detailed carvings on the stairs seemed to make her feel worse, and their silent faces hinted at secrets that would surely come out as they stayed longer. The house was alive and watching them. Its old mind came to life when they arrived, and its first nighttime symphony was a prelude to the trouble that was to come.

An Uninvited Guest

The dawn that broke over Blackwood Manor was dull and weak, as if the sun didn't want to shine its full light on the old stone. Eleanor had trouble sleeping, and when she woke up, the ghost of the night's disturbing symphony was still echoing in the quiet corners of her mind. Even though the air in the bedroom seemed still, there was a constant, sad draft. It whispered through the windows that looked like they were closed, a sad sigh that snaked its way through the halls, a clear sign of the house's constant unrest. Thomas, who was next to her, didn't know what was going on. He was in a deep, peaceful sleep that only the very tired could understand. But for Eleanor, the night had been a crucible, turning a vague feeling of unease into a more clear sense of fear.

She got out of bed and walked on the worn Persian rug, which felt soft and familiar in the strange place. The grand staircase, which could be seen from the door, was no longer hidden in the darkest shadows of night, but it still had an air of dark mystery. The carved banister, which had been polished to a silky sheen by generations of hands, seemed to soak up the pale morning light. Its intricate details hinted at secrets that were still hidden. Eleanor was drawn to the study, which Thomas had said would be her safe space for art. There, surrounded by the smell of old paper and polished mahogany, she found comfort in her sketchbook and pencils again.

She sat down at the big oak desk, and the heavy leather of her chair creaked softly in protest. Her fingers were still a little stiff from the stress of the night, but they picked up a charcoal pencil. She wanted to capture the imposing front of Blackwood Manor and put its Gothic beauty on the clean white page. But when she started to move her hand, something strange happened. Not all of the house she drew was the one she had seen. The lines of the front seemed to move and change, and the strong gables looked almost like they were moving. She drew in a window that she knew for sure wasn't there. There was only solid stone where a small, arched window should have been high up on the west wing. She frowned. Was it all in her head? She was probably just imagining things because she hadn't slept and things had been going wrong all night.

But the strange thing kept happening as she went on. A side wing that had looked like a solid, plain building on their tour started to grow under her pencil, adding fancy turrets and impossibly narrow, winding staircases that spiraled up into the sketched sky. The hallways in her drawing turned and twisted in ways that didn't make sense from an architectural point of view. They led to rooms she had never seen before, rooms that felt both familiar and strange. A big ballroom appeared on the first floor, with imagined chandeliers dripping with ghostly light. She knew this room didn't fit with the rest of the manor's known layout. As she drew more, Blackwood Manor became more complicated and maze-like on the page, like a nightmare map of a house that seemed to have a life and will of its own, a life that was much more complicated and creepy than its physical structure suggested.

She stopped and stared at the drawing, feeling more and more confused. It was like her mind was revealing a hidden structure, a secret layer of life that lay beneath the stone and mortar of the manor. The complexity was too much to handle, with a huge web of hidden spaces and impossible shapes. It was beautiful in a creepy way, like a dark, complicated tapestry made of shadow and suggestion. But it was also very disturbing. These weren't just random ideas from an artist's mind; they felt like revelations, like she was seeing into a hidden reality that her waking mind wouldn't accept.

Thomas came into the study, and his usual quick manner was a nice change from Eleanor's growing anxiety. He moved with purpose as he carried two steaming mugs of tea. "Good morning, my dear," he said in a warm voice, but there was a hint of tension around his eyes, which showed that he hadn't slept well either. "Still doing it? I thought we could work on the library this morning. "Think of all the things you could do with those shelves!"

Eleanor nodded and pushed the sketchbook away with a firm gesture. "Of course." The library sounds great. She didn't want to look him in the eye because she didn't want to show how upset her drawings had made her. "I was just thinking about some ideas for the inside design."

He put a cup of tea on her desk and touched her fingers. He joked, "If you're not careful, you'll have us living in a maze." His smile was a little too forced. He looked at the sketchbook and a look of interest crossed his face, but he didn't ask any more questions. He wanted to keep up the appearance of normalcy and focus on the things that were real and possible, like the renovations, the improvements, and the change of this big, old house into their perfect home.

Thomas started to feel strange as they walked through the quiet halls. It was a small but constant feeling of being trapped, a growing fear of small spaces that didn't seem to fit with the manor's huge size. At first, the hallways seemed big and grand, but now they felt smaller, and the high ceilings were pressing down on him. The dark, rich paneling on the walls made them look like they were leaning in, and the detailed carvings of mythical beasts and stern-faced ancestors made them look like they were leaning out. Their silent gazes followed him with an unsettling intensity. He kept looking around, his eyes darting from one shadow to the next, and a chill ran up his spine.

He thought it was because they were tired and because the job was so big. Changing Blackwood Manor was a huge job, and the mental toll of such a project should not be underestimated. For Eleanor's sake, he had to look strong and determined. He was the realist, the one who kept them grounded in reality, and he couldn't let the sneaky whispers of unease that seemed to come from the very walls of the house get to him.

They got to the library, which was a beautiful room with bookshelves that went all the way to the ceiling on every wall. This showed how much the people who lived there before them were interested in learning. The smell of old paper and leather bindings filled the air, a comforting smell that made Thomas feel better for a moment. He ran his hand along a row of leather-bound books, but the titles were too faded to read. "Remarkable," he said quietly, clearly impressed. "Think about the history that is in these walls."

But Eleanor was drawn to the windows. Even though Thomas had told her before that it wasn't there, she could still feel it: that constant, subtle draft. There wasn't a strong wind; instead, there was a soft, almost invisible stream of air that seemed to come from nowhere and everywhere at once. It was cold and had a faint, almost floral smell mixed with something else that smelled like damp soil and musk. She ran her hand over the complicated latch of a tall, leaded casement window. It was cool, solid, and looked like it was airtight. But the draft stayed, and a ghostly breath touched her cheek.

"It's strange, isn't it?" she said, her voice low. "This draft. I can't seem to find where it came from.

Thomas waved his hand in a dismissive way as he was busy looking at the binding of a very large book. "Old houses, Eleanor." They have their own strange habits. There might be a loose pane of glass somewhere, or the stonework might not be as sealed as it looks. "Don't worry about it." He stood up straight and looked at all the books. "We'll have to be very picky about which ones we keep. Think about how much space we could make if we got rid of some of these. "Maybe a reading nook here and a small writing desk there..."

He stopped talking when he saw Eleanor's face. The small feeling of unease that had been following him all morning now seemed to be in her eyes. "Are you okay, sweetheart?" he asked, his voice getting softer. "You seem... busy."

Eleanor made herself smile. "I guess it's just the size of it all," she said, looking back at the windows and the draft that was hard to find. "It's so big, so... powerful. It will take some time to get used to. She knew it was more than that, though. The drawings, the constant drafts, and the creepy creaks and groans of the night were all parts of a puzzle that wouldn't fit together, a pattern that her logical mind couldn't accept. The lawyer's words, the strange parts of the contract, and Mrs. Gable's strange behavior all started to come together into a disturbing story that couldn't be denied.

They spent the morning making a list of books, and their hands were covered in dust from years of use. But even while I was studying, the house kept bothering me in small ways. A light smell of lavender that was strangely strong in one corner of the library and then went away completely. A soft thud came from somewhere inside the walls. It wasn't an animal and it wasn't the house settling down. And always, that ghostly draft, a constant, chilling reminder that Blackwood Manor was not just a building, but a living thing that seemed to breathe and sigh and force its will on its residents.

Thomas ignored every oddity in his determined search for practicality. The draft was a structural flaw, the thuds were probably from old pipes, and the smells were probably from perfumes that had been left behind by previous tenants. He was building a fortress of logic against the strange things that were coming closer, refusing to think that their dream home could be something much deeper and more disturbing than they had ever thought. He talked about insulation, drafts, and structural surveys, and Eleanor watched as his mood changed in small, unsettling ways. The way his eyes would sometimes stay on something, unfocused, as if he were seeing something just outside of their shared reality. The slight shake in his hand as he reached for a book. He was trying to keep up the appearance of being completely rational, but deep down, he was starting to feel claustrophobic and terrified. It looked like the house wasn't just a bunch of rooms and hallways; it was a living, breathing thing with its own secret plan that was slowly but surely starting to happen around them. And the scariest truth, the one they both refused to accept, was that their dream home might really be a trap that was very real and very dangerous. Eleanor's drawings were not just a figment of her imagination; they were a premonition, a visual premonition of the impossible architecture that lay hidden behind the manor's deceptively solid walls. Blackwood Manor wasn't just a house; it was a maze, and they had willingly walked into its depths, not knowing how complicated and suffocating the design was.

Chapter 2: The Shifting Walls

The Breakfast Rooms Betrayal

When the morning light finally broke through the constant darkness of Blackwood Manor, it didn't do much to calm the unease that was still there. Eleanor had trouble sleeping, and the dreams of moving hallways and whispered worries stuck to her like the damp seep from the old stone. She got up with a tired sigh, feeling the weight of her unspoken fears on her. Thank goodness Thomas was still asleep, deep in a dreamless sleep. This was very different from how she woke up. She got dressed quietly, the silk of her nightgown brushing against her skin, and then she went to the breakfast room, hoping that a meal would make things feel normal again.

She pushed the heavy oak door open and was greeted by the familiar smell of old wood and beeswax. The tall, mullioned windows that usually gave a wide view of the overgrown gardens let in weak, watery sunlight. But as her eyes got used to the dim light, a knot of fear grew in her stomach. There was something wrong. Very wrong. There was a window in the eastern wall, which should have been a smooth stretch of weathered stone. A small, impossibly narrow window, no bigger than a ration book, was set in the middle of the old stone. There was nothing to see outside. A solid, gray brick wall with a dirty surface that showed no signs of a garden or the green grounds they had seen when they first arrived. It was like a part of the outside had been changed for no reason, with a patch of homey-ness added to the manor's imposing front, and a window that only showed a glimpse of an artificial void.

Eleanor walked slowly toward it, her heart racing against her ribs. She ran her shaking hand over the cool glass, looking for any sign of a seam, any sign that it was a temporary change, a trick of the light, or maybe some strange decorative addition. But it was definitely solid; it was a real window that looked out onto a real, if confusing, wall. There was no reason that made sense. The gardens were big and surrounded by a high stone wall. But this brick building was completely new to them, and it made them feel very uneasy. It looked like the manor's dimensions were warped, like they were out of place.

She looked at the other wall, which had always been a solid, imposing wall of dark, polished wood that separated the breakfast room from what Thomas thought was a pantry or storage area. There was now a door where solid wood had been. The opening was rough and not polished, and it led into a dark area. There were thick, old cobwebs on the edges of the frame that looked like creepy lace. The thin strands of silk shone faintly in the little light that came from the breakfast room. The air that came through the opening was stale and heavy with the sickly sweet smell of dust and decay. It smelled like a place that had been forgotten and sealed off for a long time.

Eleanor felt sick all of a sudden. The house wasn't settling. This had nothing to do with drafts or creaking wood. They were actively and purposefully changing their new home. The manor wasn't just old; it was alive, changing, and, it seemed, actively reshaping itself around them, making new spaces, swallowing old ones, and trapping them in its constantly changing architecture.

At that moment, Thomas walked into the room. His usual quick energy was a sharp contrast to Eleanor's frozen fear. He had two steaming mugs of coffee in his hands and was concentrating on the room. But right away, his eyes were drawn to the strange things. He stopped in his tracks, his eyes going from the new window to the door that wasn't there. His mouth dropped open a little, and he looked completely confused.

He set the coffee mugs down on the table with a clatter and said, "What in God's name…?" He walked to the window, and it was clear that his architect's mind was having a hard time processing what he saw. He tapped the glass and then the brickwork outside. His lips moved as he silently recalculated the basic rules of architecture, angles, and dimensions. He turned to Eleanor and said, "That's… impossible," his voice full of disbelief. "That wall… it's part of the old garden boundary, the one with the broken cherubs. This brickwork isn't the same as it was before. And the window? There was never a window here. "No."

He went to the new door and held his hand over the dusty threshold. "And this… I don't get it. This was a strong wall. When we were planning the kitchen remodel, I looked over the blueprints myself. There was no space, no passage, or anything else behind it. "Nothing." He looked into the dark, his face twisted in a grimace of disgust. "Looks like an old-fashioned cupboard of some kind." Full of… who knows what.

Eleanor watched him and felt a deep sense of hopelessness. Thomas, the practical man with plans and a strong sense of structure, was clearly upset. His logical mind was fighting against the clear proof that his senses were giving him. The house went against logic and even the laws of physics. "It's like," she said, her voice barely above a whisper, "the house is… changing its shape." Like a strange, living thing, it grows new rooms.

Thomas ran a hand through his hair, and his usual calmness was starting to fray. "Don't be silly, Eleanor," he said, but his voice didn't sound as sure as it usually does. "Houses don't change their shape. There has to be a reason. Maybe… maybe the blueprints weren't right. It's possible that the original plans were never changed for this old house, which has been changed by many generations. Or maybe… He stopped talking and looked around the breakfast room. His eyes narrowed as he noticed the small differences in the size of the room, like how the walls seemed to have moved a little and the ceiling looked a little lower than he remembered.

He carefully stepped through the door and into the dark, dusty room. Eleanor held her breath and tried to see him. Her hand reached out as if to pull him back. There was a muffled cough coming from inside the closet. "It's… just a small storage space," he said, his voice a little muffled. "And very dusty. There are cobwebs all over the place. "Smells like a tomb." He came back to the door and brushed off his jacket. His face was dirty. "We'll have to close this up. It's bad for your health and not useful at all.

But Eleanor knew he wouldn't close it up. He couldn't do it. Not right now. Not when it was such a big break in how they thought the manor worked. This wasn't just a strange structure; it was a sign of something much worse. The house was actively showing its will and presence by changing its own shape. Each change was a small act of control, a silent message that they were not in charge of this area, but were just guests who had to follow its whims.

“But Thomas,” she said softly, her eyes on the dark opening, “why would there be a closet there?” What was it used for? And the window… it looks out over the old stables, right? Or at least, according to the lawyer’s notes, where the stables used to be.”

Thomas frowned, and a hint of worry came back to his eyes. He said, “The solicitor’s notes were a little vague about the outbuildings,” and then he looked back at the strange window. “He talked about a fire in the late 1800s that burned down most of them. But that wall of bricks… it doesn’t make sense. It looks like it’s been… stuck on. Or maybe the house has taken over some other land? He shook his head; the idea was clearly silly. Blackwood Manor had its own huge estate, which was miles away from any other property.

He walked over to the coffee mugs, and his hands were still shaking a little. He picked up his own, looking far away. “It’s the stress, Eleanor,” he said, his voice a little too loud and forced. “The move, the size of this project. It’s having an effect on both of us. Our minds are messing with us. We need to think about the practical things. On turning this house into a home.”

Eleanor nodded, but she felt a cold, creeping fear in her stomach. She knew it wasn’t stress. It wasn’t a trick of the mind. The house was getting different. It was actively changing its own structure and form to fit something or maybe to hide something. The window that looked out on a brick wall and the new door that led to a forgotten closet were not just random events. They were planned changes, acts of architectural sabotage. The manor wasn’t just a place to live; it was a maze, a living thing that was slowly, but surely, rewriting its own reality and trapping them in its ever-deepening, ever-changing depths. The coffee’s warmth didn’t do much to warm her up, even though it was hot. She looked at Thomas and saw the forced smile and the flicker of doubt in his eyes. She knew that their dream of a peaceful country estate had turned into a nightmare. The house had begun its quiet siege, and the breakfast room, which had once been a sign of their new beginning, was now the first place to fight.

A Maze of Memories

It wasn't just a metaphor that Blackwood Manor was like a maze; it was a scary, real thing. Eleanor and Thomas were caught in its confusing embrace. At first, they were fascinated by its gothic beauty, but that quickly turned into a nagging worry. It seemed like the house had a mind of its own, with its architecture changing and being unpredictable, making fun of their efforts to make things more orderly and familiar.

One morning, their usual search for breakfast turned into a confusing trip into the unknown. The hallway that led from their rooms to the dining room had changed overnight in a way that was both small and big. What had once been a straight path with portraits on the walls whose eyes seemed to follow them everywhere had turned into a long, winding path like a snake. The walls, which used to be a steady, if dark, shade of gray, now had patches of different textures on them. Some had rough, unpolished stone, while others had sickly, peeling wallpaper with faded roses that seemed to move in the dim light. With every hesitant step, Eleanor's heart raced against her ribs. She felt like a mouse stuck in a maze that kept changing, and with each turn, she lost her sense of direction.

"Thomas," she whispered, her voice tight with fear that she couldn't hide anymore. "Do you... do you feel this?"

Thomas, who usually focused on things that could be seen and measured, had a similar look of confused fear on his face. He stopped and ran his hand over the wall's cool, damp stone. "It's... it's longer," he said in a low voice. "The hallway. It feels... stretched. And the sizes... they don't seem right. He waved his hands in a vague way, as if his architectural instincts were against what was impossible. "It feels like the space between the walls has grown. Or maybe the walls themselves have been "pushed outwards."

They kept going, and the quiet of the manor made their footsteps sound louder, each one a nervous echo in the heavy stillness. The portraits that had once looked like they were just watching now looked like they were sneering, with painted lips that curled into silent, mocking smiles. They walked past a door that should have led to the library, a room they had spent a lot of time in the day before. The ornate mahogany door was gone, and in its place was a smooth, dark wood-paneled wall that looked like it had never been there. There was no seam, and there was no sign that a door had ever been there. It was like the house had just taken it in and swallowed it whole.

"The library," Eleanor said, her voice full of disbelief. "Where... where did it go?"

Thomas walked up to the spot and ran his fingers over the wood grain's intricate patterns. He pushed against the panels to see if there were any hidden latches or mechanisms. Nothing. The room seemed to have disappeared from existence, or maybe it had just moved to a different dimension. "It's... it's gone," he said, his voice flat and not as calm as usual. "Not locked, Eleanor." Gone.

The farther they went, the more confusing the trip got. They thought the corridor would eventually take them to the grand staircase, but it ended suddenly at a narrow door with iron bands that was bolted shut from the outside. They had never seen this door before. The iron bands were thick and rusty, and the wood was dark, scarred, and old. There was a small, dirty window high up in the door that let in only a little bit of light.

"This... this can't be happening," Thomas said quietly, looking at the locked door as if it were a personal insult. "This wasn't here yesterday." We walked this way a dozen times. It was a straight shot to the main hall. He looked at Eleanor with wide eyes, realizing something scary that was just starting to dawn on him. "The house is different. It's actively changing itself around us.

Eleanor's breath caught. The paranoia that had been a small fire inside her began to grow into a raging fire. People laughed at their first attempts to map the manor because of its oddities, hidden alcoves, and secret passages. But this was more than just strange. This was a planned act of spatial manipulation, a hostile takeover of their surroundings.

They decided to go back the way they came, a last-ditch effort to get back to something familiar. But the way back was just as dangerous. The winding hallway looked different now. What had looked like a solid wall, a dead end they had come across before, now showed a narrow opening that was only big enough for one person to get through. The air that came out of it was thick with the smell of dust and mildew, which made it seem like there were forgotten places in the manor that hadn't been touched in hundreds of years.

Thomas paused, torn between his usual practicality and a growing sense of dread. "Should we...?" he started, looking from the door to Eleanor.

"We have to," she said, her voice strong even though her hands were shaking. "We need to know what's going on." We can't just... take it.

Thomas took a deep breath and pushed himself through the small space, with Eleanor right behind him. They stepped into a huge, empty space that felt completely strange. They had never seen that room before and had no idea it existed. The ceiling was so high that it was impossible to see, and the walls were lined with rows and rows of shelves filled with what looked like old furniture covered in dust sheets. It was a storage room that had been forgotten, big and scary.

"This... this is huge," Thomas said in a low voice that echoed in the vastness of the room. "It has to go all the way across the east wing. "What did we miss?"

Eleanor looked at the dusty old things. In one corner, a grandfather clock stood still, its pendulum stopped, and cobwebs covered its face. In the middle of the room stood a huge four-poster bed with worn-out and faded hangings. It was a tomb for things that had been lost, a reminder of lives that had come and gone. But the fact that it was so big and seemed to have come out of nowhere was very scary.

They walked through the maze of aisles, their footsteps muffled by the thick layer of dust. There were more hidden treasures and silent witnesses to the manor's history around every corner. They were in what looked like an empty ballroom. The floor, which had once been shiny, was now scuffed and dirty, and the chandeliers were covered in ghostly cobwebs. The air was thick and still, and it smelled faintly of death.

Eleanor thought, "It's like the house is giving birth to new rooms," and she shivered. "Or maybe it's just showing parts of itself that have always been there but were hidden."

Thomas shook his head and furrowed his brow in thought. "No, Eleanor.

This isn't just about rooms that aren't visible. The hallways were different. The library was gone. This... this is something else. "It's like the house's plans are always changing."

A distant noise, a faint scraping, and then what sounded like a muffled thud cut short their exploration of the new room. They froze, straining their ears. The sound seemed to come from the far end of the big room, from a part that was in deeper shadow.

"Did you hear that?" Eleanor whispered and put her hand on Thomas's arm, digging her fingers into it.

Thomas nodded and looked around in the dark. "It sounded like... movement."

They moved slowly toward the sound, their hearts beating in time with each other. As they got closer, they saw that the shelves in this part of the store weren't full of furniture; they were full of old books with faded, brittle spines. And behind a very tall stack, a small, hunched person was having trouble with what looked like a loose floorboard.

The housekeeper was Mrs. Gable. She was as old and worn as the manor itself, with a face full of wrinkles and sharp, knowing eyes. As they got closer, she looked up with a hint of surprise in her eyes, but then her usual stoic look came back.

"Mrs. Gable?" Thomas shouted, his voice full of relief and confusion. "What are you doing here?" We... we didn't know this room was here.

The housekeeper looked from Thomas to Eleanor, her eyes staying on Eleanor's pale, worried face. She slowly straightened up, and her joints creaked like the old wood in the manor. "This old house," she said, her voice rough, like dry leaves scraping against stone, "has a lot of secrets." Many places forgotten, even by those who live within its walls."

"But… how did you get here?" Eleanor pushed on, still shaken by how impossible their situation was. "We came through a small opening from the main hallway, but it's different now."

Mrs. Gable's lips turned up in a small, mysterious smile. She said in a mysterious way, "The paths here are not always what they seem, madam." She pointed to the floorboard she had been working on. "This… this leads to the old servant's passages. A network that goes under the main house. Good for moving around without being seen or for "hiding things that are best kept out of sight."

"Passages for servants?" Thomas said it again, and his mind was already racing with ideas for buildings. "Under the house? We weren't told anything like that.

"Sir, not all of the house's history is written down in neat plans," Mrs. Gable said, her eyes steady. "Some of it is… lived. Felt. It is a house that remembers, and it has ways of letting people know. She stared straight at Eleanor, and her old eyes seemed to see through the younger woman's rising fear. "This house," she said, her voice dropping to a near whisper, "doesn't like to be confined." It gets bigger and changes. It remembers what it wants to and forgets what it wants to.

Eleanor felt a twinge of worry when the housekeeper said that. Her eyes showed a deep understanding and a familiarity with the manor's strange behavior that was almost like she was part of it. Was Mrs. Gable just a long-time worker who knew the house's quirks, or was she something else? Did she know the manor's most secret and dark secrets?

"So, these passages… they link different parts of the house?" Eleanor asked, her voice barely audible.

Mrs. Gable corrected, "They connect what the house wishes to connect, madam," putting a little extra emphasis on the word "wishes." "Sometimes, a door that was there yesterday won't be there today. And a wall that seemed solid may have a passage you never knew about. Don't try to map it out too strictly. It will only make things more confusing, and maybe even get you to a place you don't want to be.

Thomas ran a hand through his hair, getting more and more angry. "But that's the issue, Mrs. Gable!" We should be able to find our way around our own house. We can't have rooms and hallways disappearing and reappearing overnight.

The housekeeper smiled again, but it wasn't a warm smile. "Maybe, sir, you're trying to force your will on a house that has its own will. Blackwood Manor is different from other houses. It is... special. She stopped and looked around the dimly lit storage room. "It protects its memories. And it sometimes moves them around.

The hint was very strong in the air. The house wasn't just old; it was alive, with a memory that changed all the time and the ability to change its own structure. They weren't wasting their time trying to map its maze-like hallways; the manor itself was actively stopping them. The walls seemed to breathe, move, swallow, and show things, playing a cruel game with the people who lived there.

Eleanor couldn't shake the feeling that they were no longer in charge of their own lives as they finally made their way back to the more familiar, though still unsettling, main corridors. Mrs. Gable's vague directions somehow got them exactly where they needed to be. They were just passengers on a trip through a house that was changing its own story, and in doing so, it was slowly and permanently changing theirs. Eleanor couldn't stop thinking about the locked door, the library that had disappeared, and the storage room that seemed too big to be true. The maze wasn't just in the hallways; it was in their heads. Each confusing turn was a sign of their growing paranoia, their fading sanity, and their dawning realization that Blackwood Manor wasn't just a house, but a living thing that kept them trapped in its dangerous, changing embrace. The question was no longer whether they could get away, but whether the manor would ever let them.

The Architects Dilemma

The blueprints, which used to stand for order and reason, were now spread out on a dusty table in what had been the library just a few hours before. Or, more accurately, where the library used to be. Thomas ran his finger over the ink lines, and the exact measurements he had carefully written down now seemed like a cruel joke. The size of the room, the placement of the tall bookshelves, and the exact angle of the bay window that looked out over the overgrown gardens were all lies. He had gone back to what should have been the library entrance, but instead he found a solid wall with no decorations. There wasn't even a hint of a doorframe or a seam. It was gone, as if the house had breathed out and the room and everything in it had disappeared.

Of course, he had brought Eleanor with him. At first, she was fascinated by the manor's strange features, but that interest had turned into a deep-seated fear that was similar to his own growing dread. He needed her calmness and her ability to find peace in things that weren't real to calm his own rising panic. But even she seemed shaken by how bold the changes to the house's design were. "It's gone, Thomas," she whispered, her voice a thin thread in the heavy silence. Her eyes were wide with worry, as if they were taking in all the light in the room. "Totally gone."

This new room they were in, this fake library, was a poor copy. Yes, there were shelves, but they were rough-hewn, poorly built, and only had a few books on them that felt more like hastily put together props than real knowledge. The smell was wrong, too. It had a sharp, chemical smell that fought with the musty smell of old paper. It was a fake library, a ghost made by an architect who was too creative.

Thomas opened up another blueprint, this one showing the manor's complicated network of service corridors. He had taken on this project with the goal of making a list of every nook and cranny. It showed how much he believed in his job and in things that could be seen and measured. But Blackwood Manor seemed set on tearing down that belief, brick by painful brick. He held the paper up and looked at the world around him. The hallway they had used to get from their rooms that morning, which had somehow grown longer and twisted, was marked here as a straight, unchanging passage. His compass, which he always used when he was exploring, now looked like a toy for kids. It spun around like it didn't know what to do with the air.

"Look at this, Eleanor," he said, his voice tight with anger as he pointed to a part of the blueprint. "This says that the main staircase for the east wing should be here." Right next to the grand salon. He waved his hand around them, across a blank wall where a beautiful staircase made of dark, polished wood had been the day before. It spiraled up. "And yet..."

He walked over to the wall and put his fingers on the cool, smooth surface. There was no sign of an opening or a missing structure. It was like the stairs had been cut off and there was no sign of them being there before. He felt a tremor that was like vertigo, a feeling of being lost that went beyond just being confused about where he was. It was a basic breakdown of how he understood the physical world.

"Maybe," Eleanor said softly, looking at a part of the wall that seemed to shimmer at the edge of his vision. "Maybe the house... reabsorbs things." Like a living thing. It takes back what it doesn't need anymore or what it wants to hide.

"Reabsorbs?" Thomas laughed, and the sound was harsh in the quiet. "Houses don't 'reabsorb,' Eleanor. They are made. They are built. There are physics, engineering, and logic. This... this goes against everything. He hit the blueprint with his fist, and the paper fluttered dangerously. "This can't be done. It goes against reason.

He took out his measuring tape, which felt heavy and solid in his hand because it was made of brass. He started to measure the room he was in. His movements were quick and jerky because he needed to feel like he was anchored in something real. The sizes were almost right; they were close enough to the original library's footprint to suggest a link, but not quite right. A few feet shorter here and a few inches narrower there. The height of the ceiling was much lower than it should have been, which made the room always seem dark.

He looked up to try to figure out how far away the ceiling was. It was a dark, cloudy area. He felt a wave of anger that didn't make sense. It seemed like there was even a disagreement about what vertical space was. He saw himself as a surveyor, trying to map out a landscape that changed with every step he took. The ground itself changed shape with every step he took.

Eleanor said, "It's not just the rooms, Thomas." Her voice was barely above a whisper, and her eyes were once again fixed on the strange shimmer. "It's the windows." Do you remember the little window in the study in the west wing? The one that looked out over the ruins of the old chapel?

Thomas nodded, his mind racing. He remembered it very well. A small window made of leaded glass that showed a sad view of crumbling stone and ivy that had grown too big.

"It's gone," Eleanor said, her voice shaking. "When we went back this morning, it was just a wall." A solid, unbroken stretch of oak paneling. And the big window in your study that looks out over the east lawn has been replaced by a narrow slit, like a "loophole" in a castle.

Thomas felt a chill of fear in his stomach. His research. He had spent hours there, working on his designs and feeling safe as a professional. He couldn't even be sure of what he could see out of his own window. The house wasn't just moving furniture around; it was changing how it looked and how it interacted with the outside world. It was a quiet act of imprisonment, a planned cutting off of ties.

He thought about what Mrs. Gable had said, how the housekeeper had said in a calm voice that the house had its own will and memory. He thought they were just the crazy thoughts of an old woman who had spent too much time in the manor's sad atmosphere. But now, her strange warnings seemed to have a scary sense of foreboding.

He picked up a piece of charcoal and started drawing on a loose sheet of paper. His usual straight lines became jagged and unclear. He tried to show the hallway as it used to be, then as it is now, then the ghost library, and finally the missing staircase. The drawings turned into a jumbled mess of lines crossing each other and angles that were impossible to see, which was a visual representation of his own mental breakdown.

He said to himself more than to Eleanor, "It's like it's fighting us." "Every time we try to understand it or put it in a box, it makes fun of us. It changes the rules. It changes the map.

He suddenly stood up and started to walk around the fake library. The air felt thick and heavy, like it was trying to keep him from moving. He could almost feel the house watching him, its unseen mind watching him fail to put things in order. He was an architect, which means he knew how to build, structure, and turn abstract ideas into solid shapes. But this house was falling apart, breaking down the very things he believed in.

He remembered a very strange thing that happened the week before. He had been looking at the manor's main hall and admiring the beautiful plasterwork on the ceiling when he saw a hairline crack that hadn't been there the day before. He had told a local stonemason named Silas about it. Silas was known for being able to understand old buildings in a way that no one else could. Silas looked at the crack and shook his head. "Sir, that's the strangest thing," he said in a low voice. "That crack... it's not a new one. It's... it's like it's always been there. But the plasterwork around it has changed. It seems like the crack erased a part of the ceiling and then the house. It just... smoothed itself over around the gap.

Thomas had thought that Silas's comment was just the silly idea of a worker who wanted to impress. But now the memory came back, and it made him uneasy. The house wasn't just moving walls; it was also changing the way it was built, leaving behind signs of its changes, like a sculptor chipping away at marble, only for the marble to mysteriously come back together.

He stopped walking back and forth and looked at a big, fancy mirror that was leaning against one of the rough bookshelves. It was a thing that should not have been in the real library. He walked toward it, and his reflection appeared: a pale, thin man with a furrowed brow who looked very focused. He looked closely at the reflection and the room behind him. The mirror seemed to show a slightly different view, with the shelves arranged in a way that was a little different and the light coming from an unseen source in a way that was strange.

"Look," he said to Eleanor, his voice low and shaky with a new kind of fear, one that was colder and deeper than just being confused. "Look in the mirror."

Eleanor walked up slowly. She held her breath as she looked into the mirror. Her reflection looked... sharper. More clear. And the room behind her reflection looked like it had a faint, ghostly outline of the original library. The bookshelves, the wallpaper pattern, and the bay window were all there, like ghosts, on top of the fake room's rough reality.

"It's... it's showing us what was," she said in a whisper, putting her hand over her mouth.

"Or what should be," Thomas said, his voice stern. "It's like the house is showing us the plan it isn't following." It makes fun of us by reminding us of its own logical form.

He reached out, and his fingers were only a few inches away from the mirror. He could almost feel a coolness coming from it, like there was something in the air that was pushing back. He was an architect who worked with solid materials, gravity, and load-bearing walls. He worked with the laws of physics that are always the same. But it seemed like Blackwood Manor worked on a completely different set of rules, ones that were set by an unseen, unknowable being.

He remembered giving Eleanor the original blueprints for the manor, which were a complicated and beautiful document with exact notes and beautiful drawings. They had thought they were the key to understanding the house and finding out its secrets. Those blueprints now looked like a child's drawing of a dragon, a naive attempt to show something much older and scarier.

Eleanor's voice was so low that it was hard to hear. "What if the house… doesn't want to be understood?" What if it doesn't make sense because it's trying to tell us something?

Thomas ran his hand over his face. The rough stubble on his unshaven chin was very different from the smooth, polished surfaces he was used to. "Tell us what, Eleanor? That we're stuck? That our reasoning doesn't matter here?

He went back to the table and picked up the original plan for the east wing. He looked closely at the detailed drawing of the stairs and the graceful curve of its design. He could almost feel how heavy the stone was and how smooth the wood was. He looked up at the empty wall, which was where the stairs should have been. He felt a deep sense of loss, not just for the building itself, but also for the ideas it stood for. He based his whole career on the idea that a building, once designed and built, would always stay the same. But Blackwood Manor showed the opposite to be true. It was a building that went against its own creation, a structure that was always changing, or maybe not changing.

He felt a rush of anger and a desperate need to regain some sense of control. He would measure once more. He would draw again. He would make his understanding fit into this impossible space. He took his measuring tape and stretched it out across the floor. He needed to set a baseline, a single point of reference that couldn't be questioned. He started in one corner of the fake library and moved slowly. He first measured the length, then the width, and finally the height of the walls. He carefully wrote down the numbers in his sketchbook as he worked, even though his hand was shaking a little.

He got to the far corner, and when he pulled out the tape measure, it got stuck on something. He looked down. A small, almost invisible line in the floorboards that wasn't there a second ago. When he pushed down on the floorboard, it gave way a little, showing a dark, narrow space below. It was another passage, another secret way that hadn't been there when he first came into the room. The house was not only changing the upper levels; it was also changing the foundations, making new paths and new ways to get stuck.

He looked into the dark and felt a cold realization come over him. His blueprints weren't maps; they were fossilized records of a past that Blackwood Manor was trying to erase. His professional knowledge and lifelong commitment to the principles of architecture were of no use here. He was like a doctor trying to treat a disease with medicines that only made it worse. The house was more than just a building; it was a mind, a malicious architect who loved breaking the rules of building, turning logic on its head, and trapping its residents in a maze that was not only made of stone and mortar, but also of their own slowly losing sanity. The architect's problem was no longer just a thought experiment; it was a terrifying reality that he was stuck in, with walls that were impossible to move.

Eleanor's Unsettling Visions

Eleanor found comfort in her charcoal and paper that was strange. It was a desperate, clawing comfort that came not from comfort but from a need to get rid of the suffocating fear that had become her constant companion. The manor was more than just a house; it was a presence, a huge, dark thing that seemed to breathe out a cloud of despair. Its strange architecture and eerie silences made it seem like it was alive. Her sketchpad, which used to be full of tentative landscapes and studies of light, was now full of growing darkness. The lines got bolder and more frantic, just like the shaking in her hands. She started to draw the house, not how it looked to them, but how it felt to her.

The windows, which used to be doors to the outside world, became empty, blank spaces in her drawings. They weren't just holes in a wall; they were hungry mouths with gaping maws that looked like they were swallowing the light. She didn't just draw the rafters as beams; she drew them as skeletal fingers that were brittle and sharp and reached down from the dark ceiling. The walls of Blackwood Manor seemed to writhe under her charcoal, which looked like twisted, suffering flesh that was groaning under an unseen weight. Every time she drew with the charcoal, it felt like she was confessing to the fear that was eating away at her. Thomas, who was too busy trying to bring order to the manor's chaos to care about her drawings, would only see an artist's morbid interest. He couldn't understand that her art had become a divining rod, digging deep into the manor's hidden depths and bringing to light its buried horrors.

It started off slowly, with a flicker at the edge of her vision. A shadow moving in the background, breaking away from the darkness of a hallway. At first, she thought it was just a trick of the light or a result of her own frayed nerves. But the glimpses kept coming, and they got stronger. These were not just figments of an overactive mind. They were shapes that were hard to see and seemed to come together from the air, but they disappeared as soon as she tried to focus on them. They were like breath on a cold mirror: there for a second, then gone, leaving only the cold behind.

She would be walking down a hallway, and the quiet of the house would make her feel like something was there, just out of sight. There was a small change in the air and a small change in the temperature. Her eyes would dart to the source, and for a heartbeat, she would see it: a tall, slender form, a figure cloaked in shadow, its features obscured, its presence radiating an ancient, palpable sorrow. Then it would be gone. Gone as if it had never been there.

These ghostly figures didn't just show up in the dark hallways. She saw them in the drawing room, where dust motes danced in the weak sunlight, making shapes in their swirling ballet. She saw them in the library—the real library, the one Thomas missed, the one that only lived on in his memories and his scattered blueprints. The air in the phantom library felt stale and wrong, and the figures seemed to stay longer, with their shadowy outlines clearer, as if the house's very essence was more concentrated there.

One afternoon, while she was drawing in the neglected conservatory, where the glass panes were thick with dirt and the only plants left were dead and dried up, she felt someone behind her. She turned, the charcoal ready to go on the paper. There was a woman standing next to a dead rose bush. She wore a long, flowing dress that seemed to soak up the little light that was there. Eleanor couldn't see her face clearly; it was just a blur of shadow. But she could feel the weight of her gaze, which made her feel very sad all the way to her bones. The woman raised a clear hand, not to say hello or threaten, but to show how deeply sad she was. Then she slowly faded into the shadows cast by the dying plants.

Eleanor's hands shook so much that she could hardly hold the charcoal. She knew, without a doubt that went beyond reason, that these were not hallucinations. They were things that happened in the past. Echoes. The house wasn't just a building made of stone and wood; it was a vessel full of the pain of the people who had lived there, and now it was sharing that pain with her. The open windows she drew were the dead people's empty eyes. The skeletal rafters were the bones of a past that wouldn't stay buried.

Thomas would gently say that these fleeting figures were caused by stress and the overwhelming nature of their situation when she tried to explain them. "It's the house playing tricks on you, Eleanor," he'd say, his voice full of worry that felt real but not enough. "It's the changes that make things confusing." "Focus on the real things, the plans, and what we can measure." But how could she measure the sadness that hung in the air? How could she draw the outlines of figures that appeared and disappeared? Her compass, like his, spun uselessly, but it wasn't pointing north or south; it was pointing to a past that was bleeding into the present.

She started to connect certain parts of the house with certain visions. Men often stood in the east wing, which now seemed to twist and lengthen with each hour that passed. Their faces were ghostly and etched with what looked like grim determination or maybe despair. They moved with a quiet purpose, as if they were still working on something they had forgotten. She sometimes saw children in the west wing, which had the study with the mysteriously changed window. They were ghostly shapes that moved quickly through the rooms, and their laughter was a ghostly echo that never quite reached her ears. They looked like they were having fun, but there was an unsettling stillness about their games, as if they weren't really happy.

The grand staircase, which had disappeared from the main hall, was a common place for her ghostly encounters. Here, she saw a kaleidoscope of shapes that made her think of times of greatness and times of sadness. Maybe a ghostly procession or a scene of people running away in fear. There was a lot of energy in the air around where the stairs should have been, and she could see them—shapeless shapes that seemed to shimmer and writhe, as if they were stuck between worlds.

Her drawings turned into a creepy diary. She drew the dark woman in the conservatory, capturing how unsettlingly still she was. She drew the people who were moving quickly through the hallways, their outlines blurred and unclear. The frantic energy of the drawings showed how hard they were to catch. She even tried to draw the kids, using a few quick, impressionistic lines to show how they looked. These weren't pictures for a kids' book; they were signs, visual signs of the manor's never-ending need for memory and pain.

She began to feel a strange connection with these ghosts. It wasn't exactly empathy, but they both felt like they were stuck. They were stuck in the house, and their lives or deaths were always echoing in their minds. And now, in a terrifying way, she and Thomas were also stuck in the house, forced to watch its ghostly residents. The house was showing itself, not through its changing architecture, but through the marks left behind by those who had been hurt inside. It was a dark confession, a sign of the pain that had been a part of Blackwood Manor's history for a long time.

One night, while Thomas carefully compared the manor's current size to its original blueprints, Eleanor sat by the fire in the drawing room. The fire cast moving shadows that looked like the people she had seen. She was drawing the outline of a specific hallway that had changed its length and angle for no apparent reason that morning. She felt a cold breath on her neck as she drew. She stopped moving, her charcoal floating above the paper. She turned her head slowly.

A man stood just behind her, his figure shimmering in the firelight. He was tall and broad-shouldered, and he wore clothes that were sad and out of date. Eleanor couldn't see his face, but she could feel a deep sense of regret coming from him, a deep sadness that seemed to come from his very being. He raised a ghostly hand, not toward her but toward the wall, as if he were pointing to something that wasn't there. Then, as if the effort of showing up had worn him out, he faded away, leaving behind a chill and the smell of wet earth.

Eleanor's heart raced against her ribs. She turned to look at the wall he had pointed to. It was a solid wall of dark wood panels that didn't stand out in any way. But she was sure, with a chill down her spine, that he had been pointing to a memory, a time and place where something important had happened. It could have been a door that used to be there, a secret passage, or even the place where something horrible happened. The house was not only changing its shape; it was also covering up its present reality with the ghosts of its past, making them relive their traumas and moments for all time.

She began to notice patterns in the ghosts, small links between the figures and the strange ways the house was built. The men in the east wing always seemed to be doing some kind of building or tearing down, and their ghostly movements were like the changes that were happening in the house. The kids in the west wing often looked like they were lost and looking for a way out when they were near rooms that had been sealed off or changed. The woman in the conservatory, who was so sad, seemed to show up when Eleanor was at her lowest point, as if the manor was sharing her own pain.

Her drawings stopped being about the people themselves and started being about the mood they created and the feelings they left behind. She drew the heavy sadness that weighed them down, the cold emptiness of their presence, and the silent screams that echoed in the empty spaces. The charcoal lines turned into dark smudges, and the paper itself seemed to soak up the darkness. She understood that her art was more than just a way to deal with her fear; it was also a way to talk to the ghost in the manor. It was a dark, unspoken conversation, a hesitant exchange of fear and hopelessness.

She started to realize that the house was a place where pain was stored, a huge, old memory bank. It wasn't just a place where ghosts lived; it was a ghost, a living thing made up of the pain of many years. And it was sharing that pain with her, leaving its dark past on her mind and making it hard for her to tell the difference between her own life and the ghostly echoes that haunted its halls. The big mouths she drew for windows weren't just scary pictures; they were the mouths of the house, telling stories of despair that were now getting into her very being. The house was hungry, and it was feeding on her fear, her sanity, and the very essence of her being. It used her art as a way to satisfy its never-ending, ghostly hunger.

The First Trap Sprung

There was an unspoken fear in the air of the manor, and Eleanor could feel the tension in her chest. Thomas, who was always practical, thought that the answer was to find a way to send out a signal, a desperate cry for help that could break the heavy silence of their gilded cage. He had been going over old schematics with a furrowed brow, muttering about wire gauges and signal strength. His voice was a low hum against the unsettling quiet. Eleanor, on the other hand, was becoming more and more interested in the edges of the house. Her charcoal was still her friend, and her sketches now showed not only ghostly figures but also the house itself as a bad force. She had seen it, a slow change that seemed to come from the plaster and stone themselves. The angles were never quite right, and the distances seemed to change in a way that made me uneasy.

Thomas said one afternoon, “I think I’ve found it.” His voice had a rare spark of hope that made Eleanor feel more uneasy than his usual resigned focus. He held up a faded blueprint and ran a dirty finger along a line. “This part here used to be the servants’ quarters. I think there was a small storage room, a pantry. It's marked here, just off the main hallway, not far from the... from where the stairs used to be. His voice broke for a moment, and the loss of their familiar path was a constant, painful wound. "If we could get to it, maybe there's an old external access point or at least a place where a radio antenna could be run without being obvious right away. Eleanor, give it a shot. We have to give everything a shot.

Eleanor nodded, and a knot of worry grew in her stomach. The "place where the stairs used to be" was now a big hole, a constant reminder of how unpredictable the house was. But Thomas's desperation was contagious, like a flickering ember in the dark. "I'll go with you," she said, her voice steadier than she felt.

"No, no," he said, showing a little bit of his old impatience. "Stay here." You know, keep an eye on things. I'll be quick. "That would change everything if I could find a way to get in touch." He smiled at her to reassure her, but his eyes, which were usually so clear and direct, showed a hint of fear. He then put on his old coat, which was a faded canvas that seemed to soak up the sadness of the manor. He walked out of the drawing room, and the heavy oak door closed behind him with a soft thud.

Eleanor watched him leave, and a tingle ran up her spine. The hallway he had walked down seemed to stretch out in front of her, the shadows getting darker and coming together. She picked up her sketchpad and charcoal, and a familiar sense of unease came over her. She started to draw the hallway, trying to show how creepy it was that the light seemed to fade away in its depths and how the walls seemed to lean in, as if they were listening.

Minutes felt like they would never end. The manor's silence, which usually made people feel uneasy, now felt alive with anticipation. Eleanor held her breath and strained her ears to hear any sound from Thomas. The grandfather clock in the hall ticked in a way that made the silence seem even more intense. Each tick was like a hammer blow against the silence. She could feel it: a change in the house's mood, a small tremor that ran through the floorboards, up her legs, and into her very core. She had learned to recognize this feeling: a sign of change, of something deep inside her changing.

Then it came. A muffled shout, then a loud, sharp clang. Thomas was the one. Eleanor's head shot up, and her heart raced. "Thomas?" She yelled, her voice a thin thread of sound in the vast emptiness. There was no answer. She quickly got up, and her sketchpad fell to the floor without her noticing. "Thomas!" She cried again, and her voice shook with fear.

She ran down the hallway, and her footsteps echoed in a scary way. The spot where Thomas had gone missing was now just a wall. A smooth, dark, polished wood paneling that looked just like the rest of the hallway. There wasn't a door. There was no sign that an entrance had ever been there. It was like the house had eaten him whole and left no trace.

"Thomas!" Eleanor's voice was full of fear and echoed off the hard surfaces of the manor. She ran her hands over the smooth wood in a panic, looking for any seam, latch, or other sign of the door that had been there just a few moments before. Nothing. The paneling was smooth, unbroken, and cold to the touch. She hit it over and over again, her fists hitting the hard surface in a desperate, pointless rhythm. "Thomas! Can you hear me? Where are you? "

There was an oppressive silence in response to her shouts. The house seemed to be holding its breath, like a predator watching its trapped prey. The air felt thicker, full of a triumphant evil. Eleanor fell to her knees, crying from fear and anger. The changing walls, the disappearing stairs, and the ghostly figures were not just random events. They were planned. The house wasn't just changing shape; it was doing something. It was a conscious, evil being, and it had just taken Thomas.

She remembered what he had said: that he was hopeful they could find a way to talk to each other and that they could find a way out. The house had heard him. It had sensed his intent and desire to break free, and it had acted quickly and brutally. He thought he was walking into a pantry, which could have saved his life, but the house sealed him inside, hiding the door he had used to get in.

Eleanor felt a deep, bone-chilling sadness wash over her. Thomas, her rock and logical counterpoint, was gone, swallowed up by the house's never-ending, ever-changing architecture. In this maze of craziness, she was completely alone. Her artistic sensibilities and efforts to capture the house's essence had been a way of gathering information about the enemy. But knowing didn't help.

She looked around the hallway, her eyes following the smooth lines of the wood paneling. It was too perfect and too the same. There was a faint shimmer in the air that she had thought was just a trick of the light or maybe a remnant of the spectral visions. Now she understood what it was: the house was changing its shape on purpose, adding and removing passages as it saw fit. The pantry had never been a pantry; it had been a trap that worked perfectly.

The realization was like a sharp knife against her mind. This wasn't just about getting lost; it was about being chased. The house was a living, breathing predator that played with them, kept them apart, and broke them down bit by bit. People saw Thomas's attempts to talk to the outside world as a direct threat, so the house took him out of the picture.

Her mind was spinning as she tried to find any thread of logic or order. She thought about the blueprints and how Thomas had measured everything so carefully. They were no longer useful. The house didn't follow the plans; it was the plans, always changing. The only map that mattered was the one that showed how evil it was and how it wanted to hurt people.

Eleanor made herself stand up slowly and with great effort. Her legs felt heavy, and her body shook with fear and a growing, desperate determination.

She couldn't afford to fall apart. If Thomas was stuck, she had to figure out how to get to him or at least figure out what had happened. She looked at the wall again, her eyes moving over its smooth surface. There had to be a way. The house was strong, but it was also a real thing, even though its shape changed.

She started to walk down the hallway, running her fingers along the walls, not just the paneling where Thomas had disappeared, but the whole hallway. She tapped, pushed, and listened. The silence was scary; it was a huge, mocking void. She thought about Thomas on the other side, maybe in a small, stuffy room where his shouts were getting weaker and his hope was fading. The thought drove her on, a deep, instinctive need to get to him.

There was a small mark on the base of the wall that looked out of place against the clean wood. She got down on her knees to look at it more closely. There was a small scratch, like something heavy had been dragged across the floor. Her heart was pounding against her ribs. This was a sign, a small flaw in the house's perfect lie. She looked for other signs on the floor as she followed the faint marks. The marks took her a few feet down the hallway to a part of the wall that looked like the rest of it.

But as she got closer, she felt a small change in the air and a faint vibration under her feet. It was so quiet that it sounded like the hum of an engine far away. She put her ear against the wood. Nothing. But the vibration didn't stop. She started to tap the wall slowly and carefully, listening for any change in the sound. Most of the wall made a strong, dull thud. But at one point, about chest height, the sound was a little different, a little more hollow, as if there were a hole behind it.

Hope, a weak and unwelcome guest, flickered inside her. She pushed on the spot, then again, harder. Nothing. She looked for a seam or a hidden catch, but the wood stayed stubbornly smooth. She was angry, but she wouldn't give up. She thought of the ghostly man who had pointed to the wall in the drawing room, his gesture pointing to something that wasn't there. Did Thomas find something like that? A secret mechanism?

Eleanor started to carefully look around the area for anything that might set her off. A loose floorboard, a strange knot in the wood, or anything else that broke up the boring perfection. She ran her fingers over the beautiful carvings on the wainscoting, looking for any bumps or other problems. She saw a small, decorative rosette carved into the wood near where she had heard the hollow sound. It was a little off, but it was such a small detail that anyone who wasn't looking for flaws wouldn't have seen it.

With shaky fingers, she reached out and gently pushed the rosette. There was a soft click that was almost too quiet to hear. Then, with a low groan of an old machine, a part of the wall slid in, revealing a narrow, dark opening. That was the way into the pantry.

She felt so much better that her knees went weak. But soon after, a new wave of fear hit. Thomas was in there. And the house had tried to keep him inside, away from the rest of the world. She looked into the dark, and her eyes had a hard time adjusting. The air that came out of the opening was cold, still, and had a faint metallic taste. It smelled like dust, rot, and something else… something that made me feel uneasy, like the smell of old blood.

"Thomas?" She whispered into the void, and her voice was barely heard. She stepped carefully into the opening, her hand outstretched to touch the rough, cold stone walls of the pantry. It was small, crowded, and completely dark. She could only hear her own ragged breathing. Behind her, the door and the part of the wall that had slid open stood ajar, a dark mouth calling her to go deeper into the unknown.

Then she heard it. A soft whimper came from the back of the pantry. It was Thomas. He was still alive.

"Thomas, it's me, Eleanor!" " she yelled, her voice breaking with emotion. "I'm here!" I found the door! "

A choked sob answered her, and then a weak voice said, "Eleanor…thank God."

She stumbled deeper into the pantry, her hands brushing against empty shelves that were covered in a thick layer of dust. The space was so small that only one person could stand in it. She could feel the walls closing in on her, like a suffocating hug. She felt her way through the dark, her heart racing with both relief and fear. The house was almost successful. It had lured Thomas into this trap so that it could keep him hidden, forgotten, and maybe even starve him or do something worse.

She saw him leaning against the back wall, breathing in a shallow and uneven way. When she got to him, his face was pale and drawn, and his eyes were wide with the same fear she felt. He was mumbling things that didn't make sense, and his words were a mix of fear and confusion.

"It… it closed," he said, his voice hoarse. "Just… slammed shut. And then there were the walls. Eleanor, they were moving. I could feel them squeezing in. "I thought…" He stopped talking and shivered violently.

Eleanor knelt next to him and put her arms around him. She could feel the tremor in his body and the cold sweat on his skin. "It's okay, Thomas. You are now safe. I found the way. "We're leaving,"

But as she talked, she felt it again: the small change in the air, the almost imperceptible vibration that had signaled the opening of the secret door. She turned around and looked at the door, her heart racing. The part of the wall was slowly and quietly closing. The soft click of the mechanism sounded like a death knell.

"No!" Eleanor screamed and got up quickly. "Thomas, we need to hurry!" "

She pushed him forward, telling him to go toward the smaller space. He fell, his legs weak, but his instinct to survive pushed him on. Eleanor pushed him through just as the wall was about to seal itself off for good. She lunged after him, her body scraping against the rough stone, and her fingers frantically searching for a grip.

She felt a sharp pain when the edge of the closing wall hit her arm, and then she was through, falling to the floor of the hallway next to Thomas. The hidden door closed with a soft, final thump, leaving no sign that it had ever been there. The hallway was once again a smooth, polished wood floor. It was as if the pantry and its prisoner had never existed.

Thomas lay on the floor, his chest heaving and his eyes wide with fear and disbelief. Eleanor looked at him, then at the wall that didn't move, and her breath caught in her throat. The house had not only set a trap, but it had also shown its true self. It was a thinking predator that could change its own structure to trap its prey. The attempt to talk and the desperate search for a way out had not led to an opportunity, but to a deadly, architectural trap. They weren't just lost in a house; they were trapped inside a living, evil being that was playing a game with their lives. The whispers of ghostly figures, the walls that moved, and the passages that disappeared were all signs of its will, its never-ending need for power and pain. And now they knew, with terrifying certainty, that it was working against them.

Chapter 3: The Growing Hunger

A Paucity of Provisions

The shelves, which used to show how smart they were, now made fun of them by getting emptier and emptier. The pantry, which used to be full of preserved fruits, jars of pickles, and sacks of flour, was now a picture of food that was disappearing. It wasn't a slow loss or a steady decrease that could be explained by their small meals. It was instead a creepy, almost instant disappearing act. Eleanor would count the jars of preserved peaches and carefully write down how many there were in her head. By the next morning, however, one, then two, then three jars were missing for no apparent reason. Thomas, always the practical one, first thought it was because of a mistake or bad memory in the manor's stuffy atmosphere. But he couldn't explain how many people had gone missing. A whole sack of potatoes, enough to last them for weeks, was gone without a trace. There was no spilled dirt, no chewed-up pieces, just an empty space where it had been.

This ghostly lack was also affecting the larder. The cured hams, which were hung up to keep their delicious flavor, looked like they were getting smaller and smaller, and their meaty girth was going down at an unnatural rate. The cheese wheels, which had been solid and substantial, now looked a lot like loaves of bread that had been left out in the sun. They were dry and shrunken, and the creamy insides were gone, leaving only a dry, crumbly emptiness. It was like the food was losing its very essence, leaving behind only empty shells.

"It's not possible," Thomas said softly one night, his voice full of confused anger as he looked into the empty larder. He held up a jar of pickled onions that was only half full. The last few were floating sadly in their vinegar brine. "We might have eaten three yesterday." This… this is less than half. And the bread… I swear, Eleanor, there was a whole loaf on the counter this morning.

Eleanor nodded, feeling a cold knot in her stomach. She had tried to ignore it and make sense of the differences, but the proof was too strong. The house wasn't just watching them suffer; it was also making them hungry. The fact that their supplies were running out so quickly made it seem like something more than just decay or an accident. It felt like they were doing it on purpose, like they were hunting. The house was eating up their supplies, not because they needed them, but because it had some hidden, insatiable hunger of its own. It was as if the walls were eating the food and getting stronger and more solid with each bite that disappeared.

The air in the manor was already full of fear, but now it was also full of hunger.

Their small rations were getting even smaller. At first, the disappearances shocked them, but now they were determined to ration their supplies and make them last as long as possible. Every piece of bread was now a planned sacrifice, and every piece of dried fruit was a valuable treasure. They started to cut their food into smaller and smaller pieces, and the act of eating became a painful reminder of how desperate they were getting.

Eleanor stared at the last jars of preserves, tracing the cool glass with her fingers. She felt a pang of sadness in her heart. These weren't just things to eat; they were memories of a time before the house showed its true colors, when there was real abundance in the world. She remembered the orchard in the fall, when the smell of ripe apples filled the air and the fruit felt good in her hands as she helped her mother get them ready for the winter. Now, those jars were getting smaller, and the bright colors were dulled by the heavy darkness. Each one was a sign of what they were losing.

Thomas, who was a scientist, had started to carefully record the disappearances. He had started a ledger that showed how many of each item there were at the start of each day and how many there were at the end of the day. His neat, accurate handwriting was very different from the phenomenon, which was chaotic and hard to explain.

"Look at this, Eleanor," he said one afternoon, his voice strained, and pointed to a page in his ledger. "The cheese. We had a full wheel that weighed at least ten pounds. At 8 AM yesterday, I wrote it down as exactly 10 pounds and 2 ounces. This morning, 9 pounds, 8 ounces. That's more than half a pound gone in one night. We didn't touch it, though. Not a sliver. He tapped the page with his finger, making his knuckles turn white. "And the flour." We lose almost two pounds every day, and we only used a cupful to bake that small loaf. "Like the house itself is hungry," it seems.

The realization hung in the air between them, a chilling echo of what Thomas had said. The house wanted food. Their supplies were running low, but that wasn't just because they were stuck there. The entity that held them captive used them as fuel. The house was stealing their food and getting stronger with each stolen bite and crumb that disappeared. It was a dark sign of what the house really wanted, a clear sign of its never-ending hunger.

The manor's silence, which had once been a passive fear, now seemed to throb with a quiet, predatory pleasure. It sounded like a predator eating or a parasite getting food from its host. Eleanor couldn't help but be fascinated by the empty shelves. She didn't just see that there was no food there; she also imagined the house's unseen mouth eating it. The empty spaces weren't empty; they were battlefields, lost lands in a war they were slowly, but surely, losing.

They started to talk about food in quiet voices, as if just saying the word could make it go away faster. The thought of a meal, which used to be a simple comfort, now made them anxious, a prelude to the inevitable disappointment of finding out. They would make a small amount, their hands shaking a little, and their eyes would scan the area for any sign of the house's involvement. And most of the time, when they came back to get their small meal, part of it would be gone, a ghostly theft that left them with a gnawing emptiness in their stomachs and a deeper fear in their hearts.

The spoilage was another strange thing that happened. The food that was left often rotted quickly and in an unnatural way. If you put a freshly picked apple on a stone slab and kept it cool, it would turn brown and mealy in just a few hours, and its skin would get an unhealthy shine. There would be a small piece of bread, carefully wrapped to keep it fresh, that was covered in a fuzzy, gray mold that seemed to spread too quickly. It was as if the house was making sure that the food was inedible and unusable, which sped up their descent into starvation even more.

Eleanor whispered one night, "It's like it's making fun of us," as she pushed away a plate with a single, shriveled fig. "It takes what it wants and then poisons the rest."

Thomas sighed and ran a hand through his messy hair. "Or maybe the spoilage is a side effect of its energy. No matter what it is, it's eating us from the inside out. It's not just that we don't have food; the house is actively keeping us from getting it.

The rationing turned into a sad routine. They carefully counted every last bit of food they had left, down to the last grain of rice and piece of dried meat. The sun no longer rose and set to mark the days; instead, the amount of food they had left in their stores did. Hunger was always there, a dull ache that slowly turned into a sharp, nagging pain. It changed how they thought, how they felt, and even how well they could focus. Eleanor's sketches' bright colors started to fade, and the charcoal lines got weaker and less sure. Thomas's careful math in his ledger became less accurate as the gnawing in his stomach made it hard for him to think clearly.

They began to dream about food, vivid, tempting dreams of feasts and plenty that made them wake up feeling even more hopeless. It was a cruel torment for them to see how different their waking lives were from their subconscious desires. Eleanor dreamed of juicy, ripe berries that tasted sweet on her tongue, but when she woke up, her mouth was dry and dusty. Thomas dreamed of huge fields of wheat that were golden and swaying in a light breeze. This was very different from the empty shelves in their prison.

The house seemed to enjoy their pain. The slight changes in its structure, the ghostly whispers, and the disappearing passages were all signs of its power and control. And now, the slow, sneaky loss of their food supply was another weapon in its arsenal, a way to mentally torture them and break their spirits. It was a starvation of the body, but more importantly, it was a starvation of hope. Every empty shelf and every spoiled piece of food showed that the house had won, and they were a grim sign of the price it would have to pay in the end. Their small supplies ran out, just like the house's never-ending hunger. This was a chilling sign of what it really wanted: not just their food, but their very essence, their will to live. The rationing wasn't just a practical move; it was a desperate plea, a useless attempt to outlast something that seemed to get stronger from their lack.

The Scent of Decay

The smell. It had started out as a small problem, like a faint smell of dampness in the cellar or a hint of mildew in the east wing. Now, it was a thick, suffocating fog that covered the whole manor. It was no longer just happening in one place; it was everywhere, hitting their senses all the time. Eleanor was breathing through her mouth in a useless attempt to get rid of the thick, sticky air. Thomas's senses were dulled by hunger and despair, but he could still smell the strong smell that kept reminding him of how bad the house was.

It was the smell of decay, but not the clean, dead decay of things that have been left alone for too long. This was a living rot, a lively decay that gave off an unsettling energy. It smelled like wet earth, but not from outside; it came from inside the walls, as if the foundations were crying out rich, black soil. It smelled like still water, not from a broken pipe, but from a hidden, internal source of decay. And underneath it all, there was a low, sneaky undertone of something that wasn't quite rot or mold, but an old, unidentifiable smell of hunger and voracious eating.

They realized with growing horror that this was the house's breath. Its breath was this horrible exhalation, and its inhale was the quiet siphoning of their dwindling supplies. The smell was a sign of its vital essence and proof of its ancient, never-ending hunger. It got into everything: their clothes, their hair, and even their tongues, which tasted bitter after eating it. They tried to hide it by burning dried herbs, but all that did was make the smell even worse by adding a sickeningly sweet, acrid smoke that fought with the smell that was already there. They opened the windows, but the air that came in from the overgrown gardens wasn't any cleaner. It had its own smells of overripe plants and the distant promise of rot, which were less strong but still unsettling.

Eleanor scrubbed her hands so hard that they bled and got raw, but the smell of decay still seemed to be there, like a greasy film on her skin. Even in the short times of quiet she could find, she could smell it. It was like a wave that made her recoil and gasp for air that was never really clean. It was like being stuck inside a huge, rotting organism, and the smell of this horrible perfume made its inner workings clear.

Thomas, who was trying to put the unexplainable into categories with his scientific mind, called it a "bio-chemical miasma," a complicated mix of organic decay sped up by an unknown outside force. He thought it was a result of the house using up energy, a visible and smelly sign of its constant feeding. "It's like a predator after a kill," he said one night, his voice hoarse from the dry, hot air. "The smell of its food, which lingered in the air, was a promise of what it had eaten and what it would eat again."

The decay wasn't just a smell; it also started to show up in other ways. When food wasn't just disappearing, it was going bad faster than normal, which was hard to explain. Within hours, a crisp apple with taut, shiny skin would get dark, bruised spots and its flesh would get soft and mealy. A loaf of bread that had just been baked the day before would be covered in a thick, soft mold. The texture that used to be so inviting was now a fuzzy, strange landscape of gray and green. It was as if the house was actively ruining their food because it didn't like what they were giving it, making sure that even the scraps it left behind were not edible.

One morning, Eleanor found a pear that had been half-eaten on the kitchen counter. It was whole the night before. Now, it was a dried-up, blackened shell, and the flesh that was left was a dark, unappetizing pulp. It wasn't just the rot; it was the way it had rotted. The speed, the strange change in color, and the way the skin seemed to cling to the rotting flesh as if it didn't want to let go of its prize. It was a joke. The house had eaten all it could and then ruined the rest, leaving behind a foul-smelling proof of its power.

"It's like it's giving us scraps, but poisoned scraps," she said in a shaky voice, pointing to the rotting fruit. "It's not enough to eat, but it's enough to remind us of what we're losing."

Thomas, whose face was thin and his eyes were dark from lack of sleep, nodded sadly. He had carefully recorded the rates of spoilage and compared them to normal rates of decay. The numbers were so high that they were impossible. He thought to himself, "The cellular breakdown is happening at a rate that suggests an internal catalytic agent," his voice a dry rustle. "Or, to put it another way, the house is speeding up the breakdown. It's not just eating the food; it's making it toxic. Eleanor, it's a planned act of starvation. "Not just by lack, but by pollution."

The hunger that had once been a dull ache was now a constant, sharp pain that echoed through their bodies. It changed the way they thought, felt, and saw the world around them. Sounds were far away and colors were dull. Their dreams, which used to be a safe place, were now a cruel torment, full of vivid, painful images of feasts and plenty. When they woke up, they were faced with the harsh, dry reality of their empty stomachs and the sickening smell of decay. Eleanor dreamed of a big harvest, with strawberries that had been warmed by the sun and tasted sweet on her tongue. When she woke up, her mouth was dry and tasted like dust and despair. Thomas dreamed of huge fields of golden, ripe grain that were ready to be harvested. This was very different from the empty shelves and the smell of rot that filled their waking hours.

They started to notice the decay all around them. The shadows in the corners of the rooms looked like they were getting darker and moving around in ways that weren't clear. The dust motes that danced in the slivers of sunlight that came through the dirty windows seemed to come together to make shapes that were there one moment and gone the next. The house itself seemed to be breathing this decay, letting it out into their lungs and souls.

The smell was always there, like a psychic weight that stole their strength and will. It was the smell of the house's lifeblood, which came from the fact that it was a parasite. It was the smell of its ancient hunger, a hunger that had been satisfied for hundreds, maybe thousands, of years but was now awake and focused on them. They weren't just prisoners; they were livestock that were being fattened and then slowly and carefully killed. The smell of decay was the smell of their death, a sickly sweet scent that promised a long, painful end.

Every breath was a reminder. A reminder of how hungry they were, how little food they had left, and how the house was always on the hunt. It was always there, a physical presence that showed them what had caught them. The air was thick with it, heavy and oppressive, like a blanket made of the smell of decay and an ancient, never-ending hunger. It got into their bones, made them feel cold to the core, and whispered evil promises of a certain, disgusting end. Not only were they trapped by walls and locked doors, but also by the air they had to breathe, which smelled like decay and was the breath of their prison. It was a hunger that went beyond food; it was for their very essence, their energy, and their lives. The smell was its messenger, its promise that would last, and its foul proof.

Whispers Become Voices

People used to think that the old manor's groans were just the sound of old wood settling or the wind blowing through broken windows, but now they sound more sinister. They didn't sound like simple complaints about the building anymore; they sounded like a huge, sleeping thing waking up. Eleanor stopped and tried to figure out what the symphony of creaks and groans that filled the house meant. She was desperately trying to find order, a pattern, anything to hold on to as the tide of unease rose. What had started as a faint, unsettling murmur, a barely perceptible undertone beneath the silence, was steadily growing in clarity, coalescing into something more deliberate, more invasive.

Thomas, who was always practical, didn't pay much attention to her growing worry at first. "It's the acoustics, Eleanor," he'd said, his voice weak from hunger and tiredness. "The house has a lot of strange angles and empty spaces. Sound travels in a strange way. It's just making the natural sounds louder. But even as he talked, his eyes kept darting to the dark corners, and his ears twitched at the smallest noise. The hunger that was gnawing at him and the heavy atmosphere were starting to break down his scientific detachment. He was also hearing it, but he tried to call it anything other than an auditory hallucination.

After that, the whispers got louder. They changed from unclear moans to something that was definitely a voice, but not in any language that people speak. It was a soft, hissing sound, like dry leaves skittering across stone or the hiss of a snake that wasn't there. The whispers seemed to come from the very walls of the house, from the grain of the wood in the wainscoting, from the plaster dust that fell from the ceilings, and from the depths of the worn-out carpets. They were sneaky, like secrets shared in the dark, creeping into their minds in a way that made them feel very close.

"It... it speaks," Eleanor said one night, her hand flying to her throat as a very clear string of whispers seemed to wrap around her from the fireplace. It wasn't the sound of burning embers or the wind whistling up the chimney. This was not the same. It was a quick, almost breathless string of syllables in a language that didn't have any vowels but was full of meaning that she couldn't understand but knew instinctively.

Thomas, bent over a fraying tapestry and tracing the faded threads with his fingers as if looking for a hidden clue, suddenly looked up. His face, thin and lined with worry, showed a flash of what looked like fear. "What did you say?"

"The walls," she said in a low voice, her eyes wide and fixed on the patterned wallpaper. "They're... whispering."

He got up slowly, and his joints made a series of small clicks that sounded like the house's own internal conversation. He went to the wall and put his ear against the cool, old paper. For a long time, all they could hear was their ragged breathing and the wind howling far away. Then he pulled back, and a muscle in his jaw twitched. "I hear something." Like noise. Or a weak radio signal."

"It's not static, Thomas," Eleanor said, her voice getting more and more desperate. "It's a language." It's telling us things.

The whispers, which used to come and go, now seemed to make a constant sound tapestry throughout the manor. They were strongest in the middle of the night, when the house was quietest and their own defenses were weakest. They would weave through their dreams, turning into clear, though scary, statements. Eleanor heard stories about old rituals, blood and shadow pacts, and a thirst that had been sleeping for hundreds of years but was now awake and couldn't be satisfied. The whispers talked about a "tithe," which was a price to pay or a sacrifice that the house itself wanted.

Eleanor had a dream one night about a huge, echoing room that was lit by flickering torchlight. Figures shrouded in darkness did a ritual, and their chants sounded like the low, hissing whispers she heard when she was awake. In the middle of the room, a being of pure shadow writhed. Its shape was hard to make out, but it gave off a lot of power. And then, an old, gravelly voice spoke directly into her head, "The house wants what it is owed." The body is weak, but the spirit is a feast once it is broken. They are food. They are the tenth. She woke up with a strangled scream, her body covered in a cold sweat, and the voice still ringing in her ears.

Thomas, too, was bothered by the ghostly conversation. His dreams were full of math problems and strange scientific facts that turned into something strange and scary. He saw pictures of energy flows that turned into sigils and molecular structures that changed into symbols of a powerful, ancient force that no one knows about. He heard the whispers picking apart his regrets, failures, and deepest fears. They talked about the accident that had ruined his research, the money he had lost, and the coworkers who had looked down on him. They made his guilt and self-doubt worse by turning them into huge, real things that clawed at him in the dark.

"It knows," he told Eleanor one morning, his voice hoarse. He had been looking at a broken window, and his reflection looked strange and scary. "It knows what scares us. It's using our own minds against us.

The whispers, which had once sounded like one voice, started to break apart and carry personal insults. Eleanor heard them whispering her name and turning it into accusations. They talked about how impulsive and proud she was and the choices that had brought them to this lonely place. They talked in hushed tones about the guilt she still felt over a fight she had with her sister when they were kids. The fight ended in silence that lasted until her sister died too soon. "You never said you were sorry," the whispers hissed as they crept out of the dark. "You let your pride get in the way. The house now wants a bigger apology. "More of a sacrifice."

Thomas heard them making fun of his intelligence and his scientific theories, which were now just childish nonsense. They made him think of his father's disappointed voice and harsh words about failure and not being good enough. The whispers, which seemed to come from the dust motes dancing in the little sunlight, said, "Your logic is wrong." "Your understanding is not complete. Thomas, you're a fraud. And this house… this house knows you. It sees how empty you are. It wants it.

This sneaky personalization of the whispers started to cause problems between them. Eleanor, who was already prone to strong emotions, became more and more suspicious of Thomas's silences. She thought he was listening to the whispers that talked about her weaknesses when she saw him staring off into space with a furrowed brow. "What are they saying?" she would ask, her voice full of anger. "What's going on with you?"

Thomas was tired of Eleanor's growing paranoia because he was so troubled by his own problems and hunger. He thought she didn't trust him or their ability to survive when he saw her carefully checking the locks and her eyes darting at every shadow. "Those are just sounds, Eleanor," he would say, losing his cool. "Or our minds could be playing tricks. We need to concentrate to find a way out. Not to give in to the fear they're trying to spread."

"Fear?" she would say, her voice shaking. "Or truth? You throw out things that your equations can't explain so quickly. But Thomas, this is too much for your science. This is… alive. And it's trying to tear us apart. "It's trying to get us to fight each other."

The whispers seemed to enjoy the growing gap. They would repeat Eleanor's doubts back to her, making her even more unsure of Thomas's calmness. "He doesn't get it," they'd hiss from the floorboards below her. "He doesn't understand how deep this hunger is. He hides his fear, but it grows. He will give up. And when he breaks, he won't bother you anymore.

At the same time, they would feed Thomas's anger at Eleanor's perceived craziness. "She's coming apart," the whispers would say from the dark corners of the room. "Her fear is spreading. If she doesn't trust you, you can't save her. "Her craziness will be your downfall."

The line between what the house said and their own sanity falling apart became less and less clear. Were these voices really coming from the old manor, a sign of its parasitic mind? Or were they just the broken, desperate echoes of their own minds, broken by being alone, hungry, and scared of what was happening to them? The house seemed to get stronger with every seed of doubt and paranoia they planted in each other. The whispers weren't just words; they were poison that went straight into their fragile minds to break their bond, separate them, and make them easier targets.

Eleanor started to think of Thomas's attempts to do scientific research as a way of denying reality, a desperate hold on a rational world that no longer existed in these walls. She only heard the desperate, empty words of a man who didn't want to face the supernatural horror that was all around them when he talked about checking the air quality or the strength of some beams. "You can't measure this, Thomas," she'd say, her voice full of despair that was almost hysterical. "You can't make a graph or chart of its hunger or intentions. It's very old. It's not right. And you're still trying to act like it's just "bad plumbing."

On the other hand, Thomas saw Eleanor's growing dependence on her gut feelings and her willingness to see every creak as a message as a sign that the house was getting to her. He was afraid that her crazy ideas and increasingly frantic claims that the house was evil and aware of its own existence were not insights but delusions. "Eleanor, please," he begged, his voice strained. "We have to think logically. We need to come up with a logical answer. These whispers are a sign that we are stressed and hungry. "You're not imagining them; they're not real."

"And what if they are?" she would ask, her eyes burning with a desperate fire. "What if this is how it talks to us? Of letting us know what it wants? You'd rather believe we're both going crazy than admit that this house might be alive because you're so afraid to admit you don't know everything. And hungry."

The whispers seemed to get stronger and clearer as the tension grew. They didn't just hint at threats anymore; they said them. "The pact is unbreakable," they hissed from the shadows of the grand staircase. "The thirst never ends." You have to pay the tithe. One has to break, and the other will eat. The words hung in the air, heavy and hard to breathe, each syllable a hammer blow against the fragile structure of their shared sanity. They were stuck not only by the manor's walls, but also by its invisible, sneaky tendrils of power, which used their deepest fears and their shared past as weapons. The whispers were no longer just sounds; they were the ones who were going to kill them, carefully breaking down their trust, hope, and even their grip on reality. The house wasn't just eating their food; it was eating them from the inside out, one whispered doubt, one shared fear, and one broken thought at a time.

A Flicker of Life

The conservatory, which used to be a lively place full of the smell of wet earth and strange flowers, had turned into a tomb. Eleanor found it one morning when the first light of day came through the dirty windows and showed her a scene of complete despair. The beautiful plants that had once stood up to the manor's oppressive atmosphere were now in sad piles, their leaves brown and brittle, crumbling to dust at the slightest touch. The bright greens had faded, leaving behind a sickly, even pale color. The beautiful orchids, with petals that looked like painted silk, had shriveled into paper-thin husks, and their once-beautiful blooms were now drooping and broken. The philodendrons' wide leaves, which used to open up with a lot of life, were now curled inwards, dried out, and dead, as if they had been wrung dry of every drop of water.

It wasn't a slow decline; it was an instant death. The bright ferns that had fallen from hanging baskets were now a tangled mess of brown threads, and their feathery fronds were turning to dust. The proud, tall bird of paradise, with its fiery flowers that stood for their everlasting hope, now looked thin and skeletal, with its leaves drooping like torn flags. Even the tough succulents, which are known for being strong, didn't show this kind of strength. Their thick leaves were wilted and sunken, and their flesh was see-through and rotting. It was as if a cruel, unseen hand had swept through the glasshouse, taking away all signs of life and leaving behind only the shells of what had once been alive. The air, which used to be full of the sweet, sickly smell of flowers, now had a faint, acrid smell of death, like a sad breath of stolen life. Eleanor ran a shaky finger along the stem of a dead rose. The thorns were sharp and brittle. The petals, which used to be a deep red, were now a dull, dusty maroon that stuck to the stem like dried blood. She felt a deep sense of loss, a grief that went beyond the plants being destroyed. It was a clear and undeniable sign of the manor's insatiable hunger, which went beyond the small amounts of food they had.

Thomas came into the empty room because he heard Eleanor's choked gasp. He, too, was shocked by how quickly the decay happened. "It's impossible," he said softly, his scientific mind having a hard time making sense of the proof in front of him. He picked up a leaf that had fallen and turned it over in his hands. It fell apart into dust almost right away, as if time had sped up its decay by a thousand times. "There's no visible blight or pest problem that could explain this. It feels like something is actively draining them. He looked around, and his eyes moved over the empty land where plants had died. "This isn't just neglect, Eleanor. This is... eating. The word hung in the air, a chilling echo of the whispers that now seemed to come from the air they breathed. He had thought about the manor's strange energy patterns and gravitational anomalies, but this... This was something much more basic and scary. It was life itself being eaten up in a planned way.

The emptiness wasn't just in the glasshouse. The ivy that had been clinging to the weathered stone walls of the manor for decades seemed to be giving up. Eleanor first noticed it on her morning rounds. It was a creeping feeling of unease that made her skin crawl. Parts of the ivy that used to be a thick, green carpet now looked thin and dead, with the leaves curling and turning brown. The tendrils, which had once aggressively snaked their way over every available surface, seemed to be pulling back, retracting from the stone as if recoiling from a burning touch. It was as if the plant's very life force was being sucked out, leaving it gasping for food. The parts that were still stuck to the walls looked pale and sickly. Their bright green color had faded to a dull, bruised olive.

Thomas, who was keeping careful notes of every strange thing he saw, saw it too. He was checking the mortar in one of the outer walls for signs of structural weakness when he noticed that the ivy was pulling back in a strange way. "Look," he said, pointing to a spot where the tendrils seemed to have purposely pulled away from the stone, leaving behind bare, gray spots. "It's not just dying, Eleanor. It's moving away. It is actively avoiding contact. He touched a leaf that was shriveled up, and it turned to a fine, dusty powder under his finger. "This is... amazing. The plant is really shriveling up. Like the stone is losing its life force. He stopped for a moment, his brow furrowing in thought. "Or more like, as if the stone itself is doing the leaching." It was clear and very disturbing that the manor was not just a dead building; it was an active, parasitic being that sucked life from its surroundings.

The plants in the conservatory were wilting, and the ivy was pulling back. These were more than just changes in the environment; they were signs that the manor was getting hungrier. It was a hunger that went beyond food; it was a hunger for life itself. Eleanor felt a deep sense of fear wash over her. She knew with a chilling certainty that the house was a predator. It had drawn them in not with a direct, obvious threat, but with a slow, sneaky consumption. It ate the very essence of living things, leaving behind a dead, empty shell. The plants that were dying were a silent, grim warning and a clear sign of how bad things were for them. What would stop the manor from doing the same thing to them if it could easily kill the hardy ivy and the tough plants in the conservatory? The house wasn't just falling apart; it was alive, breathing, and eating, and they were its unwilling food. The whispers, which had seemed like nothing more than auditory hallucinations or signs of their own fears, now had a terrifying new meaning. They were the voice of this hunger, the quiet words of a power that was actively and purposefully taking life from everything it could reach. The realization was like a heavy weight that made them feel like their worst fears had come true. They weren't just stuck in an old house; they were stuck in the belly of a beast, and its hunger was growing.

Thomas, always the scientist, started to come up with ideas about how this life-draining event worked. He thought about localized energy fields, a kind of weak radiation, or maybe even a biological agent that the house gave off to break down cell structures and soak up the energy that was released. He carefully put the dried leaves he had collected into specimen bags and was determined to find a logical explanation, even if it was very strange. But even as he carefully recorded the dying plants, a deep-seated fear began to creep into his scientific detachment. He was getting more and more tired, a deep, bone-deep fatigue that no amount of rest could help. His skin felt dry and papery, and his movements were slow. He stared at his hands and saw that they were losing color and becoming slightly transparent, just like the plants that were dying. Was it just the hunger and lack of good food, or was the house's effect more sneaky, reaching even them in a parasitic way? The idea made him shiver with fear. He tried to make sense of it by blaming it on stress and not eating enough, but the dying conservatory and the ivy that was slowly disappearing around him told him a much scarier truth.

Eleanor, on the other hand, didn't want to know why things happened. She had accepted that the house was alive and wanted to hurt her. The wilting plants weren't a scientific curiosity to her, they were a confession. The house was telling the truth about its hunger and need. She saw it in the way the dead sunflowers' heads hung down, the way the wilting roses' stems broke, and the way the ivy seemed to pull away from the walls it had once hugged. It was a silent, desperate cry for food, a primal scream for life. She started to feel a strange connection to the dying plants, as if they were all victims. She could also feel the house's slow drain, which was slowly taking away her own energy. At first, the whispers were about their fears and insecurities, but now they seem to have changed. They have a new undertone of excitement and a hint of what is to come. They talked about "giving back what has been taken," "sacrifice," and "renewal." They suggested that the plants' life force was just a warm-up, a first offering to the manor's true, insatiable hunger.

Eleanor stood in front of the big, dark oak doors of the manor one night as the sky turned purple and gray. She ran her hand over the smooth, cool wood and felt a deep sadness rising inside her. It felt so much like the dying plants, which were full of old, dormant life but somehow empty, as if their essence had been drained away. She thought that the manor got its strength from the ground beneath it and the air around it, and then it turned that stolen life inward to feed its own never-ending hunger. She thought that the ivy had always been a sign of strength, of how life won't give up. Its retreat showed that even nature's strength has limits when faced with such a deep, unnatural hunger. The conservatory was a hothouse of stolen life. Its lively inhabitants were now just dried-up shells, their energy sucked up by the manor's never-ending hunger.

Thomas felt a new wave of fear as he watched Eleanor quietly think. It was very disturbing that she accepted the manor's evil nature, even though it might have been a form of psychological surrender. He wanted to believe that there was a scientific reason for this, a way to fight it with logic and reason. But the plants that were dying were a strong argument against science. They were a clear and undeniable sign that the house was taking life. He saw his own reflection in a dusty window. His face was thin and his eyes were sunken. He didn't look like a man fighting for his life; he looked more like a man who was slowly losing his very essence. The whispers sounded like they were making fun of him and making him weaker. "The house is not just a building," they seemed to hiss from the dying leaves of a potted fern he had brought inside. "It is a hunger. And you, Thomas, are the next thing it eats. He flinched and looked away from his own scary reflection. The house was like a parasite, and it was eating everything, even the souls of the people who lived there. It didn't just eat life; it used it as fuel to keep itself alive, to get stronger, and to ask for more. The empty conservatory and the dying ivy were just the beginning of a much scarier story that would end with the house being destroyed.

The Cold Embrace

There was always a chill in the air at Blackwood Manor, a dampness that made the stone walls feel sad and seeped into the worn-out tapestries. This time, though, it was different. It was a cold that gnawed at me, a cold hug that seemed to come from the very bones of the house. It had started slowly, a few weeks after they got there, with a slight drop in the temperature that Thomas, with his scientific pragmatism, had blamed on the manor's age and poor insulation. He kept himself busy with drafts, sealing gaps, and getting the old heating system to work better. But his efforts were useless, like trying to melt a glacier with a candle. The cold got worse, and it felt like a real thing, like a ghostly snake wrapping around them.

It was most clear in the newer parts of the manor, where Eleanor had found the strange rooms and hallways that seemed to appear and disappear at the house's will. These were the places where the cold was a real pain. When they went into these redesigned areas, it was like stepping into a tomb. The temperature dropped suddenly and violently, stealing their breath and shaking their bones. Even with the roaring fires in the main hearths, the warmth seemed to be unable to reach these annexes because they were so cold. Eleanor was always shaking, and her teeth were chattering even though she was sweating from trying to look calm. Her fingers were always numb, and her toes hurt from the cold that felt like it was freezing her from the inside out. She wore layers of wool and wrapped herself in blankets, but the cold was sneaky; it got through fabric, skin, and deep inside her.

Thomas also felt its unyielding hold. This coldness that was creeping in was attacking his scientific mind, which usually protected him from irrational fears. He had put thermometers in different rooms and carefully recorded the readings. The information was confusing. The main hall might only be able to handle twelve degrees Celsius, but the new study would drop to almost freezing, and sometimes even below freezing, even though he kept a roaring fire going inside it. The strange thing didn't fit with any of the usual explanations. There were no drafts and no obvious holes in the structure that could explain such a sudden and deep drop in temperature. It was as if these new rooms were not only cold, but also pulling heat away from the air, the manor itself, and, he was becoming more and more afraid, from the people who lived there. He spent hours looking over architectural plans, hoping to find any signs of hidden ventilation shafts or strange structural designs that could explain what was going on, but the manor's layout stayed a frustrating mystery. When he could find them, the blueprints often didn't match up with what was really going on in the house. Rooms would appear and disappear, and hallways would move, making it impossible for him to make sense of things.

The cold was more than just a physical pain; it was a mental weapon. It made them more anxious, frayed their nerves, and made them feel alone, even when they were in the same room. They huddled together, looking for comfort in the little warmth they could share. Their breaths fogged up in the cold air. Eleanor would often put her head on Thomas's shoulder, her body stiff with cold and fear. He would wrap an arm around her, and his skin would feel strangely cold to the touch. The shared pain, on the other hand, did not lessen the growing fear. It was a constant reminder of the manor's never-ending hunger, which was made worse by the bone-chilling cold. They were the cause of this coldness, as their own body heat was being drained away and their energy was slowly being drained away, getting them ready for the house to eat them.

The whispers, which had been few and far between and easy to ignore as the creaks and groans of an old house, seemed to get louder in the cold air. They were no longer just sounds in their heads; they were the cold's breath, a sibilant chorus that spoke of emptiness, decay, and a gnawing need. They talked about "preparation," "gathering strength," and, most worryingly, "softening." The cold seemed to be meant to make them more flexible and open to the house's evil influence, which would break down their physical and mental defenses. Sometimes Eleanor could hear them whispering just barely, a faint, rough sound that seemed to come from the icy walls themselves. They talked about their life force and how it was being pulled out of them and into the very structure of Blackwood Manor. It was a slow, painful process that was both scary and strangely fascinating.

Even though Thomas was interested in science, the cold took a toll on his mind. He had always been proud of how strong he was and how he could stay calm and think clearly even when things were hard. But this constant cold was getting to him. He noticed that his thoughts were getting slower and his focus was shifting. He'd find himself staring into the flickering flames of the fireplace, his mind wandering, and his body aching with a tiredness that sleep couldn't fix. He saw small changes in his own reflection, like his skin looking paler, almost see-through, and his eyes sinking deeper into their sockets. He looked like a man who was slowly being eaten from the inside, he told himself in the privacy of his own scared thoughts. The cold wasn't just a part of the environment; it was a clear sign of how parasitic the manor was. It was the house's cold breath, its exhalation, and its hunger that made it clear, taking the warmth and life from its residents, softening them, and getting them ready for a fate worse than starvation.

Eleanor felt a dark understanding come over her as she accepted the manor's evil intelligence. It wasn't an accident that it was cold; it was on purpose. The house was a predator, and this strange coldness was how it caught its prey. It was a slow, painful bleed that drained them of their very essence, making them weaker and more open to its final claim. She would watch Thomas, who was trying to make sense of everything with his scientific mind, and her heart would break. She knew for sure, and it was a chilling certainty that went deeper than the cold, that his logic would never be able to satisfy the house's ancient, never-ending hunger. The whispers would get louder, the cold would get worse, and the house would keep eating. She pictured the manor as a huge, living thing with roots that went deep into the ground, walls that let out a cold mist, and a core that was always hungry and needed food. And they, the unwilling residents, were its unwilling gift.

The cold got into their bones and made them feel cold all over, no matter how much fire they used. They could feel it in the air they breathed, the water they drank, and the food they forced themselves to eat, even though it seemed to lose its taste and substance in the cold. They ate huddled together by the fire, which cast shadows that seemed to mock their efforts to stay warm. The food, which was not very much, didn't seem to provide much real nutrition, as if the house was stealing its life-giving properties before it could even reach their bodies. They moved more slowly and with more effort, fighting off the growing lethargy with each step. They were like bugs trapped in amber, their life force slowly fading away, making them brittle and unable to move, ready to be broken and eaten.

Thomas, who was desperate for a logical explanation, started to come up with ideas about a type of psychic vampirism that drained bio-energy. He talked about resonant frequencies and vibrational decay, but his words felt empty even to him. It was a desperate attempt to make sense of the scary truth. He would spend hours in his makeshift lab, which was just a corner of the library where he had set up his instruments, trying to find some strange energy output that could be measured as proof of the manor's power. But his devices often broke down in the strange atmosphere of the manor. Needles would jump around or stop working altogether, as if the house itself was working against him as he tried to figure it out. The cold seemed to get thicker around his equipment, wrapping around it and stopping him from doing his scientific work. It was a reminder of how pointless his logical efforts were. He was fighting an enemy that didn't make sense, an evil, ancient force that worked on rules that people couldn't understand.

Eleanor was drawn to the new rooms, not because she was curious, but because she was morbidly interested. She would stand in the middle of these cold rooms with her eyes closed, letting the cold wash over her. It was a scary closeness, a connection to the heart of the manor's hunger. She felt a strange sense of acceptance, like she was giving in to what was going to happen. The cold wasn't something to fight against; it was something to understand and deal with. She could hear the whispers coming together in the cold air, no longer broken up but making clear, if scary, statements. They talked about a coming bloom, a great awakening, and the manor finally reaching its full potential, thanks to the life it had so carefully taken. They promised an end to the hunger, a fulfillment, a final satiation, but the promise was laced with a chilling undertone of dread, for the fulfillment would come at their expense. The cold was like a predator's lullaby, a soft touch before the last, deadly bite.

The icy grip got stronger. Sleep didn't help much; it just made them feel even colder in the manor's embrace. Their dreams were filled with images of wilting flowers and skeletal trees, and they could feel ice spreading through their veins. Every morning, they woke up to a world that felt colder, darker, and heavier, and their spirits were more broken. The little light that came through the dirty windows didn't seem to be warm; it was just a pale, sickly glow that didn't help the heavy gloom. The house wasn't just cold; it was actively hostile, a living thing that was slowly and deliberately taking their lives away. The cold was its breath, and its hunger was clear. It was a chilling sign of the monstrous appetite that lay at the heart of Blackwood Manor, an appetite that was steadily growing.

Chapter 4: The Labyrinth of Fear

The Hall of Mirrors

The air in the newly revealed room was heavy, but not with the usual damp chill of Blackwood Manor. Instead, it had a strange, still density that seemed to soak up sound. Eleanor found it by accident when her hand brushed against what she thought was a solid piece of oak paneling in a hallway on the first floor that wasn't being used. Her fingers had instead sunk into an unseen seam, and a part of the wall had pulled back with a sigh of old machines, making an opening. Not a dusty storage room or a forgotten library, but a space that went against the manor's usual Gothic style.

It was a huge, echoing ballroom, but it was hidden behind a layer of neglect that made it look less grand. Dust motes danced in the weak light that came through the dirty windows high on one wall. The light showed a scene of faded luxury. The floor used to be a smooth surface for couples to dance on, but now it was dull and scuffed. However, it still had a shine that showed how beautiful it used to be. The windows were covered in tattered, faded velvet drapes that looked like dried blood. The floor was littered with the broken pieces of a crystal chandelier, which sparkled like broken ice. But the walls were what really caught their attention right away, and it was the most scary thing.

Mirrors covered every inch of the wall space that was available. Not sleek, modern panes, but old, beveled mirrors with tarnished silvering and dark spots that show their age. They were in fancy, gold-plated frames that looked like they were moving with carvings of plants and animals that had been lost to time. Eleanor and Thomas carefully walked into the room, and their reflections started to show up. They weren't just copies of their tired bodies; they were distorted, larger versions of themselves. Eleanor saw her own face staring back at her, but her eyes were wider and filled with a deep fear that she hadn't let herself feel before. Her shoulders were hunched, not because she was cold, but because she was carrying an unbearable load. Her hands, which were reflected in the glass, were clawing at the air, trying to grab onto something they couldn't see.

Thomas's reflection was just as disturbing. He clenched his jaw, and a vein in his temple throbbed with a force that he didn't feel in his own body. The sharp intelligence in his eyes was replaced by a look of desperation, as if he were about to go crazy because his scientific certainties had been shattered. He saw himself as thin, with messy hair and a lab coat that was once clean but now stained and torn. This was a clear sign that he was losing touch with reality. It felt like the mirrors knew something bad was going to happen, and each one was a different way to see their deepest fears and worries.

"This is... extraordinary," Thomas said in a low voice, which was very different from how he usually spoke with confidence. He reached out with his gloved fingers, which were only a few inches away from the glass. His reflection did the same thing, but there was a delay, a slight difference that made Eleanor shiver. The hand that Thomas saw in the mirror shook violently, but his real hand stayed steady.

"Very strange and very disturbing," Eleanor said, her eyes moving quickly from one distorted picture to another. It seemed like each mirror showed a different part of their shared fear. In one, she saw herself as a weak, old woman with a face full of regret and a broken posture. In another, Thomas was shown as a fraud, with his scientific tools all messed up and a crowd of angry faces behind him, their ghostly shouts echoing in the eerie silence.

The reflections started to change in a disturbing way as they got closer to the ballroom. The mirrors' surfaces rippled like water that had been disturbed, as if they were breathing. Eleanor suddenly stopped, and her breath caught in her throat. There was no longer just her reflection in the mirror across from her. Her mother stood right behind her, and her image was eerily clear and solid. Her mother, who had died years ago, had a face that looked like it was silently blaming her. Her ghostly lips parted as if to say things that weren't said. Eleanor fell back, gasping for breath. "Mom?"

Thomas ran to her side, his own eyes wide with fear. He looked in the mirror and only saw his own warped face. "Eleanor, what is it? There is no one there.

"But there is," she said in a shaky voice. "She's right there. Thomas, she's looking at me. "She's... she's judging me." The dark, deep eyes of the mirrored mother seemed to look right into Eleanor's soul, bringing back memories of guilt and feeling like she wasn't good enough. Eleanor's fear of letting her mother down and not living up to her expectations, a fear she thought she had buried, came back with a force that made it hard to breathe.

At the same time, Thomas was drawn to another set of mirrors. His reflection here was a creepy scene. He thought of himself as a failed scientist. His experiments had gone horribly wrong, and a huge explosion had destroyed his lab. He could hear the ghostly screams of his coworkers, people he had never even met. He saw headlines flashing by, calling him out for his arrogance and carelessness. "Thomas Ashton: A Threat to Science." "The Man Who Tried to Be God and Failed." These were not just thoughts; they were poisonous statements that fed on his deepest professional fears, the fear that his life's work would end in failure and shame.

"This room… "It's not just showing us," Thomas said, his voice tight with fear. "It's… it's making what's inside us stronger. It's making our fears and regrets real, or at least making them feel real. He had to turn away from the damning headlines, but the mirrored images kept coming back, like a shroud around his vision. He saw his father shaking his head slowly, his stern face twisted with disappointment. His father, who had never really liked his scientific work and had always thought it was a waste of time, was there. The ghostly disapproval felt like a physical blow, like a heavy weight on his chest.

Eleanor had stopped looking at her mother. The reflection had changed again. Eleanor, who was now looking in the mirror, was standing in a huge, empty void all by herself. The silence was deafening. This was her worst fear: being alone, being abandoned, which she had always been afraid of, and the worst thing that could happen because of her perceived failures. She felt like she was fading away, unseen and unheard, and that her life was pointless. The cold that came from the mirrors seemed to get stronger, seeping into her bones and echoing her inner emptiness.

"We need to leave," she said, her voice barely above a whisper. She reached for Thomas's hand, and her fingers were cold.

But the reflections moved with her. The mirrored Eleanor seemed to make fun of her attempt to escape. Her ghostly form stayed in the void, a chilling reminder of what she thought would happen to her. Thomas was also stuck. His reflection moved in the same way he did when he tried to pull away from the mirrors, but in a creepy way. The mirrored Thomas's hand reached out, not to pull him back, but to grab his throat. Its ghostly fingers wrapped around him in a tight, suffocating hug.

The teasing got worse. The reflections started to talk, and their voices came from the glass itself. They were a mix of whispers, taunts, and accusations. Eleanor heard her mother's ghostly voice, full of disappointment, say, "Eleanor, you were never good enough." Not good enough for anyone. Even though the words were ghostly, they had the weight of real condemnation and hit her self-doubt right in the gut.

Thomas heard his father's ghostly voice, full of disdain: "A fool's errand." Thomas, you've wasted your life on stupid things. And now, look at you. "Nothing." The phantom scorn was a physical attack that slowly tore down the walls of his self-esteem.

The ballroom was becoming a stage for their own personal hells. The distorted pictures and ghostly voices weren't just tricks of the mind; they were parts of their subconscious that the manor's evil power had brought to the surface and made stronger. Eleanor saw a vision of herself as an old woman who had been forgotten, with a life full of broken promises and a face full of bitter regret. The empty space in the mirror grew larger, threatening to swallow her whole. The silence made her screams louder.

Thomas felt like his peers were shunning him, his scientific reputation was in ruins, and his life's work was now just a warning story. The phantom headlines kept coming, turning into a flood of accusations that threatened to drown him. He felt a growing panic and a strong need to break the glass to stop the constant pain, but his arms and legs felt heavy and unresponsive, as if the air in the ballroom was thick with an invisible weight that kept him in place.

The reflections started to mix together, making horrible combinations. Eleanor saw her mother's accusing eyes staring out of Thomas's distorted reflection, and her ghostly lips whispered accusations of betrayal. Thomas saw his father's disappointed frown on top of Eleanor's picture of being abandoned. The ghostly disapproval made her fear of being completely alone even worse. The room was no longer a ballroom; it was a crucible of their worst fears, where their inner demons danced in a strange way.

"It's a trap," Thomas said, his voice strained. "It's feeding on our fear." The more we respond, the stronger it gets. He tried to concentrate, to get past the gut-wrenching fear, and to find a logical reason for what was happening, a flaw in the manor's psychological warfare. But the mirrored faces didn't stop, and their whispers wrapped around them like a web of despair.

Eleanor saw her own reflection crying, but not tears of sadness. They were tears of cold, stark fear. The mirror's gaze changed and met Eleanor's own. In that moment, Eleanor saw not only her fear but also a terrifying vision of their shared doom. The warped images weren't just showing them their worst fears; they were also showing them their certain death, twisted and made worse by the evil of the manor. The cold that was creeping into the room felt like it was becoming real, like an icy touch that promised death.

They were stuck in a hall of mirrors, not made of glass and silver, but of their own broken minds. Every reflection was a lie, a distortion, a poisonous echo meant to break them. The ballroom, with its dirty grandeur and evil mirrors, showed how smart the manor was and how it could use their deepest weaknesses against them. It was a place where the past, the present, and the scary future all came together, all seen through the broken glass of their worst fears. The whispers got louder. They weren't just voices anymore; they were a suffocating chorus of despair that promised an end to their pain, but only through total destruction, a falling into the cold, dark abyss that the manor so expertly conjured. They weren't just visitors; they were unwilling actors in a psychological horror play, with their souls on display, being dissected and mocked by the evil, aware reflections that surrounded them. The air got even colder, and a cold breath from the heart of the manor promised to freeze their courage, hope, and very being, leaving them as empty and twisted as the reflections that now held them captive.

The EverChanging Staircase

The oppressive silence of the mirrored ballroom finally broke, not with a scream or a loud crash, but with the quiet, sneaky creak of wood under pressure. It was the sound of the manor moving and changing shape, like a sleeping architectural beast waking up. Eleanor and Thomas had finally broken free from the suffocating grip of their mirrored fears. The raw, visceral terror had dulled their senses for a moment, letting a small part of their survival instinct come back to life. They had stumbled out of the ballroom, not through any door that could be seen, but as if the wall had suddenly disappeared, spitting them back into a hallway that felt both familiar and completely strange. The mirrors' fancy, gold-plated frames seemed to push in on them, and their distorted images were like a curse that stuck in their minds.

They had run away in a panic, trying to get away from the mental pain as quickly as possible. They were in what looked like the manor's grand entrance hall, which had big arches and old tapestries, but the air here was full of a different kind of fear. The mirrors were gone, and in their place were cold, hard stone and shadows that hung around like wet blankets. At the bottom of the main staircase, the manor's true, terrifying, physical form began to show itself in its most twisted, maze-like form.

The stairs rose up in front of them, a beautiful curve of dark, polished wood. The banister was carved with detailed, almost creepy, gargoyles that seemed to be looking down at them. A central artery that connected the different levels of the house was a classic feature of any grand manor. But when Eleanor looked up, a shiver of worry ran down her spine. Something was wrong. The angles didn't look right, and the climb was too steep in some places and too shallow in others.

"Thomas," she said, her voice barely above a whisper, "does that seem… right to you?"

Thomas blinked and followed her gaze, his scientific mind still spinning from the mirrored horrors. He ran a hand through his messy hair and narrowed his eyes to focus. He mumbled, more to himself than to her, "The perspective is… distorted." "Maybe it's just the way the light hits it or the size of the hall…" He stopped talking because he didn't want to say what he was starting to think: that this wasn't just an optical illusion.

He stepped forward slowly, and the sound of his boot on the marble floor echoed. When his foot hit the first step of the staircase, a solid slab of oak, it seemed to move slightly. It wasn't a big lurch, but a small change that was hard to notice. It was like a predator getting into a better position. Eleanor gasped and put a hand over her mouth.

"Did you see that?" she said with a gasp.

Thomas nodded, his face pale. "It moved. The step. "That moved." He took another careful step, and the second step did the same, angling itself slightly to make a small, almost unnoticeable curve where there had been a straight line. The gargoyles on the banister looked like they were grinning wider, and their stone eyes sparkled with a new evil.

"This isn't just architecture," Thomas said in a low, strained voice. "It's... moving." He took out his worn notebook and a pencil, which was a common thing for him to do to try to make sense of the mess. "I need to make a chart of this. We need to know how it works.

He took another step, and this time the third stair seemed to dip down a little, but not enough to throw him off balance. He tripped and caught himself on the railing. The gargoyle that was closest to his hand looked like it was snarling, and its carved mouth opened to show teeth that were too sharp to be real. "It's not just moving, Eleanor." It's changing. "The rise... it's not steady anymore."

He tried to step back and go back to the relative safety of the hall, but the first step he had taken was no longer there. There was a smooth, unbroken stretch of marble floor in the hall instead, as if the stairs had just pulled back that part. Eleanor screamed, a sharp, scared sound.

"Where did it go?" she yelled, her eyes wide with fear.

Thomas looked at the place where the first step had been, his face a mask of shock and growing fear. "It went away. Totally. "Like it was never there." He looked up the stairs, which now seemed to have changed shape. What had been a fairly easy climb, though scary, now twisted and turned in ways that didn't make sense. There were parts that looked like they were going up at an impossible angle and others that looked like they were going back on themselves.

"This isn't an accident," Thomas said, his voice full of a new sense of urgency. "This staircase… it's a trap." A trap that changes over time. He tried to step onto the second visible stair, but it also broke apart under his foot, sending him down with a sickening jolt. Eleanor yelled his name and reached out, but he was already falling.

But he didn't go very far. He didn't crash into a lower floor or a dark abyss. Instead, he landed with a loud thud on a part of the stairs that had appeared out of nowhere, a few feet below where he had been standing. He was on a different level now, on a landing that hadn't been there a few seconds ago. Not only had the stairs changed shape, but they had also changed the place they were going.

"Thomas!" Eleanor's voice was a desperate call from above. She was still on the same level, looking down at him with a mix of relief and complete confusion.

"I'm… "I'm fine," he said back, his voice rough. He forced himself to stand up, even though his body hurt from the sudden fall. He looked around the landing. It was small and cramped, and there were more of those creepy gargoyles with carved eyes that seemed to follow him around. He looked up at Eleanor, and something that shouldn't have happened happened. The stairs that used to be between them were gone. There was now a solid, unbroken wall where it used to be. The plaster and wallpaper were the same age as the rest of the hall.

"Eleanor?" He yelled, and his voice sounded strange. "Are you able to hear me?"

There was a pause, and then her voice, weak and strained, came through the wall. "Tom? Where are you? I can't see you! The stairs are gone! "It's a wall!"

"I'm here!" he yelled back, putting his hands on the cold plaster. "I'm on a landing! The stairs changed shape! It... it put me here!"

"Deposited you? What are you saying? Her voice was full of rising fear. "There's just a wall!" "I can't get to you!"

Thomas felt a deep, cold fear wash over him, much worse than the fear he had felt in the ballroom. This wasn't a mental torture; it was a physical separation, a cruel game of moving things around that the manor itself was playing. He hit the wall, which was pointless. "It's messing with us, Eleanor! The stairs... they know what they're doing! "It's trying to pull us apart!"

He looked back at the landing. The stairs he had come up on seemed to be the only way forward. They were narrow and dangerous and led up into the dark. He knew for sure that every step would be a risk, and it scared him to death. He took a deep breath and the musty air filled his lungs. "I have to keep going," he said to himself, getting ready. "I need to find a way to get back to you."

He started to rise, and his heart raced against his ribs. Every step was a prayer. He reached out and touched the banister with his hand. The stone faces of the gargoyles seemed to twist and turn. He climbed higher, and the stairs started to twist and turn again, but this time not in a smooth curve, but in sharp, jarring angles. He felt like he was moving through the insides of a huge, ugly monster.

He got to another landing, this one bigger and more open. It looked out over what looked like a big hall, but the angles were all wrong. He could see bits of the outside world through a tall, arched window, but the sky was a strange, bruised shade of purple. And then he saw it. A part of the stairs that was impossibly long and steep seemed to go on forever, leading to nowhere. It was a ghostly part of the stairs, a trick of the eye meant to lead the unwary to their death.

He pulled back and stumbled back. He had to be careful. He took out his notebook again, and his hand shook as he tried to draw the changing buildings. But it was a fight he couldn't win. While he was drawing, he could see the steps below him slowly changing shape. A flight of stairs that had gone up now curved down, and if he hadn't seen it in time, he would have fallen straight down.

"It's not just changing," he said in a whisper, his anger and fear fighting inside him. "It's… it's actively working against any effort to chart it. It's a moving target, a living maze meant to confuse and kill. He thought of the mirrored ballroom, where their biggest fears had been made bigger and reflected. This was not the same. This was the manor's most basic, physical evil: its ability to change reality itself, to bend space and time within its walls.

He looked around the landing in a panic. There had to be a way for him to go back over his steps and find Eleanor again. But the stairs didn't give any comfort. It kept up its unpredictable dance, moving around with a slow, deliberate cruelty. He saw a part of the stairs that looked like it went right to where Eleanor had been standing, which made him want to see her again. He took a step toward it, and a wave of desperate hope washed over him.

But as his foot got closer to the edge of the landing, the whole section of stairs pulled back, folding in on itself like a creepy origami creature. It disappeared into the wall with a soft sigh of wood and dust. The stairs were gone, and all that was left was the cold, hard stone.

"No!" he yelled, his voice full of despair. He was stuck, cut off from Eleanor, floating in a sea of changing buildings. He felt panic rising in him, a basic need to break through the walls and scream until his lungs gave out. But he knew for sure that doing those things would only make the manor's evil worse. The stairs weren't just in the way; they were a predator that was playing with its prey.

He made himself breathe and think. Even though the world around him was changing, he had to stay calm. He looked at his notebook, where the messy writing showed how hard he had tried to make a map. He threw it away. There was no reason for this, and no pattern to be found. The only thing to do was give in to the madness, let the stairs take him where they wanted to go, and hope that there was a way back to Eleanor somewhere in the stairs' constantly changing design.

He focused on the last flight of stairs, the ones that seemed to lead up into the dark. They looked unstable and uneven, as if they had been put together quickly. He was aware that this was his only choice. In a strange way, he had to trust the stairs to take him somewhere, anywhere, that might bring him back together with Eleanor.

He stepped down, and the stairs creaked in a scary way. He kept his eyes on the steps right in front of him and wouldn't look at the impossible angles, the illogical curves, or the sheer drops that seemed to yawn just out of the corner of his eye. He wasn't making a plan anymore; he was trying to get through a nightmare. Every step was a leap of faith into the unknown. The stone voices of the gargoyles on the banister seemed to whisper, forming a scary chorus of doubt and despair. He could almost hear them, their taunts echoing the fears he had tried to push down: Lost… alone… stuck forever.

He kept going, even though the air got colder and thicker. The manor was alive, and the staircase was its heart. It was a huge thing that fed on confusion and despair. He could feel it there, a heavy presence in the air, an evil mind that was happy about his situation. He was no longer a scientist studying a strange event; he was a mouse caught in a cosmic, architectural trap.

All of a sudden, a part of the stairs in front of him just disappeared. It disappeared into nothingness, leaving a huge hole that went down into complete darkness. Thomas came to a sudden stop, and his heart raced. He was only a few inches away from death. He slowly backed away, breathing heavily. The manor was playing with him, pushing him to the edge, not to kill him right away, but to break him, to make him into a trembling, scared wreck.

He looked back at the path he had taken, but it had changed as well. The stairs he had just come down were now a solid wall. There was no way to go back. He was definitely stuck, caught in the manor's complicated web of lies. He fell onto the nearest step, his head in his hands, feeling the weight of being alone. He thought about Eleanor and how scared and helpless she was. Did she get away from the ballroom? Or was she now stuck in a different part of this architectural hell?

He looked up once more. The stairs started to move again, as if they knew he was sad. A new path, made up of wide, shallow steps, began to appear in front of him. It led down to what looked like a cellar or an underground passage. It was a call to action, a trap. Part of him screamed to ignore it and find another way, any way that wasn't dictated by the stairs. But the other part, the one that was desperate, saw it as the only choice. He was lost on the path.

He got up, his legs heavy with fear, and stepped onto the first of the new stairs. It felt strong enough, but that didn't mean much in this house. He started to go down, and the darkness surrounded him. The gargoyles' whispers faded into the heavy silence of the manor's depths. He was walking deeper into the maze, which was always changing, and he had no idea how to get out or if he would ever see Eleanor again. The stairs, which were the main part of the house, had turned into a huge, unpredictable thing that was a death trap that promised only a never-ending, confusing descent into madness.

The Nursery of Lost Innocence

The oppressive silence of the mirrored ballroom finally broke, not with a scream or a loud crash, but with the quiet, sneaky creak of wood under pressure. It was the sound of the manor moving and changing shape, like a sleeping architectural beast waking up. Eleanor and Thomas had finally broken free from the suffocating grip of their mirrored fears. The raw, visceral terror had dulled their senses for a moment, letting a small part of their survival instinct come back to life. They had stumbled out of the ballroom, not through any door that could be seen, but as if the wall had suddenly disappeared, spitting them back into a hallway that felt both familiar and completely strange. The mirrors' fancy, gold-plated frames seemed to push in on them, and their distorted images were like a curse that stuck in their minds.

They had run away in a panic, trying to get away from the mental pain as quickly as possible. They were in what looked like the manor's grand entrance hall, which had big arches and old tapestries, but the air here was full of a different kind of fear. The mirrors were gone, and in their place were cold, hard stone and shadows that hung around like wet blankets. At the bottom of the main staircase, the manor's true, terrifying, physical form began to show itself in its most twisted, maze-like form.

The stairs rose up in front of them, a beautiful curve of dark, polished wood. The banister was carved with detailed, almost creepy, gargoyles that seemed to be looking down at them. A central artery that connected the different levels of the house was a classic feature of any grand manor. But when Eleanor looked up, a shiver of worry ran down her spine. Something was wrong. The angles didn't look right, and in some places the climb was too steep and in others it was too shallow.

"Thomas," she said, her voice barely above a whisper, "does that seem… right to you?"

Thomas blinked and followed her gaze, his scientific mind still reeling from the mirrored horrors. He ran a hand through his messy hair and narrowed his eyes to focus. "The view is… distorted," he said softly, more to himself than to her. "Maybe it's just the way the light hits it, or the size of the hall…" He stopped, not wanting to say what he was starting to think: that this was more than just an optical illusion.

He took a step forward, but it was shaky, and his boot echoed on the marble floor. When his foot hit the first step of the staircase, a solid slab of oak, it seemed to move slightly. It wasn't a big lurch, but a small change that was hard to notice. It was like a predator getting into a better position. Eleanor gasped and put a hand over her mouth.

"Did you see that?" she said with a gasp.

Thomas nodded, looking pale. "It moved. The step. It moved." He took another careful step, and the second step did the same, tilting slightly to make a curve that was almost invisible where there had been a straight line. The gargoyles on the banister looked like they were grinning wider, and their stone eyes sparkled with new evil.

"This isn't just architecture," Thomas said in a low, strained voice. "It's... active." He took out his old notebook and pencil, which he often did to try to bring order to chaos. "I need to make a chart of this. We need to know how it works."

He took another step, and this time the third stair seemed to go down a little, not much, but enough to make him lose his balance. He tripped and caught himself on the railing. The gargoyle that was closest to his hand looked like it was snarling, and its carved mouth opened to show teeth that were too sharp. "It's not just moving, Eleanor. It's changing. The ascent... it's not always the same."

He tried to back up to the hall, where it was safer, but the first step he had taken was now gone. There was a smooth, unbroken stretch of marble floor in the hall instead, as if the stairs had just pulled back that part. Eleanor screamed, a sharp, scared sound.

"Where did it go?" she yelled, her eyes wide with fear.

Thomas stared at the place where the first step had been, his face showing shock and growing horror. "It went away. Completely. As if it had never been there." He looked up the stairs, which now looked like they had moved. What had been a fairly simple, if scary, climb now twisted and turned in ways that didn't make sense. There were parts that looked like they were going up at an impossible angle and others that looked like they were going back on themselves.

"This is no accident," Thomas said, his voice sounding more urgent than ever. "This staircase... it's a trap. A living, evolving trap." He tried to step onto the second visible stair, but it, too, fell apart under his foot, sending him down with a sickening lurch. Eleanor screamed his name and reached out, but he was already falling.

But he didn't go very far. He didn't crash into a lower floor or a dark abyss. Instead, he landed with a loud thud on a part of the stairs that had appeared out of nowhere, a few feet below where he had been standing. He was on a different level now, on a landing that hadn't been there a few seconds ago. The stairs had not only changed shape; they had also changed where they were going.

"Thomas!" Eleanor's voice from above was a desperate cry. She was still on the same level, looking down at him with a mix of relief and complete confusion.

"I'm... I'm okay," he said back, his voice rough. He got up, even though his body hurt from the sudden fall. He looked around the landing. It was small and cramped, and there were more of those creepy gargoyles with carved eyes that seemed to follow him around. He looked up at Eleanor, and something that shouldn't have happened happened. The stairs that used to be between them were gone. There was now a solid wall where it had been, with the same old plaster and faded wallpaper as the rest of the hall.

"Eleanor?" he yelled, and his voice sounded strange. "Can you hear me?"

There was a pause, and then her voice, weak and strained, came through the wall. "Thomas? Where are you? I can't see you! The stairs are gone! It's a wall!"

He yelled back, "I'm here!" and pushed his hands against the cold plaster. "There's a landing! The stairs changed shape! It... it dropped me off here!"

"Deposited you? What do you mean?" Her voice was getting more and more panicked. "There's just a wall! I can't get to you!"

Thomas felt a deep, cold fear wash over him, much worse than the fear he had felt in the ballroom. This wasn't a mental torture; it was a physical separation, a cruel game of moving things around that the manor itself was playing. He hit the wall, which didn't help. "It's messing with us, Eleanor! The stairs... they're alive! They're trying to keep us apart!"

He looked back at the landing. The stairs he had come up on seemed to be the only way forward. They were narrow and dangerous and led up into the dark. He knew for sure that every step would be a risk, and it scared him to death. He took a deep breath and the musty air filled his lungs. "I have to keep going," he said to himself, getting ready. "I have to find a way back to you."

He started to rise, and his heart raced against his ribs. Every step was a prayer. He reached out and touched the banister with his hand. The stone faces of the gargoyles seemed to twist and turn. He climbed higher, and the stairs started to twist and turn again, but this time not in a smooth curve, but in sharp, jarring angles. He felt like he was moving through the insides of a huge, ugly monster.

He got to another landing, this one bigger and more open. It looked out over what looked like a big hall, but the angles were all wrong. He could see bits of the outside world through a tall, arched window, but the sky was a strange, bruised shade of purple. And then he saw it. A part of the stairs that was impossibly long and steep seemed to go on forever, leading to nowhere. It was a ghostly part of the stairs, a trick of the eye meant to lead the unwary to their death.

He pulled back and stumbled back. He had to be careful. He took out his notebook again, and his hand shook as he tried to draw the changing buildings. But it was a fight he couldn't win. While he was drawing, he could see the steps below him slowly changing shape. A flight of stairs that had gone up now curved down, and if he hadn't seen it in time, he would have fallen straight down.

"It's not just changing," he whispered, frustration and fear warring within him. "It's... it's actively sabotaging any attempt to chart it. It's a moving target, a sentient maze designed to disorient and destroy." He remembered the mirrored ballroom, the way their deepest fears had been amplified and reflected. This was different. This was the manor's most basic, physical evil: its ability to change reality itself, to bend space and time within its walls.

He looked around the landing in a panic. There had to be a way for him to go back over his steps and find Eleanor again. But the stairs didn't give any comfort. It kept up its unpredictable dance, moving around with a slow, deliberate cruelty. He saw a part of the stairs that looked like it went right to where Eleanor had been standing, which made him want to see her again. He took a step toward it, and a wave of desperate hope washed over him.

But as his foot got closer to the edge of the landing, the whole section of stairs pulled back, folding in on itself like a creepy origami creature. It disappeared into the wall with a soft sigh of wood and dust. The stairs were gone, and all that was left was the cold, hard stone.

"No!" he yelled, his voice full of despair. He was stuck, cut off from Eleanor, floating in a sea of changing buildings. He felt panic rising in him, a basic need to break through the walls and scream until his lungs gave out. But he knew for sure that doing those things would only make the manor's evil worse. The stairs weren't just in the way; they were a predator that was playing with its prey.

He made himself breathe and think. Even though the world around him was changing, he had to stay calm. He looked at his notebook, where the messy writing showed how hard he had tried to make a map. He threw it away. There was no reason for this, and no pattern to be found. The only thing to do was give in to the madness, let the stairs take him where they wanted to go, and hope that there was a way back to Eleanor somewhere in the stairs' constantly changing design.

He focused on the last flight of stairs, the ones that seemed to lead up into the dark. They looked unstable and uneven, as if they had been put together quickly. He was aware that this was his only choice. In a strange way, he had to trust the stairs to take him somewhere, anywhere, that might bring him back together with Eleanor.

He stepped down, and the stairs creaked in a scary way. He kept his eyes on the steps right in front of him and wouldn't look at the impossible angles, the illogical curves, or the sheer drops that seemed to yawn just out of the corner of his eye. He wasn't making a plan anymore; he was trying to get through a nightmare. Each step was a blind faith, a leap into the unknown. The gargoyles lining the banister seemed to whisper, their stone voices a chilling chorus of doubt and despair. He could almost hear them, their taunts echoing the fears he had tried to suppress: Lost… alone… forever trapped.

He pushed onward, the air growing colder, thicker. The manor was alive, and its heart was this ever-changing staircase, a monstrous entity that fed on confusion and despair. He could feel its presence, a palpable weight in the air, a malicious intelligence that delighted in his predicament. He was no longer a scientist exploring a strange phenomenon; he was a mouse caught in a cosmic, architectural trap.

Suddenly, a section of the stairs ahead of him simply ceased to exist. It dematerialized into nothingness, leaving a gaping chasm that stretched downwards into absolute darkness. Thomas skidded to a halt, his heart leaping into his throat. He was mere inches from oblivion. He backed away slowly, his breath coming in ragged gasps. The manor was toying with him, pushing him to the brink, not to kill him outright, but to break him, to reduce him to a quivering,

The west wing of the manor was a different kind of silent. It was not the absence of sound, but a heavy, pregnant stillness, as if the very air held its breath. Eleanor found herself propelled by an unseen current, her feet moving with a surety that belied her terror. Thomas was nowhere to be seen. The last she remembered of him was his descent into the shifting maw of the staircase, his desperate shout swallowed by the house's insatiable hunger. Now, she was alone, adrift in the manor's labyrinthine corridors, each turn more disorienting than the last. The stone walls, cool and damp to her touch, offered no comfort, only the chilling sensation of being enclosed, of being swallowed whole.

A faint melody, thin and reedy, began to weave its way through the oppressive silence. It was a lullaby, impossibly sweet and achingly sad, a child's tune played on a forgotten music box. It seemed to emanate from everywhere and nowhere, a ghostly echo that tugged at a forgotten corner of Eleanor's heart. It was a sound that spoke of innocence lost, of comfort stolen. The melody drew her onward, a siren song of sorrow, pulling her towards an unknown destination.

The corridor opened into a room that seemed to exist outside the manor's architectural chaos. It was bathed in a soft, diffused light that held no discernible source, a perpetual twilight that softened the edges of reality. This was a nursery, frozen in time. The walls were adorned with faded, whimsical wallpaper depicting playful animals engaged in nonsensical activities, their bright colours muted by decades of neglect. In the centre of the room stood a crib, its delicate white paint chipped and peeling, a desolate island in a sea of antique toys.

Eleanor's breath hitched. The air in the nursery was heavy with a profound melancholy, a sorrow so potent it felt like a physical weight pressing down on her chest. It was as if the very essence of childish joy had been wrung out of this space, leaving behind only the residue of despair. She felt an overwhelming urge to weep, a deep, primal grief that wasn't entirely her own. It was the sorrow of forgotten children, of dreams extinguished, of lives cut short. The room felt imprinted with their spectral presence, their silent cries echoing in the quietude.

Scattered across the worn Persian rug were the remnants of childhood. A wooden rocking horse, its paint worn smooth by countless imaginary journeys, stood sentinel near the window. Its glass eyes seemed to gleam with a hollow sadness. A collection of porcelain dolls, their painted smiles fixed and unnerving, lay strewn about, some missing limbs, others with cracked faces that seemed to mimic expressions of silent anguish. A small, tarnished silver rattle lay half-hidden beneath a plush, threadbare bear, its once-bright surface dulled by time and neglect.

As Eleanor's gaze swept across the room, she could have sworn the toys shifted. The rocking horse seemed to sway, almost imperceptibly, a phantom rider guiding its silent gallop. The dolls' heads tilted, their vacant stares following her movements. The bear's button eyes seemed to glint with a fleeting awareness. It was a trick of the light, she told herself, a product of her frayed nerves and the manor's oppressive atmosphere. Yet, the feeling persisted, a chilling certainty that she was not alone in this desolate sanctuary. These were not mere objects; they were vessels, imbued with the lingering echoes of their former owners.

The lullaby, which had seemed to fade upon her entry, now swelled again, a haunting counterpoint to the room's silent despair. It was coming from the direction of the crib. Hesitantly, Eleanor approached the ornate bassinet. The mattress within was stained and flattened, the once-pristine white linen now a dingy grey. A single, tattered baby blanket was folded neatly at the foot, as if a small occupant had recently departed, leaving their comfort behind. There was no music box, no visible source for the ethereal melody. It simply was, a mournful lament that seemed to weep from the very wood of the crib.

She reached out a trembling hand, her fingers hovering just above the faded fabric of the blanket. A wave of intense sorrow washed over her, so profound it stole her breath. Images flashed through her mind, fragmented and fleeting: a tiny hand reaching out, a desperate cry unheard, the chilling finality of silence. These were not her memories, but they resonated with a terrifying familiarity. The nursery, she realized with a dawning horror, was a repository of lost innocence, a place where childhood had been cruelly, irrevocably shattered.

This wasn't just a room; it was a wound in the fabric of the manor, a place where tragedy had seeped into the very walls, leaving an indelible stain. The toys, the crib, the lingering melody – they were all testament to lives that had been snuffed out before they could truly begin. The playful animals on the wallpaper seemed to mock the grim reality of the room, their painted smiles a cruel reminder of the joy that had been absent.

Eleanor felt a prickle of fear, not the sharp, immediate terror of the mirrored ballroom, but a deeper, more insidious dread. This was the chilling realization that the manor didn't just prey on adult fears; it had a particular appetite for the vulnerability of children. The thought sent a shiver down her spine, a premonition of what awaited her and Thomas. If this was a glimpse into the manor's past, what horrors did it have in store for their present?

She turned her attention back to the crib. The lullaby seemed to shift, its melody becoming more agitated, a frantic plea woven into the sorrow. Was the manor itself crying out, lamenting its own dark history? Or was it a warning, a desperate attempt by the residual spirits of children to communicate their fate? The toys seemed to lean in, their vacant eyes fixed on her, as if waiting for her to understand.

Eleanor knelt beside the crib, her gaze sweeping over the doll scattered on the floor. One doll, in particular, caught her eye. It was dressed in a faded blue dress, its porcelain face smudged with dirt, but its eyes, a startlingly bright blue, seemed to hold a spark of life, a flicker of defiance. As Eleanor looked at it, the doll's head slowly, deliberately, turned towards her. A tiny, almost inaudible whisper escaped its painted lips, a sound that was lost in the ethereal lullaby. Eleanor leaned closer, straining to hear. Was it a name? A plea? A warning?

The air grew colder. The toys seemed to crowd around her, their silent forms radiating an unseen energy. The rocking horse began to move, a slow, rhythmic creak that echoed the child's lullaby. The dolls' porcelain smiles seemed to widen, their fixed expressions taking on a sinister leer. Eleanor's heart hammered against her ribs. She felt a growing sense of claustrophobia, as if the walls were closing in, the weight of the room's sorrow threatening to crush her.

She had to leave. She had to find Thomas. But the nursery, with its potent aura of tragedy, held her captive. It was a place designed to ensnare, to drown its visitors in a sea of melancholic despair. The lullaby intensified, swirling around her, a vortex of forgotten sorrows. She closed her eyes for a moment, trying to block out the overwhelming emotions, but it was no use. The grief of this place was like a contagion, seeping into her very soul.

When she opened her eyes again, the doll in the blue dress was no longer on the floor. It sat upright in the crib, its bright blue eyes fixed on Eleanor, a silent, watchful presence. The lullaby abruptly ceased, leaving behind an unnerving silence. The toys were still. The rocking horse was motionless. The room felt drained, the oppressive atmosphere momentarily lifted, replaced by a chilling stillness.

Eleanor scrambled to her feet, her legs unsteady. She backed away from the crib, her gaze locked on the doll. It made no move, no sound, yet its silent presence was more terrifying than any of the manor's manifested horrors. It was a tangible manifestation of the house's hunger for innocence, a chilling testament to its capacity for cruelty.

She turned and fled the nursery, the faded animals on the wallpaper blurring into a kaleidoscope of mocking colours. The melody was gone, but the sorrow it represented clung to her like a shroud. She didn't know where she was going, only that she had to escape the spectral embrace of the nursery, this monument to lost childhood. The west wing, she realized, was not just a physical space; it was a realm of profound emotional torment, a testament to the manor's ability to weaponize grief and despair. She had glimpsed the house's capacity for tragedy, and the knowledge was a cold, hard knot in her stomach, a terrifying premonition of the fate that awaited them. The labyrinth of fear had opened a new, more sorrowful, path, and she could only pray that Thomas had found his way through its darkness, and that they could find each other before the manor claimed another lost soul. The scent of dust and decay mingled with a faint, almost imperceptible, sweetness, like wilting flowers, a perfume of grief that clung to her as she ran, her footsteps echoing a desperate flight from a place where innocence went to die.

The Sound of Dripping

The oppressive silence of the mirrored ballroom finally broke, not with a scream or a loud crash, but with the quiet, sneaky creak of wood under pressure. It was the sound of the manor moving and changing shape, like a sleeping architectural beast waking up. Eleanor and Thomas had finally broken free from the suffocating grip of their mirrored fears. The raw, visceral terror had dulled their senses for a moment, letting a small part of their survival instinct come back to life. They had stumbled out of the ballroom, not through any door that could be seen, but as if the wall had suddenly disappeared, spitting them back into a hallway that felt both familiar and completely strange. The mirrors' fancy, gold-plated frames seemed to push in on them, and their distorted images were like a curse that stuck in their minds.

They had run away in a panic, trying to get away from the mental pain as quickly as possible. They were in what looked like the manor's grand entrance hall, which had big arches and old tapestries, but the air here was full of a different kind of fear. The mirrors were gone, and in their place were cold, hard stone and shadows that hung around like wet blankets. At the bottom of the main staircase, the manor's true, terrifying, physical form began to show itself in its most twisted, maze-like form.

The stairs rose up in front of them, a beautiful curve of dark, polished wood. The banister was carved with detailed, almost creepy, gargoyles that seemed to be looking down at them. A central artery that connected the different levels of the house was a classic feature of any grand manor. But when Eleanor looked up, a shiver of worry ran down her spine. Something was wrong. The angles didn't look right, and in some places the climb was too steep and in others it was too shallow.

"Thomas," she said, her voice barely above a whisper, "does that seem… right to you?"

Thomas blinked and followed her gaze, his scientific mind still reeling from the mirrored horrors. He ran a hand through his messy hair and narrowed his eyes to focus. "The view is… distorted," he said softly, more to himself than to her. "Maybe it's just the way the light hits it, or the size of the hall…" He stopped, not wanting to say what he was starting to think: that this was more than just an optical illusion.

He took a step forward, but it was shaky, and his boot echoed on the marble floor. When his foot hit the first step of the staircase, a solid slab of oak, it seemed to move slightly. It wasn't a big lurch, but a small change that was hard to notice. It was like a predator getting into a better position. Eleanor gasped and put a hand over her mouth.

"Did you see that?" she said with a gasp.

Thomas nodded, looking pale. "It moved. The step. It moved." He took another careful step, and the second step did the same, tilting slightly to make a curve that was almost invisible where there had been a straight line. The gargoyles on the banister looked like they were grinning wider, and their stone eyes sparkled with new evil.

"This isn't just architecture," Thomas said in a low, strained voice. "It's… active." He took out his old notebook and pencil, which he often did to try to bring order to chaos. "I need to make a chart of this. We need to know how it works."

He took another step, and this time the third stair seemed to go down a little, not much, but enough to make him lose his balance. He tripped and caught himself on the railing. The gargoyle that was closest to his hand looked like it was snarling, and its carved mouth opened to show teeth that were too sharp. "It's not just moving, Eleanor. It's changing. The ascent… it's not always the same."

He tried to back up to the hall, where it was safer, but the first step he had taken was now gone. There was a smooth, unbroken stretch of marble floor in the hall instead, as if the stairs had just pulled back that part. Eleanor screamed, a sharp, scared sound.

"Where did it go?" she yelled, her eyes wide with fear.

Thomas stared at the place where the first step had been, his face showing shock and growing horror. "It went away. Completely. As if it had never been there." He looked up the stairs, which now looked like they had moved. What had been a fairly simple, if scary, climb now twisted and turned in ways that didn't make sense. There were parts that looked like they were going up at an impossible angle and others that looked like they were going back on themselves.

"This is no accident," Thomas said, his voice sounding more urgent than ever. "This staircase… it's a trap. A living, evolving trap." He tried to step onto the second visible stair, but it, too, fell apart under his foot, sending him down with a sickening lurch. Eleanor screamed his name and reached out, but he was already falling.

But he didn't go very far. He didn't crash into a lower floor or a dark abyss. Instead, he landed with a loud thud on a part of the stairs that had appeared out of nowhere, a few feet below where he had been standing. He was on a different level now, on a landing that hadn't been there a few seconds ago. The stairs had not only changed shape; they had also changed where they were going.

"Thomas!" Eleanor's voice from above was a desperate cry. She was still on the same level, looking down at him with a mix of relief and complete confusion.

"I'm… I'm okay," he said back, his voice rough. He got up, even though his body hurt from the sudden fall. He looked around the landing. It was small and cramped, and there were more of those creepy gargoyles with carved eyes that seemed to follow him around. He looked up at Eleanor, and something that shouldn't have happened happened. The stairs that used to be between them were gone. There was now a solid wall where it had been, with the same old plaster and faded wallpaper as the rest of the hall.

"Eleanor?" he yelled, and his voice sounded strange. "Can you hear me?"

There was a pause, and then her voice, weak and strained, came through the wall. "Thomas? Where are you? I can't see you! The stairs are gone! It's a wall!"

He yelled back, "I'm here!" and pushed his hands against the cold plaster. "There's a landing! The stairs changed shape! It... it dropped me off here!"

"Deposited you? What do you mean?" Her voice was getting more and more panicked. "There's just a wall! I can't get to you!"

Thomas felt a deep, cold fear wash over him, much worse than the fear he had felt in the ballroom. This wasn't a mental torture; it was a physical separation, a cruel game of moving things around that the manor itself was playing. He hit the wall, which didn't help. "It's messing with us, Eleanor! The stairs... they're alive! They're trying to keep us apart!"

He looked back at the landing. The stairs he had come up on seemed to be the only way forward. They were narrow and dangerous and led up into the dark. He knew for sure that every step would be a risk, and it scared him to death. He took a deep breath and the musty air filled his lungs. "I have to keep going," he said to himself, getting ready. "I need to find a way to get back to you."

He started to rise, and his heart raced against his ribs. Every step was a prayer. He reached out and touched the banister with his hand. The stone faces of the gargoyles seemed to twist and turn. He climbed higher, and the stairs started to twist and turn again, but this time not in a smooth curve, but in sharp, jarring angles. He felt like he was moving through the insides of a huge, ugly monster.

He got to another landing, this one bigger and more open. It looked out over what looked like a big hall, but the angles were all wrong. He could see bits of the outside world through a tall, arched window, but the sky was a strange, bruised shade of purple. And then he saw it. A part of the stairs that was impossibly long and steep seemed to go on forever, leading to nowhere. It was a ghostly part of the stairs, a trick of the eye meant to lead the unwary to their death.

He pulled back and stumbled back. He had to be careful. He took out his notebook again, and his hand shook as he tried to draw the changing buildings. But it was a fight he couldn't win. While he was drawing, he could see the steps below him slowly changing shape. A flight of stairs that had gone up now curved down, and if he hadn't seen it in time, he would have fallen straight down.

"It's not just changing," he whispered, his fear and anger at war with each other. "It's… it's actively sabotaging any attempt to chart it. It's a moving target, a sentient maze designed to disorient and destroy." He remembered the mirrored ballroom, where their deepest fears had been amplified and reflected. This was not the same. This was the manor's most basic, physical evil: its ability to change reality itself, to bend space and time within its walls.

He looked around the landing in a panic. There had to be a way for him to go back over his steps and find Eleanor again. But the stairs didn't give any comfort. It kept up its unpredictable dance, moving around with a slow, deliberate cruelty. He saw a part of the stairs that looked like it went right to where Eleanor had been standing, which made him want to see her again. He took a step toward it, and a wave of desperate hope washed over him.

But as his foot got closer to the edge of the landing, the whole section of stairs pulled back, folding in on itself like a creepy origami creature. It disappeared into the wall with a soft sigh of wood and dust. The stairs were gone, and all that was left was the cold, hard stone.

"No!" he yelled, his voice full of despair. He was stuck, cut off from Eleanor, floating in a sea of changing buildings. He felt panic rising in him, a basic need to break through the walls and scream until his lungs gave out. But he knew for sure that doing those things would only make the manor's evil worse. The stairs weren't just in the way; they were a predator that was playing with its prey.

He made himself breathe and think. Even though the world around him was changing, he had to stay calm. He looked at his notebook, where the messy writing showed how hard he had tried to make a map. He threw it away. There was no reason for this, and no pattern to be found. The only thing to do was give in to the madness, let the stairs take him where they wanted to go, and hope that there was a way back to Eleanor somewhere in the stairs' constantly changing design.

He focused on the last flight of stairs, the ones that seemed to lead up into the dark. They looked unstable and uneven, as if they had been put together quickly. He was aware that this was his only choice. In a strange way, he had to trust the stairs to take him somewhere, anywhere, that might bring him back together with Eleanor.

He stepped down, and the stairs creaked in a scary way. He kept his eyes on the steps right in front of him and wouldn't look at the impossible angles, the illogical curves, or the sheer drops that seemed to yawn just out of the corner of his eye. He wasn't making a plan anymore; he was trying to get through a nightmare. Every step was a leap of faith into the unknown. The stone voices of the gargoyles on the banister sounded like whispers, a scary chorus of doubt and despair. He could almost hear them, their taunts echoing the fears he had tried to hide: Lost... alone... trapped forever.

He kept going, even though the air was getting colder and thicker. The manor was alive, and the staircase was its heart. It was a huge thing that fed on confusion and despair. He could feel it there, a heavy presence in the air, an evil mind that was happy about his situation. He was no longer a scientist studying a strange event; he was a mouse caught in a cosmic, architectural trap.

All of a sudden, a part of the stairs in front of him just disappeared. It disappeared into nothingness, leaving a huge hole that went down into complete darkness. Thomas came to a sudden stop, and his heart raced. He was only a few inches away from death. He slowly backed away, breathing heavily. The manor was playing with him, pushing him to the edge, not to kill him, but to break him, to turn him into a trembling, broken man. He could hear a new sound, a small change in the creepy music of the house. He hadn't heard it before, or maybe he had, but the groaning wood and the gargoyles' whispers had hidden it.

Drop.

It made a soft, rhythmic sound that was clear and planned. He leaned his head to one side to try to figure out where it came from. A soft, rhythmic plinking seemed to be coming from somewhere above and to his left.

Drip.

The sound again. He thought it was the sound of water, maybe a leaky pipe or condensation forming. But there was something about it, a strange resonance, that made him stop. It wasn't the clear, sharp sound of water falling. It had a thick, sticky quality that made his skin crawl.

He took a careful step forward, and the dripping sound seemed to fade away, blending in with the low hum of the manor. He stopped, and it came back, a ghostly echo just out of reach. He tried to concentrate on it and let it lead him, but it was as if the sound was alive and was actively avoiding his efforts to find its source.

Drip, drip, drip.

It was a maddening rhythm, like a metronome that wouldn't stop ticking away at his already frayed nerves. It wasn't loud at all, but it kept going, which was scary. It was the sound of something slowly falling apart, of something that wouldn't go away seeping into the very walls of the house.

He kept going, even though the stairs kept changing shape in a creepy way. The sound of dripping followed him. Sometimes it sounded like it was right above him, and other times it sounded like it was coming from the walls themselves, from the cold, indifferent stone. He tried to tell himself that it was just water, which is a common problem in old, falling apart buildings. But the way the sound changed made it seem less likely. At times, it sounded thicker and heavier, like sap or blood that was flowing slowly.

Drip. Drip. Drop.

The repetition was starting to make it hard for him to stay focused. With each plink, he got more and more excited about the next drop. It was a kind of torture that was always there, reminding him of how alone he was and how evil the manor was. He looked at the gargoyles that were on the railing. Their stone eyes seemed to be watching him, and their mouths were always sneering. He thought about how they would cry, and how their tears would make that same annoying, thick sound.

He yelled, "Eleanor!" in a hoarse voice. "Can you hear me?"

The only thing that answered was the dripping, which was a mocking, rhythmic response to his need. He kept climbing, his senses on high alert. The stairs were a dangerous, moving beast, and now they were making noise as well. He stopped for a moment and listened hard. There was a dark slit in the plaster on the wall to his right, and it looked like the dripping was coming from there.

He moved closer to it, his heart racing. He thought this was it. A leak, a broken pipe, or something else ordinary to break the spell of the supernatural. He reached out his hand, ready to feel for wetness. But when his fingers got close to the opening, the dripping stopped all of a sudden. The quiet that came after was worse than the noise itself. He held his breath and listened. Nothing.

He stepped back, and the dripping started again, this time with a single, clear drop coming from a completely different direction, as if it were coming from the floor above. It was just a game. The house was playing a cruel, auditory trick on him to drive him to the edge of insanity. He wasn't exploring a house anymore; he was stuck in a living maze, with every part of it meant to confuse, isolate, and torture him.

He made himself move so he could keep going up. He was scared, and his stomach felt like a cold, tight knot, but the need to find Eleanor and get away from this architectural nightmare kept him going. The sound of dripping water became his constant companion, a ghostly pain that flickered at the edges of his hearing and was always just out of reach and sight. He thought it might be pooling somewhere in the dark, a dark, unidentifiable liquid that was seeping through the rotting wood and plaster, a physical sign of the manor's slow decay. He was no longer just trying to find his way through a physical maze; he was now stuck in an auditory one. The maddening sound was always there, eating away at his sanity with every drop. The west wing of the manor was quiet in a different way. There was no sound, but a heavy, pregnant stillness, as if the air itself were holding its breath. Eleanor felt like she was being pushed by an invisible force, and her feet moved with a confidence that belied her fear. There was no sign of Thomas. The last thing she remembered about him was how he fell down the stairs and how the house's never-ending hunger swallowed his desperate scream. She was now alone, lost in the manor's maze-like hallways, where each turn made her feel more lost. The stone walls were cold and damp to the touch, and they didn't make her feel better; instead, they made her feel like she was being swallowed whole.

A thin, reedy melody started to break through the heavy silence. It was a lullaby, so sweet and sad that it hurt. It was a child's song played on a music box that had been forgotten. It sounded like it came from everywhere and nowhere, like a ghostly echo that pulled at a part of Eleanor's heart that she had forgotten about. It was a sound that said innocence was lost and comfort was taken away. The melody was like a siren song of sadness that pulled her toward an unknown place.

The hallway led to a room that looked like it belonged in a different part of the manor's architectural mess. It was bathed in a soft, diffused light that had no clear source. It was always twilight, which made the edges of reality softer. This was a nursery that had been frozen in time. The walls were covered in faded, silly wallpaper that showed animals doing silly things. The bright colors had faded over the years because no one had taken care of them. In the middle of the room was a crib with chipped and peeling white paint. It looked like a lonely island in a sea of old toys.

Eleanor's breath caught. There was a deep sadness in the air of the nursery, so strong that it felt like a weight on her chest. It felt like the very essence of childlike joy had been sucked out of this space, leaving only the remnants of sadness. She felt like she had to cry, a deep, primal sadness that wasn't all hers. It was the sadness of children who had been forgotten, dreams that had been shattered, and lives that had been cut short. The room felt like it was haunted by their presence, and their silent cries echoed in the stillness.

There were pieces of childhood all over the worn Persian rug. A wooden rocking horse, its paint worn smooth from all the make-believe trips it had taken, stood guard by the window. The glass eyes looked like they were sad and empty. There were porcelain dolls with painted smiles that were fixed and creepy. Some of them were missing limbs, and others had cracked faces that looked like they were in pain. A small, tarnished silver rattle was half-hidden under a plush bear that had seen better days. Its once-bright surface had lost its shine over time.

Eleanor could have sworn that the toys moved as she looked around the room. The rocking horse looked like it was swaying, almost without anyone noticing, as a ghostly rider led it on its silent gallop. The heads of the dolls turned, and their blank stares followed her every move. The bear's button eyes looked like they were aware of something for a moment. She told herself it was just a trick of the light, caused by her frayed nerves and the manor's oppressive atmosphere. But the feeling didn't go away; she was sure she wasn't alone in this empty place. These weren't just things; they were vessels that still held the echoes of their previous owners.

The lullaby, which had seemed to fade when she came in, now grew louder, a haunting contrast to the room's silent sadness. It was coming from the crib. Eleanor walked slowly toward the fancy bassinet. The mattress inside was stained and flat, and the once-white linen was now a dirty gray. There was a single, worn baby blanket folded neatly at the foot, as if a small child had just left and left their comfort behind. There was no music box, and the beautiful music came from nowhere. It was just a sad song that seemed to come from the wood of the crib itself.

She reached out with a shaking hand, and her fingers hovered just above the blanket's worn fabric. A wave of deep sadness hit her, so strong that it took her breath away. She saw images in her mind that were broken and fleeting: a small hand reaching out, a desperate cry that went unheard, and the cold finality of silence. These weren't her memories, but they felt eerily familiar. She realized with growing horror that the nursery was a place where childhood had been cruelly and permanently broken, a place where innocence had been lost.

This wasn't just a room; it was a hole in the manor's structure where tragedy had seeped in and left a mark that would never go away. The toys, the crib, and the music that kept playing were all signs of lives that had been cut short before they could really start. The animals on the wallpaper looked like they were making fun of how serious the room was. Their painted smiles were a cruel reminder of how happy it used to be.

Eleanor felt a twinge of fear, not the sharp, immediate fear of the mirrored ballroom, but a deeper, more insidious fear. This was a scary realization: the manor didn't just feed on adult fears; it also liked to prey on kids who were weak. The thought made her shiver, as if she knew what was going to happen to her and Thomas. If this was a look back at the manor's past, what terrible things did it have in store for them now?

She looked back at the crib. The lullaby seemed to change, with the melody getting more frantic and a desperate plea woven into the sadness. Was the manor itself crying out, mourning its own dark past? Or was it a warning, a last-ditch effort by the spirits of children who had died to tell their story? The toys looked like they were leaning in, their empty eyes fixed on her as if they were waiting for her to get it.

Eleanor knelt next to the crib and looked at the doll that was all over the floor. There was one doll that really stood out to her. It wore a faded blue dress and had a dirty porcelain face, but its eyes, which were a very bright blue, seemed to hold a spark of life and a hint of defiance. The doll's head slowly and deliberately turned toward Eleanor as she looked at it. A soft, almost inaudible whisper came from its painted lips, but the ethereal lullaby drowned it out. Eleanor leaned in closer to hear better. Was it a name? A request? A warning?

The air got colder. It looked like the toys were all around her, and even though they were quiet, they gave off a strange energy. The rocking horse started to move, making a slow, rhythmic creak that sounded like the child's lullaby. The porcelain smiles on the dolls' faces seemed to get bigger, and their blank stares turned into creepy grins. Eleanor's heart beat hard against her ribs. She felt more and more claustrophobic, as if the walls were closing in on her and the sadness in the room was about to crush her.

She had to go. She needed to find Thomas. But the nursery, which had a strong sense of tragedy, kept her there. It was a place meant to trap people and drown them in a sea of sad despair. The lullaby got louder and louder, a whirlwind of old sorrows. She shut her eyes for a moment to try to block out the strong feelings, but it didn't work. The sadness of this place spread like a virus, getting into her very soul.

The doll in the blue dress was gone from the floor when she opened her eyes again. It sat up in the crib, its bright blue eyes on Eleanor, watching her without saying a word. The lullaby stopped suddenly, leaving behind a strange silence. The toys were quiet. The horse that rocks back and forth was still. The room felt empty, and the heavy mood was gone for a moment, replaced by a cold stillness.

Eleanor got up quickly, but her legs were shaky. She stepped back from the crib and stared at the doll. It didn't move or make a sound, but its quiet presence was scarier than any of the other horrors that had happened in the house. It was a real sign of how much the house wanted innocence and how cruel it could be.

She turned and ran out of the nursery, and the old animals on the wallpaper turned into a rainbow of mocking colors. The song was gone, but the sadness it stood for stayed with her like a shroud. She didn't know where she was going, but she knew she had to get away from the nursery, which was a monument to lost childhood. She realized that the west wing was not just a place; it was a place of deep emotional pain, proof that the manor could use sadness and grief as weapons. She had seen how the house could bring about tragedy, and the thought of what would happen to them made her stomach drop like a rock. The maze of fear had opened a new, sadder path, and all she could do was pray that Thomas had made it through its darkness and that they could find each other before the manor took another lost soul. The smell of dust and decay mixed with a faint, almost imperceptible sweetness, like flowers that were dying. It was a perfume of grief that followed her as she ran, her footsteps echoing a desperate escape from a place where innocence went to die.

Eleanor's frantic footsteps echoed through the quiet halls of the west wing. Then, a new sound started to intrude, sly and persistent. It started slowly, with a faint drip... drip... drip that seemed to blend in with the heavy silence. Eleanor first thought it was just the sound of her own panicked breathing or maybe the ghostly sounds that haunted the manor. But the sound got louder, not in volume but in how steady and regular it was.

It wasn't the loud, clear sound of water. This sound was softer and more viscous, like thick syrup falling from a great height or maybe a slow ooze. Drip. Drip. Drip. It seemed to come from everywhere and nowhere, a presence that made her fear grow stronger. It was the sound of something wet and living slowly moving through the old fabric of the manor.

She stopped and put her hand on the cold, wet stone wall, trying hard to find the source. As she concentrated on the sound, it seemed to change and fade away. When she stopped paying attention, it came back from a different direction. She realized with a jolt of icy fear that it was just another cruel game the manor played. It was a sound meant to torture, to weaken her will, and to whisper about decay and corruption in the dark.

She pictured it gathering in the dark, a thick, dark fluid leaking from the walls, the ceiling, and even the floorboards. Was it just water, a sign of how old and neglected the manor was? Or was it something much worse, something that belonged to the evil that lived in these walls? The idea made her shiver, a deep-seated disgust that fought with her need to get away.

Drip. Drip. Drip.

The maddening rhythm went on and on, an unending auditory hallucination that drove her crazy. She tried to run away from it, to get away from the annoying noise, but it stuck with her, like an invisible friend. She couldn't help but look forward to each drop. Her muscles tensed and her breath caught in her throat. It was a mental attack meant to make her paranoid and fray her nerves.

She turned a corner and her heart raced as she saw something that made her blood run cold. A dark, shiny stain on the fancy wallpaper was spreading and looked like it was alive. A single, thick droplet of dark liquid fell from the center and hit the wooden floorboards below with a soft, sickening splat.

Drip.

The sound was no longer just in her ears; it was a picture of her fear. The liquid wasn't water. It was dark, almost black, and had a thick sheen that caught the little light that came through the dirty windows. It smelled like old blood mixed with the sickly sweet smell of decay.

Eleanor recoiled, letting out a strangled cry. This wasn't just rot; something was actively bleeding inside the manor's walls. She now understood that the sound was the house itself crying or maybe bleeding out all the terrible things that had happened there. The dripping wasn't just water; it was the manor's evil spirit's lifeblood, a thick, constant reminder of all the pain it held.

She ran away from the stain, her eyes darting around the hallway, looking for any sign of Thomas and any way out of this horrible nightmare. But the dripping followed her, a constant, echoing reminder of the terrible things that were happening behind the scenes. It sounded like it was coming from the air around her, like a sonic plague that was everywhere. She could hear it dripping from the ceiling and walls, and she imagined with a shudder that it was coming from the gargoyles that still seemed to be watching her from the shadows.

The sound made her more anxious, turning the already confusing hallways into a tight space. Every shadow seemed to move with the drip, and every creak of the old house sounded like the start of another thick drop. The manor was alive, and it was crying, bleeding, or both. It was a slow, painful process that got into her very soul. She was stuck in a maze of fear, and the sound of something much worse than water dripping over and over again drove her crazy.

The Phantom Gardener

The suffocating hug of the west wing had changed; its oppressive stillness was now broken by a faint but constant sound. Drip. Drip. Drip. Eleanor had come to associate the sound with the manor's constant decay: a thick, sticky plinking that seemed to come from the stones themselves. Her heart, which was still racing from the scary experience in the nursery, sped up. Thomas was gone, eaten up by the unpredictable stairs, and she was left alone to deal with the manor's twisted horrors. The west wing, which was full of sadness and memories of lost childhood, felt like a wound. Now, a new and disturbing image began to form in her mind, which was very different from the still sadness of the nursery.

She was pushed through a hallway that seemed like it had just been carved out of stone. The walls were wet, and the plaster was still fresh and stuck to the rough stone underneath. This was a big change from the old, crumbling grandeur of the rest of the manor. It was as if the house was a living, breathing thing that changed and rearranged itself according to some unknown will. As she turned a sharp, new corner, she stopped breathing. A few moments ago, there had been a solid wall. Now, there was a huge hole, a jagged tear in the manor's fabric that showed a view of unsettling beauty and decay.

Eleanor's eyes fell on a scene that made no sense at all through this rough, unfinished opening. There was a garden, or what was left of one, bathed in the strange, bruised twilight that filled the manor's skies. But this wasn't just any garden. It was a wild, untamed area where nature's tendrils had been given an unholy power. Dark, swollen berries hung from thick, twisted vines that snaked their way up the stone front of the manor. Their woody tendrils dug into the house's very foundations. Roots as thick as a man's arm had broken through the walls in some places, their pale fingers pushing through cracks in the plaster, a quiet, sneaky invasion. Even from this far away, the air smelled heavy with damp earth, rotting leaves, and a faint, sickly sweet smell, like fruit that was too ripe and about to rot.

And then she saw him.

In the thick weeds, a hunched and shadowy figure moved with a slow, deliberate grace. He was working in the garden, and his movements were so slow that it seemed like time had stopped for him. His shape was hard to make out because it was shrouded in shadow, so it was impossible to see any details. He looked less like a person and more like a part of the slow decay, like an extension of the manor's growing wildness. His back was to Eleanor as he cut back a huge, thick vine with a pair of dull shears. He had an aura of deep stillness around him, a silence that didn't mean peace but an old, sad acceptance. He worked with a purpose, but his movements were so slow and disconnected that they seemed to be outside of time.

Eleanor felt a shiver of fear that was different from the immediate terror of the mirrored ballroom or the suffocating sadness of the nursery. This fear was colder and more basic. The figure was a ghost gardener taking care of a garden that was trying to take back the house and pull it back into the ground where it had been built. The vines that crept through the broken panes of the new window and the roots that probed the foundations weren't just signs of neglect; they felt like acts of reclamation. And this ghostly figure, this quiet guard, was making sure that the process was not rushed or chaotic, but a slow, sure decline. Eleanor realized with a sickening certainty that he was a symbol of the manor's slow, inevitable encroachment, its patient, consuming embrace.

The person stopped, the shears hanging loosely in his hand. He turned his head, which was such a small movement that Eleanor almost missed it. Even though his face was still in the dark, she felt a strong, steady gaze on her, which made her feel cold and aware that he had seen her. There was no curiosity or anger in the look; it was just a deep, ancient knowledge that she was stuck. It was the look of a guard, someone who kept people out of a place that didn't want them there. He didn't directly acknowledge her, beckon her, or threaten her, but the message was clear: she was seen and not free.

The air around the figure seemed to get thicker and blend in with the shadows. The vines that were closest to him seemed to move, as if they were following his silent order. They got braver, their tendrils reaching deeper into the manor. Their leaves made a dry, whispering sound that sounded like a sigh of satisfaction. Eleanor could see through the broken window pane that the house seemed to vibrate slightly, as if it was responding to the gardener's presence and silent care.

Eleanor felt an irresistible pull, a sickening interest that fought with her desire to run away. She wanted to know more about this ghostly figure in the dying garden, this silent protector. He was a physical representation of the manor's slow, creeping death and its desire to consume. He wasn't trying to hurt her on purpose, like the mirrors in the ballroom had played with her fears or the nursery had taken advantage of her compassion. His presence was much more dangerous; it was a quiet sign that she was trapped. He was the living proof of the manor's slow victory, a sign that everything inside its walls would eventually die, rot, and be eaten by the hungry earth.

The gardener went back to work, moving just as slowly as before. He cut a thick bunch of berries off a vine, bowing his head in a sign of quiet respect. He didn't throw them away; instead, he held them in his hand like they were valuable jewels. Eleanor was spellbound as he brought them to his lips and tilted his shadowed face up a little bit. He didn't eat them; he just breathed in their strong, rotten smell, which was a way for him to connect with the wild growth around him. It was a ritual of giving up, a quiet way to show that the garden was in charge of everything.

She then saw that the vines closest to the hole in the wall were growing at a speed that was almost impossible to see. They moved and stretched, and their thorny tendrils slowly made their way deeper into the hallway where she was standing. The air was thick with their smell, which made the sweetness of decay even stronger and more suffocating. The gardener seemed to be an agent of the manor's desire to grow, to pull everything within its reach into its green, decaying mouth while he stood watch in silence.

He wasn't just taking care of the garden; he was planning its invasion. His slow, careful movements weren't meant to keep things in order; they were meant to help the inevitable reclamation along. He was making sure that the house wasn't just falling apart, but that it was being taken apart piece by piece and absorbed by the wilderness that was creeping in. His presence was a terrifying reminder of the manor's lasting power, a silent promise that getting away was not only hard, but impossible. He was the living proof of the house's slow but sure victory, and his quiet work was a terrifying sign of her own fate.

Eleanor felt a twinge of desperation. Thomas was lost in the manor's changing architecture, and she was faced with a silent guardian who was the living embodiment of the house's parasitic nature. She couldn't fight him or talk sense into him. He was a force of nature, or rather, a force of unnatural nature, working with the manor's evil will. The garden was more than just an outside threat; it was also an inside threat, a sign of the decay that was getting into the house and, by extension, into their lives.

She looked at her hands and thought they would be stained with the thick, black liquid she had seen before, or maybe they were already covered in tiny, new vines. But her hands were clean and free of dirt. But she felt deeply contaminated, like something was wrong with her spirit that settled deep in her bones. The spectral gardener's gaze, though unseen, felt like a brand on her soul, a sign that the manor owned her.

The gardener, who looked like he was done with his pruning, straightened up. He didn't turn all the way to her, but Eleanor could tell that something had changed, a small sign that he knew she was still there. He raised a hand, not to say hello or warn, but in a slow, deliberate way that took in the vines that were creeping in and the crumbling facade of the house. It was a sign of belonging, responsibility, and total control. He was the lord of this empty land, the quiet judge of its slow, painful death.

Eleanor knew, with a chilling certainty, that she couldn't stay here, exposed in this newly formed hallway, quietly watching the manor's insidious disintegration. She had to find Thomas and get out of this place before the ghostly gardener or the house itself decided that she was an annoyance that needed to be cut back, taken in, or just let die in the growing darkness.

She slowly backed away, never taking her eyes off the shadowy figure and the plants that were getting closer. The vines looked like they were reaching out to her, their tendrils stretching out like greedy fingers. The sweet, rotting smell got stronger and almost took over. She felt sick and had a strong urge to run away from the manor's insatiable hunger.

As she walked away, the jagged hole through which she had seen the garden started to glow, and the edges became fuzzy, as if the manor was actively closing itself up and fixing the breach. The gardener's shadowy figure stayed there, a silent silhouette against the backdrop of wild decay. His presence was a chilling reminder of the manor's unyielding power. Eleanor's last look at him was when the opening closed, the rough plaster reformed, leaving only a faint, wet stain and the sickeningly sweet smell of decay. The ghostly gardener of the manor wasn't just taking care of the grounds; he was also making sure that the house and everything inside it were slowly and carefully taken back by the darkness. He was the quiet guard of their prison, a living reminder of the manor's slow, certain victory. The sound of dripping, which had briefly stopped in her shock, came back with a new urgency, a clear sign that the manor's decay was not just an outside show, but a terrifying reality inside. She was still stuck, and the maze of fear had just shown her another, scarier part of its design.

Chapter 5: The Pact of Sacrifice

The Whispered Ultimatum

The air in the west wing got thicker, and it wasn't just the smell of wet decay; it was also filled with a strong, evil energy. It coiled and throbbed, a quiet start to the noise that was about to start. Eleanor's heart was still racing from seeing the ghostly gardener, and she could feel a change in the air. It was as if the manor had let out a deep, guttural breath that made the dust motes dance in the weak light and sent a shiver down her spine that had nothing to do with the cold. Thomas, who had come back as quietly as he had left, stood next to her. He was not as calm as usual, and his eyes were wide with worry, just like hers.

After that, the whispers started. Not the faint, disjointed whispers she had heard before, which were echoes of people who had lived there before. These were not the same. They were clearer and more insistent, and they sounded like they were coming from all over the walls at once, not just from certain spots. It seemed like the whole building, from its deepest foundations to its highest gables, had found a voice. The sound was a sibilant tide, a rising chorus of ancient, hungry whispers that slithered into her ears and burrowed into her mind. They talked about need, an unquenchable void, and a desperate desire that had been growing for centuries.

"It wants… something," Thomas whispered, his voice strained and his eyes darting around the hallway as if he were looking for the source of the noise.

Eleanor nodded, but she couldn't put into words the fear that was building in her stomach. The whispers were coming together, and their separate threads were weaving together to make one strong statement. The separate cries for help, the sad cries, and the faint echoes of children's laughter all faded away, leaving behind a single, chilling command. It was a voice that spoke with the weight of ages, a voice that had an authority so old and strong that it was impossible to understand.

The voice said, "A sacrifice is needed," and it wasn't sound; it was a vibration that went through bone and marrow. It was a clear and terrible statement that seemed to rip through the very fabric of reality. It was so bad that the walls shook and the stones groaned under the weight of it. Eleanor felt a wave of cold wash over her, and she was sure that this was not a request but a demand. The house, this huge thing she was just starting to understand, was more than just a bunch of old rooms and ghosts. It was a living thing that needed food.

"Give up?" Eleanor said, her voice barely a tremor against the house's strong demand. The word sounded strange, savage, and like something from a long-gone, bloody past. But there it was, echoing in the heart of this empty manor, a terrifying ultimatum spoken with an ancient, predatory authority.

The whispers came back, this time not as a chorus of demands but as a scary explanation of how hungry the house was. They talked about how it was hungry not only for warmth, light, and life, but also for essence, spirit, and the spark that brought a soul to life. It was a hunger that had grown over the years, a hole that had gotten bigger with each soul it had eaten. The spectral gardener's presence, the creeping vines, and the constant decay were all signs of this unending need. The house wasn't just falling apart; it was actively eating itself and, by extension, its residents in a desperate, never-ending search for food.

Thomas held Eleanor's arm tightly, making his knuckles turn white. "It wants a life," he said, and the horror grew on his face as he realized what he had said. "It wants one of us."

The sentence hung in the air like a tombstone's inscription, cold and final. Eleanor's head spun. There were no ghosts or hauntings in this story. This was a basic deal, a twisted agreement made by a horrible being. The manor was not just a place where bad things happened in the past. It was a living, breathing predator that had set a trap and was now demanding payment for their intrusion, for being inside its walls.

"Why?" Eleanor asked in a whisper, her voice breaking. "Why does it need a sacrifice?"

The whispers didn't directly answer her question, but they did give her a scary setting. They talked about a balance that had been upset, or an equilibrium. They suggested that the house was about to fall down, and that time and decay were threatening its very existence. The growing wildness, the ghostly unrest, and the strong feeling of hopelessness were all signs that it was about to fall apart. The whispers suggested that the sacrifice was not just a way to calm the beast down, but a last-ditch effort to keep it alive, to give it the life force it needed, and to keep its miserable existence going. It was a frightening discovery: the house wasn't just a prison; it was a dying being that was desperately trying to stay alive by eating anyone who dared to enter its domain.

"Don't go there, Eleanor," Thomas said in a hurry. "It's not asking for a sacrifice; it's demanding one. It gives us a choice, but there isn't really a choice."

He was correct. The ultimatum was harsh, clear, and gave no real choice. The house was giving them a terrible choice: one of them had to be sacrificed to stop its destructive growth, or else the house would keep falling apart, taking them both and the very foundations of the manor with it. The meaning was clear: if they didn't give it what it wanted, it would take what it wanted anyway, and its hungry mouth would get bigger with each passing second. The choice was not between life and death, but between a quick, painful death as the chosen victim or a slow, painful death as the house consumed them both.

Eleanor looked at Thomas. She saw the same dawning horror in his eyes, the same desperate fight to understand what was happening. They were stuck in a nightmare that was so twisted and wrong that it didn't make sense in the world they knew. This wasn't just a ghost; it was a bad spirit, a sentient decay that didn't see them as people but as fuel, as offerings to keep its terrible existence going.

Eleanor said, "It wants us to choose," and the words tasted like ash in her mouth. "It wants us to choose who dies."

The house seemed to hum with excitement, a low, resonant thrum that shook the floorboards, traveled up Eleanor's legs, and settled deep in her bones. For a moment, the whispers stopped, as if the being was waiting for them to fully understand how horrible their situation was and how heavy the decision they had to make was.

Eleanor's voice got sharper as she said, "This is not a choice, Thomas." "This is a trick. It's trying to make us hate each other." She thought of the nursery, the ghostly kids, and the sadness that hung over those rooms. The house took advantage of feelings and weakness. And what could be more vulnerable than the thought of giving up a loved one?

Thomas's jaw got tight. "But what choice do we have? If we refuse, it will… it will consume us both. And then what? It will just keep going." He pointed vaguely at the walls and the heavy air that seemed to be closing in on them. "This place is falling apart. It needs something important to hold it together."

His words were heavy. The logic, no matter how horrible, was clear. The house was dying and needed a new life. Their lives. It was a moral abyss to think about who would live and who would die. It was a place where sanity fell apart and humanity died.

Eleanor said, "We can't," her voice strong but shaky. "We can't be the ones to make that choice. To choose who should die would be just as bad as the house itself." She thought of the ghostly gardener and how he worked silently and without stopping. He was a sign of the house's desire to fall apart, and now they were being asked to help it fall apart by picking the victim.

Thomas replied, his eyes pleading for understanding, "What if refusing means we both die?" "What if our noble refusal seals our fate? Is it better to die together or let this thing keep going in its destructive cycle?" His eyes moved over the peeling wallpaper, the water-stained ceiling, and the shadows that always seemed to be in the corners of the room. "It's a twisted deal, Eleanor. It's giving us a chance to live, but at a terrible cost."

Eleanor looked around the hallway. The new walls were still wet and smelled a little bit like dirt. She saw the vines creeping in through cracks that weren't visible, and the shadows got darker, as if they were trying to swallow the little light that was there. The house was alive, like a hungry beast, and it had made them a deal. A deal to give up something. Not only was the demand for a life horrifying, but the way it was framed as a negotiation, a sick form of salvation offered at the highest cost, was even worse.

Eleanor said softly, "It's not salvation, Thomas." "Either way, it's damnation. But if we give in to its demands and choose one of us to die, then we've really lost. We become part of its evil." She took a deep breath, and the heavy air filled her lungs. "We need to find a different way. There has to be a different way."

But the house didn't seem to have any patience for that kind of disobedience. The oppressive energy in the hallway grew stronger, a silent force that threatened to crush them. The whispers started up again. This time, there wasn't just one voice; there were many. It was a loud mix of sneaky suggestions, each one a subtle push, a tempting whisper of escape for one person at the cost of the other. They painted vivid pictures of how they would survive and how they would gain freedom by killing the other person. A voice whispered that Eleanor had escaped and that her life would go on, while Thomas's spirit kept the manor going. Another voice said that Thomas was safe and sound and walking away, leaving Eleanor to face the house's last, all-consuming embrace. It was a mental torture meant to break them, plant seeds of distrust and fear, and finally force them to act.

"It's trying to break us," Thomas said, his voice strained and his eyes on Eleanor. "It wants us to see each other as the enemy." He reached out, not to touch her, but to try to close the gap of fear that the house was trying to create between them. "We can't let it do that, Eleanor. No matter what happens, we face it together. We don't... we don't choose."

Eleanor nodded, and they made a weak agreement to fight the house's sneaky manipulation. But the whispers didn't stop. They kept attacking their resolve, each one a poisoned dart aimed at the heart of their trust. They talked about instinct, self-preservation, and the way things are supposed to be, twisting these basic urges into reasons to betray. The house was a master manipulator. Its ultimatum wasn't just a demand for a life; it was a test of their humanity. It was a sick game where the prize was survival and the cost was their souls.

"The pact," Eleanor whispered, and the word had a horrible finality to it. "It's a pact of sacrifice, and it wants us to willingly enter it." She felt a deep sense of despair wash over her. How could they get out of a deal where one wrong move could mean death? How could they outsmart a being that was slowly killing them? The whispers kept coming, a never-ending wave of fear and desire. Eleanor knew that the real horror of the manor wasn't its ghosts or its decay, but how it could turn their own fears and desires into weapons against them, making them face the darkest parts of their own hearts. The house wanted a life, a sacrifice, and by doing so, it made them face the terrifying thought that the worst monster of all might not be the house itself, but the darkness that lay within them, awakened by its evil ultimatum.

The Price of Survival

The spectral announcement had stopped, and the silence that followed was so deep that it hurt Eleanor's ears and made her heart beat faster. The air felt heavy, thick with unspoken fears, even though the house's scary order had stopped vibrating. Thomas stood next to her with a look of growing fear on his face. His eyes were fixed on something beyond the peeling wallpaper and the shadows that were creeping in. He looked like he had gotten older in just a few scary minutes.

"The tithe," he whispered, and even though the words were barely audible, they broke the heavy silence like a shard of ice. "The deed... there was a clause." A "tithe of residency."

Eleanor's forehead wrinkled. She had barely skimmed the old, moldy document because she was too focused on the manor's obvious, immediate decay. "A tithe? What does that mean?

Thomas looked at her with wide eyes, showing the same fear she felt. "It means that the house doesn't just take us in. It needs a gift. A gift. "Not just an accident, but a planned act." He swallowed hard, and his throat worked. "The deed... it's a deal. A deal made a long time ago. It needs a life, either given freely or taken, to stay alive. A "tithe of residency" for those who are brave enough to live there.

The effects hit Eleanor like a physical blow. They weren't just stuck in a decaying, living structure that would slowly take away their life force. They were being given a terrible choice, a cruel split that turned the idea of survival on its head. The house wasn't just a predator; it was a careful bookkeeper who demanded its due, its pound of flesh, which they had to give up.

Eleanor said, "So, it's not enough that it will kill us." The words tasted like bile. "It wants us to pick who dies." To openly criticize someone. To become… executioners." The whispers, which are now silent, seemed to echo in her mind, where their evil suggestions took root in the rich soil of despair. They had given them a terrible, inhuman choice between one life and the other, and in doing so, they had forced them to face the darkest part of their own humanity.

Thomas ran a shaking hand through his hair. "It's a planned act of betrayal, Eleanor. We need to actively bring life to the house. We must condemn one of our own, or possibly another individual if there are additional parties involved. But there isn't anyone else. It's us. We have to decide who among us will be fed to this… this thing. He pointed vaguely at the oppressive atmosphere and the manor's very stones, which seemed to throb with evil anticipation. "It needs a willing surrender or a forced one." And the deed… the deed makes it clear. It's a condition of living there. A required tithe. And if they don't want to pay it…"

"Then it takes it anyway," Eleanor said, her voice empty. She realized with a sickening lurch that the ghostly gardener had been an unintentional sign of this terrible truth. He had been a part of the tithe, a soul that had already been claimed, and a silent proof of the manor's never-ending need. His ghostly presence wasn't a warning; it was a grim sign of things to come, a reminder of the blood that had already been shed in these walls to satisfy the house's ancient hunger.

"But how do we 'willingly' give up a life?" Eleanor asked, her head spinning. The idea itself was terrible. "How can anyone make themselves die, especially when there is a chance, no matter how small, that they will live?"

Thomas's eyes were unfocused, and it was clear that his mind was far away, trying to solve an impossible problem. "Maybe... maybe it's not about wanting to die." Maybe it's about accepting that it will happen. About realizing that one life must end in order to save another. And in that acceptance, in that grim resignation, there is a kind of "willingness." He looked back at Eleanor with eyes full of deep pain. "I know it's twisted logic. But this place... It has its own set of rules and a horrible sense of right and wrong. The deed is more than just a legal document; it's proof of a blood pact, an old agreement that binds us to its will.

He took a deep, uneven breath. "Consider it, Eleanor. If we don't make a choice and just stand here, the house will take us both. It will pull us down into its hunger and decay. We will be eaten up, piece by piece, until there is nothing left of us. That's one thing that could happen. The other one is that one of us gets an offer. One life is lost, and the other goes on. The house gets its tithe, and its aggressive growth stops, at least for a while. The deal is horrible, but that's what the deed says it is.

Eleanor's stomach turned. She couldn't stand the thought of either Thomas or her actively choosing to condemn the other. It was a fall into a moral pit that could never be climbed back out of. Choosing that would mean accepting the very darkness they were fighting against and joining the manor's horrible hunger. "But to choose... to make that choice... it makes us as horrible as the house itself, Thomas." It makes us into the thing we are afraid of.

"And what if not making that choice means we both have to face a much worse fate?" Thomas replied, his voice full of desperate urgency. "What if our brave defiance is just a longer way to go to nothingness? Eleanor, the house is alive. It eats. It needs food. The deed is proof that we own it and the contract for our lives. It doesn't just want us to leave; it wants us to pay for being there. It can get a payment in the form of a life. He touched the wall's rough, wet stone with his hand. "This place is dying, but it's a slow, painful death that it's putting off by eating whatever it can. The tithe is what keeps it alive. And we are its newest gift. Even if the terms of the contract don't make sense to us, we need to understand them.

He stopped and looked at Eleanor's face, looking for a sign of understanding or shared horror. "The deed... It talks about "a willing contribution to the manor's continued vitality." That's how it sounds. "Vitality." As if giving up your life is a gift. A gift that stops this monument from falling apart completely. Eleanor, it's a perversion of life. "A sacrament that is twisted."

Eleanor's mind raced as she looked for another option, a way out, anything but the harsh, brutal choice that was being offered. "But what if the tithe isn't a life? What if it could be something else? Something that isn't so... final? She thought about the whispers, the sad life of the ghostly gardener, and the sadness that filled the air. Is there another way to make a sacrifice? A sacrifice of memory, spirit, or something less real than a physical life?

Thomas shook his head, looking very serious. "The deed is clear: 'A tithe of residency.'" It means that someone is alive. A soul to take. The whispers and ghostly figures are echoes of lives that have already been lived or are fighting against the inevitable. But this agreement... this agreement needs a conscious and active giving up. It's the cost of our crime. Our intrusion has awakened it, and now it demands its due. It's not just about staying alive; it's also about keeping an old promise that we didn't mean to break.

He looked down at his hands and flexed his fingers as if he were trying to hold on to something solid, something real, in the face of this growing unreality. "I keep thinking about how to say it. "A contribution that is willing." It suggests a deliberate action. That we, the people who live there, have to give it. Not that it just takes it. It means there is a choice. A terrible choice that can't be put into words. To decide to kill one of us to save the other.

Eleanor felt a cold fear in her bones as she realized how trapped they were. The house wasn't just a passive, evil force; it was a smart negotiator that spelled out its terms in the cold, legalistic way that a contract does. The deed wasn't just a record of what happened; it was the plan for their suffering and the legal reason for the horror that was happening. "So, we have to become its agents," she said in a voice that was barely above a whisper. "To carry out the execution." To take part in this horrible ritual.

"Exactly," Thomas said, his voice strained. "We're not just victims; we could also be the ones who do it. The house doesn't want to get its own hands dirty, at least not directly. It would rather get us to do its dirty work. It wants us to hurt ourselves and each other to show that it has complete control over us. If we want to, we will always be tainted. If we say no, we will be eaten. There is no way out that is clean. We are the ones who have to pay the tithe.

He looked at Eleanor, and for a second, she saw the void in his eyes. He was a scholar, a man of reason and logic, and this irrational, primal fear was tearing apart everything he knew. "I... I have been looking for another way to look at it. Some way to get out of this. But the deed is so clear. "A tithe of residency." It's a cost of living here. A cost in life. And it must be given up. "Of my own free will."

"But 'willingly' means that there can't be consent under duress," Eleanor said, holding on to the last bits of logic. "How can any action be truly willing when the only other choice is death? It's forcing, Thomas. "That's all there is to it."

"But the house doesn't see it that way," Thomas said, his voice getting more and more desperate. "It sees it as a necessary deal. A fair trade. Your life or mine in exchange for the manor staying in business. It's a strange way to keep things safe. It's the cost of getting in and staying there. And by coming inside these walls, we have agreed to its terms without saying so. He pointed at the oppressive buildings and the clear signs of decay around them. "This place is a monument to its own survival, built on the backs of others." The deed is just the legal part of that horrible legacy.

Eleanor felt a deep sense of hopelessness. The house had not only trapped them physically, but it had also trapped them in a way that made them feel like they had no choice but to do something or nothing, which would have terrible consequences. The fear came not only from the threat of death, but also from the moral corruption it required. They would have to turn into monsters to stay alive. If they said no, they would be eaten. The pact of sacrifice was a noose, and the house had the reins, which got tighter with each passing moment.

"What do we do now?" Eleanor asked, her voice shaking. The question hung in the thick air, unanswered, showing how completely helpless they were. The weight of the deed, the "tithe of residency," felt like a heavy blanket of fear that was suffocating her. They weren't just dealing with a ghost; they were also dealing with a contract that required the highest price.

Thomas's eyes were far away, as if they were haunted. He was no longer just a man trying to stay alive; he was a man dealing with the unimaginable: the idea that he might have to actively condemn someone else in order to live. The deed, which had once been a dusty old thing, was now a poisonous snake, coiled and ready to strike, with blood from a forced sacrifice dripping from its fangs. He knew with horrible certainty that the price of staying alive was not just fear or pain, but a deep, soul-crushing act of betrayal. The house wanted its tithe, and it wanted the blood of its own choice.

Eleanors Desperate Plea

The silence that followed Thomas's grim statement was like a heavy blanket that pressed in on Eleanor from all sides. The ghostly gardener, whose ghostly form is now a chilling memory, was just a sign of a much worse horror to come. The house itself wasn't the immediate danger; it was the terrible choice it now offered. A choice between two lives, theirs, to give up as a blood tithe. The old-fashioned writing on the deed, which she had only briefly looked at in her first panic, now pulsed with a terrifying clarity, like a legal contract for their very souls.

"No," Eleanor whispered, the word getting stuck in her throat. It was small and weak compared to the heavy weight of the manor's demand. She instinctively put her hands on her chest, as if to protect her heart from the harsh truth. "No, Thomas." We can't do it. We can't even imagine it. Her pleading, wide-eyed gaze was locked on his. His eyes, which were usually calm and full of thought, now flickered with a desperate, almost feverish light. It was the light of a man who was about to fall off a cliff and into an abyss that looked like it would swallow him whole.

"Listen, Eleanor," Thomas said, his voice strained and panicked. "The deed... it's a deal. A contract that must be followed. This house is more than just a building. It's a thing. And it needs food. This "tithe of residency" is not a choice. It has to be done. He ran a hand through his already messy hair, and his movements were jerky and angry. "If we say no, if we don't pay the price..."

"Then it will take us both," Eleanor finished for him, and the words were very clear. But the idea of paying that price and taking part in the death of another person made her sick. It was a fall into a darkness that was so deep and complete that she couldn't understand it. "But Thomas, this is crazy. We're talking about killing someone. Not just killing, but giving up something. To a home. It's cruel. "That's... inhuman."

She took a hesitant step toward him, her voice softening and begging. "Do you remember what we talked about when we first moved in here? The restoration, the beauty we saw under the dirt. The past. You liked the history. And I... I saw the possibilities. The light that could come back into these old walls. We saw a home, Thomas, a safe place. Not this... this place of death. After years of studying the subtle differences in light and form, her artistic sensibilities now recoiled from the house's harsh, brutal ugliness. She didn't see life as something to be bought and sold. Instead, she saw it as a beautiful, complicated tapestry with each thread and color being important.

For a brief moment, Thomas's eyes met hers, and she saw a flash of the man she had known, the man who had held her hand through so many shared dreams. But the fear that was coming quickly took over. "But the history, Eleanor," he said, his voice low and full of despair. "The past is full of blood. The deed shows that. This house hasn't always been empty. It has eaten. It has asked for. And the people who owned it before must have paid. Or they were eaten. "We're just the most recent entry in its sick ledger."

"And what if the deed is a lie?" Eleanor pushed harder, her desperation giving her a weak strength. "What if it's a trick to get us to fight each other?" The whispers, Thomas... they were sneaky, weren't they? They took advantage of our fears. This... this is just another level of that pain. The house is trying to break us and make us its willing tools of destruction. She shook her head very hard. "I won't let it happen. I won't let this monster poison our love or our humanity. "We need to find another way."

"Another way?" Thomas echoed, and a hollow laugh came out of his mouth. "What else can we do, Eleanor? The deed is a legal document. It is binding. It's the cost of living here. It needs a "tithe of residency." It needs a life. A willing giving up. The text suggests that. The spectral pronouncements confirmed that. He pointed around them at the hall's oppressive, crumbling grandeur. "This place is a parasite." It grabs hold of those who dare to live in it and drains them. But this... this is not the same. This is a planned gift. "A sacrifice to make it happy."

"But 'willing'..." Eleanor's voice was strong and demanding. "How can it be willing when the other choice is death? That's not being willing, Thomas; that's forcing. A gun in the head. It's a twisted way of thinking that isn't meant to get us to make a real sacrifice. We can't believe it. We need to keep what makes us human. We need to keep in mind who we are and what we promised each other. She reached out and touched his arm, her fingers shaking. "I love you, Thomas." More than anything, I love you. I can't stand the thought of losing you. But the idea of you killing someone or me killing someone is worse than death. "That's a death of the soul."

He pulled away slightly, his gaze darting around the room as if searching for an escape route that didn't exist. "What if my love for you and my desire to protect you are what make me choose?" What if I think it's the only way to keep you alive? Isn't that a kind of willingness? A sacrifice of my own soul and morals for yours? The words were said with a chilling certainty, a horrifying reason that made Eleanor feel even more afraid. He was already making excuses, already looking for reasons to stay in the cruel structure of the house.

"No," Eleanor said, her voice getting stronger as the fierce protectiveness that filled her grew. "That's not a sacrifice, Thomas. That's giving in. That means this place is telling you what to do and how to feel. It turns love into something horrible. The house wants us to think that the only way to stay alive is to destroy. But that's its story, not ours. We need to fight back with something more powerful. Because we won't let ourselves be corrupted. She moved closer, making him look at her. "Think about the people who made this place. Did they do it with good intentions? Did they fill it with love or something darker? It seems like all this decay and evil is the result of their choices. And we can choose something else. "A choice that ends the cycle."

"But the deed, Eleanor!" Thomas's voice got louder and cracked with pain. "It's ironclad." It is a legal paper. A blood contract from hundreds of years ago. It has strength. It has some weight. It has bound others before us, and it will bind us if we don't follow its rules. He shut his eyes, as if just thinking about it was too much for him. "I can feel it." The stress. The house is waiting. "It's patient, but it can't get enough food."

Eleanor shook her head, and her eyes were full of defiance and fear. "I don't care about the action. I care about you and me. About the life we live and the life we've made. This house can't say that. It can't make us put out the light inside us. The whispers were meant to cause trouble, make us doubt each other, and make us doubt ourselves. This demand for a sacrifice is the hardest test of all. And if we give in to this darkness and fail, then this house has really won. It will have eaten us up, not just our bodies but also our souls.

She took his hands and held them tightly. "Look at me, Thomas. Look at me closely. Can you see fear? Yes, I'm scared. But do you see hopelessness? Do you see giving up? No. I see defiance. I see hope. I hope we are stronger than this. We hope that love and our shared humanity can protect us from this old evil. The house wants a "tithe of residency." What if we look at it in a different way? What if we give something else? Something that recognizes us but doesn't kill us?

"Like what?" Thomas asked, his voice tired. "What can we give a house that wants blood? A work of art? A poem? What about our memories? Eleanor, it doesn't want art. It wants the essence. It needs a life force to keep its structure from falling apart.

"Maybe it wants more than just food," Eleanor said, her mind racing as she tried to find any glimmer of hope. "Maybe it wants to be recognized. Acknowledgment of its strength. But not if it means giving up our own morals. What if we promised to protect it not by giving up something, but by fixing it? To promise to fix it and restore its lost beauty, not as a bribe, but as a real gift of our skills, time, and effort. "To give it life back, not take it away."

Thomas looked at her with a furrowed brow and a hint of doubt in his eyes. "But the deed says there is a "tithe." A payment. Not a work of love. It talks about a cost, a price that must be paid. Eleanor, restoration is work, but it's not giving up your life.

"But what if the deed's beautiful phrase 'vitality' doesn't just mean blood?" Eleanor kept saying it, and her voice got louder. "What if its 'vitality' is also about being alive and not being forgotten? What if we are giving it a chance to live on by working to restore it? What if we are giving it a chance to be remembered for its beauty instead of its evil? I know this is a strange way of looking at things, but we're dealing with a strange thing. And maybe a strange answer is needed. She held his hands tightly. "Don't let this place get to you, Thomas. Don't let it make you do something that would stay with you forever, even if you lived through it. We are not just renters. We are people who can love, care, and do good things. That should be our defense. "Our refusal to take part in its cruelty is our rebellion."

Finally, he looked her in the eye, and Eleanor saw a flash of his old self fighting the fear that had taken over him. "You really think that? "Really?"

"I have to," Eleanor said, her voice steady. "Because the other option is too awful to think about. The other option is that we lose ourselves. This house wants us to be monsters, and we become them. I won't be that. And I won't let you do that. We'll find a different way. We have to. She took a deep breath and made up her mind. "If the house asks for a tithe, we will give it a tithe of our art, our dedication, and our strength as a group. We will try to fix it and make it beautiful again, as a sign of how strong we are and how we refuse to be broken. I know it's a long shot. But it's a shot that keeps our spirits alive. "It's a shot that keeps us alive, not just as survivors, but as ourselves." She let go of his hands, and her own hands shook a little, but she kept looking at him, a beacon of desperate hope in the dark. "Please, Thomas. Don't give up. This house shouldn't take away our humanity. Let's give it a shot. "Let's try to calm it down with something other than blood."

The Ghost of Temptation

The air in the grand hall got colder, not because of the cold air coming in through an open window, but because of a creeping fear that seemed to come from the stones themselves. Eleanor's breath caught as a new figure began to take shape in front of her. It wasn't the ghostly gardener from before, and it wasn't the dark, heavy darkness that had almost swallowed her. This ghost was... classy. The ghostly outlines of a man in clothes that looked like they came from a different time— a high-necked cravat, a finely tailored frock coat—appeared with an almost aristocratic grace. They were now in shades of spectral gray and translucent mist. His features, though not very clear, had a hauntingly beautiful quality that was disarming. But beneath this ghostly refinement, Eleanor felt a deep, gnawing despair, a desperation that was like her own.

He drifted closer, and his shape disturbed the air, making a ripple in the heavy silence. His eyes, which looked like tarnished silver pools, were fixed on her. There was no malice or clear threat in their eyes, just an unsettling emptiness, a huge, empty space where a soul should have been. When he opened his mouth, his voice was a soft whisper that barely disturbed the air, but it echoed deep inside Eleanor's bones. It was a voice that promised comfort and dripped with the sweetness of an impossible answer.

"You are trapped," the ghostly man said in a voice that sounded like dry leaves rustling. "I was too. This house... It ties us together. It eats. And it won't be denied. You want to find a way out, don't you? "Is there a way out of this terrible choice, this impossible equation?"

Eleanor's heart raced against her ribs. This was a new temptation, a new way that the house was being evil. This wasn't a demand that was too strong; it was a seductive whisper, a gentle push in the direction of her most desperate wants. She instinctively pulled back, and a knot of suspicion grew in her stomach. "Who... who are you?" she was able to ask, even though her voice shook even though she tried to keep it steady.

The ghostly figure gave a sad, faint smile. "I was a resident. A long time ago. I got caught up in it too, just like you. The deed... it is a cruel contract, isn't it? It gives you a safe place to stay, but you have to give up your soul in return. I also thought I could negotiate and find a way to get around its harsh demands.

He waved his hand around the hall, and it went through a heavy oak table like it was smoke. "But this house… it's really old. It is smart. It plays on our deepest fears and our most desperate hopes.

He moved closer, and his ghostly shape seemed to glow with a faint light from within. "You think you can talk to it and that your 'restoration' will satisfy its hunger. Maybe a noble thought. But wrong. It wants essence, not work. It wants a life, not work. And it won't be calmed down by just feelings.

Eleanor felt a chill of fear spread through her. He spoke with such certainty and tired acceptance. Was he just a part of the house's elaborate trick, a carefully planned illusion meant to break her will? Or was he really a ghost of a past victim, a warning that looked like an offer? "You say you were stuck," she pushed, her mind racing. "Did you find a way out?"

The ghost's eyes blinked, and for a brief moment, they looked like they recognized something or remembered something painful. "There is… a passage. A hidden way. Only a few people know. For those who know how to use it, it's a way to get away. He stopped, and the air around them became thick with excitement. "It needs a… transfer. A change in who has to bear the burden. The house needs a tenth. A source of life. But it doesn't have to be yours. Or his.

Eleanor's breath caught in her throat. A move? A change in the burden? The words were like a siren song, playing on her strong desire to protect Thomas and save them both without having to deal with the horrible things that would happen if they did. It was so easy to believe what he said and hold on to the hope that there was another way, one that didn't involve them becoming killers. But she remembered the whispers and sneaky suggestions that had first tried to make her hate Thomas. This was the same game, but it was a more advanced version.

"What do you mean, 'transfer'?" she asked in a voice that was barely above a whisper. She made herself keep eye contact with him, looking for any sign of dishonesty in his ghostly gaze.

"The house demands a sacrifice," he said again, this time in a low, compelling voice. "A life to keep it strong, to make sure it stays alive, and to fulfill the contract." But the contract is old, and contracts can be changed. Reinterpreted. If you offer a new life force that is willing and belongs to the house in a different way, then the original agreement can be kept. You could go. He could go. No cost. "Unburdened."

His ghostly hand, thin and ghostly, reached out to her as if to comfort her, but Eleanor pulled away. The meaning was very clear and scary. He wasn't giving them a way to get away without anyone knowing. He was giving one of them a way to get away by killing the other, or maybe by helping the death of an innocent third party, if that were even possible. This was not freedom; it was a deal with a different devil that twisted it.

"You talk about sacrifice," Eleanor said, her voice getting harder. "Whose life do you want us to give up? Another victim? Is that what this house makes? "Not just despair, but a never-ending cycle of betrayal and death?"

The ghost's sad smile came back, along with a flash of something that could have been amusement or just the tired acceptance of a shared fate. "Victim? Give up? These are just names. The house needs food. It's a matter of business necessity. You want to keep your lives, your love, and your future safe. This is a way. A quick and clean way. Eleanor, think about it. No more fear. No more hard decisions. Only peace. No more pain. You and he walked away from this dark place, leaving its darkness behind forever.

He painted a picture of freedom, of a life free from the manor's curse, and it was a very appealing picture. His words were like balm to her frayed nerves because she was so tired of her current fight, the constant fear, and the moral dilemmas. She could almost feel the pressure easing and the weight lifting.

But then she remembered what Thomas had said: he had begged her to find a way to save their souls and their humanity. This ghost, which was a physical representation of the house's cunning, was offering a shortcut, a golden path that went straight to the heart of the darkness they were fighting.

Eleanor's voice was steady, but her stomach was churning. "Where does this 'secret passage' go?" And what does "transfer of burden" mean? Sir, you talk in riddles. Is this a way to get away or a way to keep the house's evil going?

The ghostly figure turned his head, and his see-through body wobbled a little. "It goes away from here. To a life free from the work and demands of this place. The house needs a price, though. It always has. It is a part of what makes it exist. Your deed requires a tenth of your life to be given up as a sacrifice. But the house is very old. It has had a lot of owners and contracts. It keeps track of… and it changes. It can take a different offer, a replacement. Someone who has no right to be here, no agreement with you, but whose life force can feed its ancient hunger. A new gift. A willing one."

His silver eyes seemed to look right through her, looking for her most vulnerable spots. "Think about it, Eleanor. You walk out of these doors with the man you love. The sky is clear and the air is clean. No more ghostly whispers or scary announcements. Only freedom. Yes, the house will still be there, but it won't have a hold on you anymore. The deed will be done, but not by you. It will be done by the person you leave in your place. It's a simple trade. One life for another. "But not your life."

Eleanor felt a shiver run through her. This was the house's last trap. It wasn't just about making them kill one another. It was about giving people a third choice: they could get rid of their guilt by blaming someone else. It took advantage of their desperation to stay alive and turned their love for each other into a possible weapon of great cruelty. The ghostly man, with his sad eyes and seductive words, was the perfect messenger for such a bad idea. He was the ghost of temptation, whispering about salvation while hiding in the shadows of damnation.

"And who is this 'someone'?" Eleanor yelled, her voice full of cold anger. "Where can we find this... replacement? Do we trick an innocent person into coming to this house? "Do we betray someone who trusts us?" The idea was horrible. It went against everything she and Thomas stood for and everything she believed in.

The ghost's face stayed calm, almost sad. "The house has ways of giving. It takes what it needs. You only have to be willing to accept the offer. To let the passage open. To make the exchange possible. I understand that this is a hard choice. But is it harder than watching the man you love die? Or, even worse, being the one who destroys him? Eleanor, this house is taking advantage of your love. It wants to turn your biggest strength into your biggest weakness. Don't let it. Take this offer. "It's the only real way out."

He reached out his hand again, and this time Eleanor could feel a faint, ghostly warmth coming from it. It was a false attraction that made her want to give in. It was the warmth of false hope, the promise of an end to suffering, a seductive illusion meant to keep her from seeing how wrong it was. His voice was soft and silky as he whispered, "The passage awaits." "The load can be moved. You are free. You just have to pick freedom instead of guilt. Over what you think is right."

Eleanor looked at him, her mind a storm of mixed feelings. Desperation and disgust fought with each other. The desire to escape and the strong desire to protect Thomas fought with her basic sense of right and wrong and her deep belief in the sanctity of life. This house was a predator, and its methods were getting more and more advanced. It had gone past ghostly gardeners and strange warnings. Now, it was using the very essence of human temptation, using the echoes of past victims to offer twisted paths to salvation, paths that always led to deeper damnation. She knew with a terrifying certainty that this ghostly man was not a friend, but a sign of the house's clever plan to break its residents by giving them a choice that was so painful and morally wrong that either way would lead to their death. This was the ghost of temptation, and its whispers were the most dangerous thing of all.

The Weight of Choice

The spectral gentleman's words hung in the cold air, each syllable a tiny shard of ice that stuck to Eleanor's bones. Liberty. A life without limits. The phrase echoed in the empty chambers of her despair, like a siren song promising an end to the constant pain. But the cost… The price was so morally wrong and so bad that just thinking about it made her stomach turn with nausea. This wasn't an escape; it was a Faustian deal, dressed up to look like a way out.

"You talk about a transfer," Eleanor finally said, her voice hoarse and rough, struggling to get through the heavy blanket of fear that felt like a burial shroud around her. "A replacement. One who is willing. She laughed, but it was a brittle sound that wasn't funny. "Sir, 'willing' is as strange to me as sunlight in this house." Who would willingly give themselves to this… this thing? Her eyes moved over the grand hall, which now seemed bigger, with deeper shadows and a silence that was full of unseen horrors. The ghostly man, who looked like he was tragically resigned, was just a pawn, a mouthpiece for the manor's ancient, never-ending hunger.

The ghost's sad smile flickered, and there was a ghostly light in his dirty silver eyes. "The house has its own quiet ways of getting people to do what it wants, Eleanor. It has a way of getting what it needs. Not always through direct threats, but through the subtle nudging of circumstance and the whispers of desperation that bring out a person's deepest wants and weaknesses. Sometimes, "willing" just means not having the will to fight against an overwhelming tide. He waved his hand again, and his transparent hand went through a picture on the wall. The stern-faced ancestor's painted eyes looked like they were crying ghostly tears. "You are bound by the deed. It calls for a sacrifice. But the house, with its endless, ancient cunning, lets people see things in new ways. A way out, if you will. One that takes the burden off of those who already have it, those who claim it through contract, and puts it on someone who is... untainted. "Unclaimed."

Eleanor shook her head slowly and on purpose, like a woman who was drowning and fighting against a strong current. "And this 'wild' soul, this 'unclaimed' life... where do we find them? Do we bring them here? Are we giving them false safety, a trap that looks like safety? Are we turning into the monsters we fear, reflecting the harshness of this place in our own? The disgust was a physical pain, a burning mark on her conscience. She thought of Thomas, whose face was filled with despair as he quietly begged them to find a way to keep their humanity and not let the darkness around them stain them forever. This ghost's offer was the opposite of that request.

"The house provides," the ghost said again, his voice a soothing balm that didn't calm the storm inside her. "It has its own economy of souls." You just have to be open to what it has to offer. To agree to the trade. Eleanor, think about it. No more the nagging worry about what the next day will bring. No more the painful math of who has to die and who has to suffer. The fresh, clean air outside, the warmth of the sun, and the fact that you are free. Thomas is free. The deed is done. The house has its share. The load has been moved. There is no going back. "A beautiful answer."

Nice. The word was a horrible joke. There was nothing graceful about betraying someone like that, throwing them into the abyss on purpose to save yourself. But as the ghost spoke, a desperate, sneaky thought began to creep into her mind, like a tiny seed of compromise planted in the dry ground of her tiredness. She saw Thomas's face, which was pale and drawn, and the horrors he had already seen in his eyes. The weight of their shared situation was heavy on him. Could she send him to the horrors of the deed and the bloody consequences of their contract when this other option was available? Was her own moral purity worth the chance that he would destroy her?

"What if," Eleanor started, her voice barely above a whisper and the words stuck in her throat, "what if there is another way?" A way that doesn't include this? She couldn't bring herself to say how horrible the phantom's offer really was.

The ghostly man's sad face grew sadder, and his transparent body seemed to sag with the weight of age. "Many people have looked for 'another way,' Eleanor. A lot of people have tried to reason with the house, outsmart it, and bargain with its old, unfeeling core. All of them have failed. This house is not a puzzle to solve; it is a natural force that needs to be calmed down. And its demands are non-negotiable. The deed is a promise. And promises must be kept, no matter how cruel they are. He stopped for a moment, and his ghostly body shook, as if the memory of his own fight was a real pain. "I, too, looked for another way. For years, I looked for a way out, a loophole, or a clause that had been missed. I thought I was smart and tough. And finally... His voice faded away, leaving behind a cold silence.

Eleanor felt a cold fear creep into her. His words were a clear and scary proof that the house would not give in. He wasn't offering a way out; he was offering a way out that looked like a clever way to avoid it. The house seemed to respond when it sensed their hesitation and internal conflict. A low groan came from deep inside the manor, as if it were coming from the very foundations of the building. The air got heavier and thicker, pressing down on Eleanor and Thomas like a weight. The oppressive atmosphere, which had been with them all the time, got worse and worse until it was almost too much to handle, like a blanket of dread and despair that suffocated them.

A door that hadn't been there a few minutes before creaked open across the hall, showing not a familiar room but a new, scary one. Inside, Eleanor could see figures, effigies made of what looked like dried leaves and twisted twigs, their shapes twisted into horrible parodies of human suffering. They didn't say anything or move, but their blank, unsettling stares made it seem like they were watching her. This was a silent sign of the horrors that lay beneath the surface of this cursed place. The house was speeding up its plans, and its changes were happening more often and more violently. It was a constant attack meant to break their will and shatter their composure.

Thomas moved next to her, found her hand, and held it tightly, as if he were desperate. When he looked into Eleanor's eyes, she saw the same fear and pain that was tearing her apart. "We can't," he said softly, his voice barely audible, as if he were trying to stop the madness from taking over. "We can't do this, Eleanor. Not like this."

His words were a weak shield against the attack, a desperate reminder of their shared humanity. But the house was great at psychological warfare and knew how to use even the strongest ties to its advantage. The new room, with its creepy statues, seemed to be full of dark energy that made Eleanor's deepest fears grow. The constant stress, the lack of any other options, and the nagging feeling that time was not on their side all started to wear down their will. The ghost's offer, which had once been unthinkable, now seemed to call out with a desperate, though dark, logic.

"But what do we have to choose from, Thomas?" Eleanor whispered back, the question coming from her deepest fear. "The deed… it needs a life. If not ours, then… She couldn't finish her thought because the implications were too terrible to say. The weight of their possible decision and the terrible effects of either choice were pressing down on them, threatening to crush them both. The house had thrown them into a moral abyss, forcing them to face the darkest parts of their own desires, fears, and ability to protect themselves.

The ghostly man watched them with a blank face, silently watching their inner pain. He didn't offer any comfort or judgment; all he had was the chilling proof of his own past failures and surrender. He was the house's evil temptation, the ghost of a lost soul whispering about how salvation could come through damnation. The newly revealed room, with its creepy dolls, seemed to get closer. Its ghostly presence seeped into the air they breathed, a constant, unsettling reminder of how much they had to pay for not making a decision. Every second that passed, every creak of the house, and every flash of a ghostly figure made their situation worse. The pact of sacrifice was coming, and the house, sensing their wavering, was ready to collect what it was owed, either through their own terrible actions or through the devious plans of its ghostly messengers. The weight of choice was no longer a burden; it was a crushing, suffocating force that threatened to take away the last bits of their hope and humanity.

Chapter 6: The Predator Awakens

The Houses Full Intent

The silence that had once been heavy now crackled with a real threat. Eleanor and Thomas stood still, holding hands, as if they were trying to hold on to something in a sea of rising fear. The spectral gentleman's words, even though he had disappeared as quietly as he had come, kept echoing in the back of Eleanor's mind: a cruel deal, a poisoned chalice that looked like salvation. But it seemed that the house was tired of the polite way ghosts talked to each other. It was no longer happy with small psychological attacks or slowly breaking their will. A new, terrifying phase had begun. There was an active, evil intelligence that made it clear: Blackwood Manor was no longer just a house; it was a predator, and they were its prey.

The first open act was a violent slamming of the grand hall doors, which made a loud noise that echoed through the stone and wood and shook the air. It wasn't the random creak of an old house settling; it was a strong, planned closing, as if a giant hand had slammed them shut. The sound was followed by a sickening lurch that made Eleanor feel dizzy for a second and made her stagger. Thomas's grip got stronger, and his knuckles turned white. "What was that?" he said, his eyes wide with fear.

"It's… it's changing," Eleanor said in a shaky voice. The previous signs—quick shadows, whispers without bodies, and scary apparitions—had been scary and unsettling, but they had also been almost ghostly. This was different. This felt real, physical, and like a show of raw, untamed power.

The expensive Persian rug under their feet started to ripple, as if to confirm her scary realization. It wasn't a gentle draft; it was a deep, natural movement, like the muscles flexing that you couldn't see. The complicated patterns changed, and the bright dyes got darker and swirled around as if the fabric were alive. Eleanor felt a shiver of fear run down her back. It wasn't just a building; it was a living thing, and its limbs were now trying to catch them.

"On the floor!" Thomas screamed, his voice a raw shout of fear. He pulled Eleanor back just as a part of the rug in front of them seemed to bend and twist, showing not the polished oak underneath, but a swirling void of blackness that made a low, guttural growl. The sound was deep, echoing, and completely not human. It talked about a hunger that had been hidden for a long time and was now free.

They moved back even more, their backs pressing against the cold, hard stone of the fireplace. The shadows in the corners of the hall, which were once just dark spots, started to get deeper, longer, and more together. They didn't just look like a lack of light anymore; they looked like something bigger and more evil. Eleanor watched in horror as tendrils of shadow broke free from the walls and twisted and turned like snakes. They twisted and turned with an unnatural energy, forming vague, huge shapes that looked like they were changing and reforming with every quick breath they took.

"It's hunting us," Thomas said, his face pale and sweat dripping down his forehead. "It's really hunting us."

Eleanor could only nod; she was so scared that her throat was tight and she was about to choke. "The house has its own subtle ways of persuasion," the ghostly gentleman said. Now it sounded like a cruel, ironic joke. This was not subtle at all. This was a full-on attack. The predatory nature of Blackwood Manor, which had been hinted at for a long time in its creepy atmosphere and whispers that seemed to come from nowhere, was now clear in its terrifying, unvarnished glory. The building itself had become a tool of its will, a maze not meant for living in but for trapping people.

A heavy oak table, covered in the dusty remains of a feast that had been forgotten for a long time, suddenly scraped across the floor with a sound like grinding teeth. It moved so quickly that Eleanor didn't even notice it was blocking a doorway. It was a planned move to block their way out. The air got thick and heavy with a sweet, earthy smell that Eleanor linked to wet soil and something much worse: decay.

The shadows kept doing their evil work, closing in on them and making their shapes more solid. One very scary shadow broke away from the wall next to a huge grandfather clock whose pendulum had stopped long ago. It stretched and twisted, becoming a strange, vaguely human-like shape. Eleanor couldn't see any features on it, but she felt like it was watching her and judging her. It moved in a way that made me uneasy; it didn't walk or crawl, but flowed across the floor, its shadowy tendrils reaching out and testing the air.

His voice was hoarse as he told Thomas, "Don't let it touch you." He took a heavy brass candlestick off the mantelpiece. The weight of it was only a small comfort against the terrible feeling of fear. But the candlestick seemed to get smaller in his hand, and the darkness made its metallic shine less bright.

The house seemed to enjoy how scared they were. A low, humorless laugh came from hidden corners, as if the walls themselves were laughing. It was a symphony of evil, the music that went along with their growing nightmare. The manor's hunger, which had been hard to find before, had finally found its voice. It was a creepy, rasping sound that promised death.

Eleanor's mind raced as she tried to find any logical reason or explanation, but there was none. This wasn't a ghost; it was an active, smart evil. The house was alive and breathing, and it was now trying to eat them. The deed, the ghostly man's strange offer, and the moral dilemma they had just faced all seemed like things that didn't matter anymore. Survival was the most important and immediate threat.

"We need to go," Eleanor said, her voice getting more and more urgent. "We can't just stay here." She pointed to a narrow hallway that led off the main hall. They had avoided it until now because they thought it was too small and easy to miss. Now, it was their only chance.

The house itself seemed to be working against them as they moved. The floorboards under their feet creaked and moved, threatening to break. An ornate chandelier hung above, its crystals glowing in a sickly way and swaying dangerously, as if it were about to fall. Every step was a risk, and every breath was a way to fight the oppressive air.

They got to the hallway, which was dark and twisted and seemed to go on forever. The heavy oak table that had been blocking the other door slid back with a loud thud as they stepped into it, its job done. The ghostly shapes of shadow came together again, pooling in the grand hall. Their silent, watchful presence was a chilling reminder of the predator's gaze.

The hallway didn't give them any rest. The walls seemed to be closing in, and the ceiling seemed to be pushing down. The air got colder and smelled like old, wet things that had been left behind. Eleanor saw that the tapestries on the walls, which used to show peaceful scenes, now looked like they were bending and twisting, and the people in them were making faces of silent pain. Were these just tricks of the light, or were they a sign of the house's power, a sign of the pain it had caused over the years?

"It's like a maze," Thomas said, his breath catching in his throat. "It's meant to confuse us and tear us apart."

"It's feeding on our fear," Eleanor said in a voice barely above a whisper. The ghostly man had talked about the house's "economy of souls." Maybe this was how it worked: it scared people, drove them to the edge of insanity, and then took them when they were at their weakest.

Suddenly, a part of the wall in front of them disappeared, not crumbling but just going away, revealing a small, round room. There was nothing in the room except for a single, twisted tree growing from the center of the floor. Its branches were bare and skeletal, reaching up toward the ceiling that couldn't be seen. The tree gave off an air of ancient despair, a sadness that hung over them like a shroud.

"What is this place?" Thomas asked, his voice a mix of fear and tiredness.

Eleanor felt a chill that went deeper than any physical cold. She remembered an old story about Blackwood Manor that people thought was just a story. It said that there was a hidden room in the house where its deepest sorrows were kept. Was this it? And why did they learn about it now?

The tree's bare branches started to twitch, as if in response. They started to sway slowly and on purpose, not because of a breeze, since there wasn't one, but because of an internal, ghostly movement. From the ends of the branches, glowing orbs of light started to appear, coming together to form vague shapes. They were see-through, otherworldly, and looked like they were crying silent tears.

"Spirits," Eleanor whispered, sensing the faint echo of souls that were stuck. These weren't the big, scary ghosts of the spectral gentleman; they were smaller, weaker remnants of lives that had ended long ago. They moved closer, their sad eyes fixed on Eleanor and Thomas.

"They're… they're drawn to us," Thomas stammered, reaching for Eleanor's hand without thinking.

The house wasn't just trying to trap them; it was trying to make them feel like they were in a lot of trouble. It was telling its darkest secrets and most horrible tragedies, hoping to drown them in a sea of sadness. The ghostly figures cried out in a soft, sad voice that made their nerves tingle. They reached out, and their thin forms brushed against Eleanor's arm. She felt a deep sense of loss and unfulfilled desire wash over her. The house was putting its own old sadness and grief on them.

"Don't let it," Eleanor said, her voice strained. "Don't let it get to you, Thomas. We need to fight this. She focused, pushing away the feelings that were trying to get in, and holding on to the idea of freedom, of a life outside these cursed walls.

The tree's branches twisted even more, and the light orbs grew brighter, coming together to form clearer shapes. Eleanor could now see faces—pale, thin faces that showed a pain that would never go away. They were the faces of the people who had died, been forgotten, or been killed by Blackwood Manor's never-ending hunger. The house was showing them its harvest, which was a scary sign of its power.

The floor of the room started to shake more violently all of a sudden. The ghostly shapes screamed, and their shapes flickered like candles going out. The roots of the tree were thick and twisted, and they seemed to be writhing and writhing, pushing up through the floor and threatening to trap them. This wasn't a safe place; it was a trap inside of a trap, a carefully planned scene of despair meant to break their spirit.

"The wall!" Eleanor yelled and pointed to a part of the round room where the twisted roots hadn't completely broken through the floor yet. There was a faint outline there, a subtle seam that hinted at another passage that was hidden behind the illusion of the bare tree.

They rushed toward it, pushing through the ghostly mist of crying souls, their hearts racing. Thomas pulled hard and was able to open a hidden panel. The sound of wood breaking echoed through the room, drowning out the spirits' sad cries for a moment.

They fell through the opening and landed on a dusty, long-forgotten landing. The chamber closed behind them with a sickening, final click. The gnarled tree and its sad ghosts were once again hidden from view, leaving only the heavy silence of the manor.

They had gotten away, but for how long? The house was alive, and its predatory instincts were fully awake. It had shown them how strong it was, how hungry it was, how it could use its own architecture as a weapon, and how troubled its past was. Blackwood Manor was no longer a still thing; it was a moving, evil force, a hungry beast ready to eat them whole. The chase was really on. Eleanor knew with a cold certainty that the house would not stop until it had taken them. It was no longer a mystery what it wanted; it was a clear, scary declaration of war. Every creak, whisper, and shadow was now a planned move in its deadly game. Not only were they stuck inside, but they were also being hunted, and the predator was just starting to taste its prey. The air around them got heavy, thick with the house's full, predatory intent. It was no longer waiting; it was actively chasing them. Every change it made brought it one step closer to eating them. They were stuck in the mouth of a monster, and all they could think about was how long they could last before it finally let them go. The house was no longer just watching them suffer; it was the cause of it, and its true, horrible nature was finally and terrifyingly revealed. The quiet hints and ghostly whispers were just teasing. The beast was now free, its hunger never-ending and its will unbreakable. They weren't just visitors; they were its food, and it wouldn't stop until it had eaten them all. The hunt had gotten more intense, and the stakes had risen to the highest level of survival. Blackwood Manor, the huge predator, was getting closer with every painful second.

Thomass Failed Escape

The frantic energy that had driven Eleanor and Thomas through the manor's twisting hallways had faded for a moment, leaving them with a gnawing tiredness and the cold certainty that their short break was just that: short. The hidden passage had given a tantalizing glimpse of escape, a narrow seam in the house's suffocating embrace, but the way it had sealed itself off completely was a grim reminder of how completely the manor controlled everything. They were still under its control and still at the mercy of its cruel and unpredictable will. Thomas leaned against the cold, wet stone of the newly revealed landing, breathing heavily and looking around for any sign of an exit or a weakness. The air here was even more still, and it smelled like wet dirt and something else, something that smelled like old blood.

"We're still in," he said in a voice that was barely a whisper, as if he was afraid the stones would hear him. "It... it didn't let us go. "Not really." He ran a shaking hand over the rough-hewn stones of the landing, and the desperate hope that had flared up inside him moments before sputtered and died. The illusion of escape had been a cruel tease, a short-lived promise meant to make them feel safe before tightening its grip again. The house was like a master predator playing with its trapped prey.

Eleanor also felt the heavy burden of their ongoing imprisonment. The rush of adrenaline that had come and gone left her feeling very tired, as if it had settled deep into her bones. There was a cold, watchful presence in the manor that seemed to fill every molecule of air. It wasn't just a building; it was a living thing, and its evil intelligence was so strong that it felt like a heavy weight on them. "It's playing with us," she said, her voice empty. "Every escape that seems real is just another turn of the screw."

Thomas pushed away from the wall and looked at a low, arched opening at the end of the landing. It was dark, and the heavy darkness almost swallowed it up, but it was the only way to move forward. This opening, unlike the sealed passage they had just come out of, allowed them to move around, explore more, and maybe even find a real way out. "There," he said, pointing with a shaky but determined finger. "That has to go somewhere." We can't stay here.

They walked toward the archway with a shared, unspoken understanding.

The floor was uneven and covered in trash that made a scary noise every time they stepped on it. As they got closer to the opening, the air got noticeably colder and smelled strongly of mold and still water. It was a smell that came from the ground, from things that had been buried and forgotten, a stench from below that promised darkness and decay.

"Cellar?" "Eleanor said, her voice full of fear. The word brought to mind dark, damp places that had been forgotten, where things writhed in the dark all the time.

Thomas nodded, his jaw set. "Has to be." "It's the only way down from here." He took a deep breath, but the cold air didn't help his racing heart. "Maybe there's a window." "A way out to the grounds." The hope that was so strong, even though it was broken, wouldn't die completely. Outside, in the world beyond these cursed walls, there was hope, a chance to finally break free from the manor's tight grip.

They went through the archway and into an even darker place. The oppressive atmosphere got worse, and the only sound was the drip, drip, drip of water somewhere in the dark. The air was thick and sticky, and it felt like they were breathing in the very essence of the manor's old sadness. Thomas fumbled around in his pocket and pulled out a small, worn-out lighter. The weak flicker of its flame pushed back the thick darkness, revealing a steep stone staircase that led down into an abyss. The walls of the cellar were slick with a dark, thick moisture, and the steps were old and uneven, making them dangerous because of the dampness.

"Be careful," Eleanor said, and her hand instinctively reached for Thomas's arm. The weak flame made the rough-hewn walls look like they were dancing, which made the descent feel even more dangerous. Every step was a risk, a test of their balance and courage. The silence was deep, like a heavy blanket that seemed to soak up all sound. But Eleanor could feel the house breathing around them, and its presence was a real, heavy weight.

The metallic smell in the air got stronger as they went down, mixing with the smell of wet earth and another smell, something sharp and bad, like a chemical that had been forgotten. The light from Thomas's lighter flickered and didn't do a good job of lighting up the rough stone walls. He held it close and looked at every inch of the staircase as it went down. He was looking for anything, like a crack, a weakness, or a sign that this hidden world wasn't as solid as the rest of the manor.

Their feet hit a cold, packed-earth floor at the bottom of the stairs. The cellar was huge, and the light from the lighter couldn't reach the end of it. The shadows twisted and turned, tricking their eyes and making the corners that weren't there seem to be full of life. The size of the room was scary, as if it held a secret depth that they were just starting to understand.

Thomas took a step forward, his steps unsure, and held the lighter high. He was looking for a way out of this dark place, a window, or any other way out that might help them get out. The cellar seemed to go on forever, with the rough-hewn stone walls disappearing into the dark. It was cold and damp outside, and the sound of water dripping echoed like the earth was crying.

"Anything?" Eleanor whispered, her voice tight with rising anxiety. It felt like the darkness was closing in on them, and the feeling of being trapped was stronger here than anywhere else in the manor.

Thomas shook his head and let his shoulders droop a little. "Nothing." "Just... more walls." He walked toward what he hoped was an outside wall, but the ground was uneven, so his steps weren't very steady. He ran his hand over the cold, wet stone, looking for any bumps or signs of a window or door that might lead to freedom. The walls were so solid that it was hard to believe they had been built that way.

Then, his fingers touched something else. Not stone, but glass. A small, dirty window set low in the wall was almost hidden by the darkening sky.

"Here!" He shouted, his voice hoarse with a sudden rush of desperate hope. "A window!" "

He ran toward it, with Eleanor right behind him. The pane was small, no more than a foot square, and it was covered in layers of dirt and what looked like dried mud. Eleanor could only see a vague outline of a gray, overcast sky outside through the thick layer of dirt. It wasn't much, but it was a link to the outside world, a possible lifeline.

Thomas got to work right away, forgetting how tired he had been before and feeling a strong, primal need to get away. He took out the heavy brass candlestick he had gotten earlier. The weight of it in his hand made him feel better. He hit the glass with his knuckles to see if it was real. It felt old and fragile. "It has to break," he said, his voice tight with excitement.

He lifted the candlestick and aimed it at a corner of the window. He swung with all his strength, and the heavy brass hit the glass with a loud crack. There were cracks all over the surface that looked like spiderwebs. He swung again and again, and with each blow, his movements became more frantic. With one last, desperate smash, a piece of glass broke, leaving a small, jagged hole in the pane.

A cold, wet breeze blew in, bringing with it the smell of wet dirt and rotting leaves. The smell of freedom and the outside world filled Eleanor's lungs with a desperate hope. Thomas smiled, his face covered in dirt and sweat. It was a wild, almost crazy look. "I knew it!" I knew there had to be a way out! "

He started to work on the broken pane, making the hole bigger with his hands, even though the sharp edges of the glass cut into his skin. He grunted as he worked hard to break up the last pieces. His muscles were straining. The hole was still small, just big enough for a child to crawl through, but it was there. A real chance.

"Go!" He pushed Eleanor gently toward the opening and told her to go. "Go! Get out! "

Eleanor hesitated. She looked back at Thomas, the darkening cellar, and the heavy weight of the manor that seemed to press down on them even here. "What about you?" "She asked, her voice shaking.

"I'll be right behind you!" He insisted, his eyes bright with a desperate, almost feverish determination. He was only thinking about how to get out of their prison and make a way out. He scraped away at the last bits of glass, and the sound of his work echoed in the small space.

Eleanor felt a strange sensation on her skin as she got ready to squeeze through the opening. There was a faint vibration coming from the walls of the cellar. At first, it was very quiet, but it got stronger. The packed-earth floor under her feet felt like it was moving.

Her eyes were wide with fear as she looked at Thomas. "Thomas, the walls..."

He stopped what he was doing and tilted his head to listen. The water was no longer dripping. The cellar was no longer quiet. It was filled with a low, grinding sound, a deep rumble that seemed to come from deep within the earth. The air became heavy and thick, making it hard to breathe because of the oppressive pressure.

And then it happened. The little, jagged hole that Thomas had worked so hard to make started to get smaller. The stone around the glass and the edges of the glass seemed to flow together, as if an unseen force was changing the very material of the cellar. The pieces of broken glass were pulled back into the wall, closing the hole with a strange, fluid motion. The window was gone in a matter of seconds, and the same wet, unbroken stone wall was there instead.

Thomas stared with his mouth open, and the brass candlestick fell from his limp fingers and hit the floor with a loud crash. His face, which had been full of fierce joy at the thought of being free, was now a mask of disbelief and despair. "No… no, it can't be…" he stammered, reaching out with a shaky hand to touch the wall, which was now smooth.

But the manor's cruel teasing wasn't over yet. The grinding noise got worse and turned into a sickening groan. The walls of the cellar, which had seemed strong and unbreakable just a few moments before, started to push in. At first, the stone moved slowly, but then it moved with an unstoppable force, squeezing the air out of the cavernous space.

"Thomas!" Eleanor screamed, her voice full of fear. She lunged at him and grabbed his arm. The floor beneath them was sloping, and the packed earth was moving and shifting like a living thing.

Thomas fell, his eyes wide with fear, and he stared at the walls that were closing in on him. "It's not possible," he said, his voice a hoarse whisper. He really thought he had found a way out, a weak spot in the manor's strong armor. He had seen the light, tasted the air of freedom, and now it was being taken away and replaced with a tomb that was too small to escape.

The walls kept going down, and the space between them got smaller and smaller at an alarming rate. The space they were in was quickly getting smaller, and the heavy pressure made their chests hurt and their lungs burn. The stones groaned and moved, making a sound that showed how strong and unnatural they were.

Thomas fought against the walls that were closing in on him. His movements were frantic and wild. He hit the stone with his fists, which were raw and bloody, but it was like hitting bedrock. The house was alive and crushing them, making fun of every effort they made to fight back. The short burst of defiance and the last-ditch effort had only gotten them deeper into its trap.

The cellar, which had once been a possible way out, had turned into a vise that was getting tighter on purpose.

"It's getting closer!" Eleanor yelled and pulled Thomas toward the small amount of space that was left. The air was getting so thick that it was hard to breathe. They couldn't breathe because the smell of wet earth and something chemical that made them sick filled their noses. The darkness, which had only been a lack of light before, now felt like a real thing that was pushing in on them and suffocating them.

Thomas, whose face was twisted with a mix of anger and fear, made one last, useless effort to push back against the stone that was closing in on him. His hands scratched at the hard surface, breaking his nails and making his knuckles bleed. But the walls kept moving forward, and the space between them got smaller and smaller with every painful second.

They couldn't get out. The short, false hope of escape had turned into the horrible truth of their ongoing imprisonment. The manor had tricked Thomas into feeling safe, which was a desperate gamble that it had planned for, and then it had sealed his fate with terrifying efficiency. The cellar window, which they thought was the weak point, was really just a trapdoor, a carefully made illusion meant to catch them more securely.

As the walls closed in, the last bits of light from Thomas's fallen candlestick went out, leaving them in complete, suffocating darkness. The grinding of stone got louder, making a deafening noise that shook the ground itself. Eleanor could feel Thomas's body against hers and hear his ragged breathing, which was a desperate counterpoint to the groaning of the manor. They were being crushed, pushed into a tiny space, and the weight of the old house was pressing down on them with all its evil power.

The house wasn't just keeping them inside; it was also tearing down their hopes, breaking their spirits, and showing them, in the most brutal and terrifying way possible, that they could never really escape from it. The predator had shown its true teeth, and its hunger was as strong as the stone that was about to grind them to dust. Their fight wasn't just against walls; it was against a living, evil force that had woven itself into the very fabric of existence. This force took pleasure in the suffering of its victims and made sure that every attempt to resist only made its deadly grip stronger. Thomas's failed escape wasn't just a failed attempt; it was a terrifying, clear example of how powerful the manor was and how it would never give up.

Eleanors Visions Intensify

The dark, oppressive cellar had been a physical sign of their despair, a suffocating blanket made from the manor's evil will. But even in that terrible prison, a different kind of darkness began to grow inside Eleanor. It was a flickering, unbidden kaleidoscope of images that clawed at the edges of her mind. It started out as a ghostly feeling at the edge of her vision, like dust motes dancing in a sunbeam that wasn't there. But it got bigger, turning into scenes that felt both very familiar and very strange.

She didn't see the manor as it is now, a crumbling relic of a bygone era. Instead, she saw it as a hungry being, its stone bones pulsing with a dark, unquenchable life. She knew with a chilling certainty that it was alive and that its hunger was a bottomless pit. The pictures changed, turning into scenes of complete destruction. She saw its tendrils, which looked like ghosts and spirits, reaching out from its roots and creeping across the green countryside. She saw them weave their way into the very fabric of existence, moving through the sleeping villages. Their buildings melted away like sugar in water, and the people living there had no idea that doom was coming.

These weren't just quick looks; they were real, scary intrusions into a future she really wanted to deny. The manor didn't just want bricks and mortar; it wanted the very essence of life: the laughter of children, the whispered secrets of lovers, and the quiet hum of everyday life. She watched whole towns, once full of life, fade away, their lights dimming and their sounds fading into a hollow silence, all of which were swallowed by the house's ever-growing, insatiable maw. It was a huge assimilation, a slow, planned eating that left behind only an echoing emptiness where life had once thrived.

Eleanor gasped, a small, choked sound that was lost in the thick, heavy air of their prison. Thomas, whose face was still wet with sweat from his own despair, turned to her with a look of confusion in his eyes. "Eleanor? What is it?

She shook her head because she couldn't put into words the horror that was happening in her mind. It was too big and scary to put into words. But then the visions changed again, making them focus on something with painful clarity. She saw people. There were countless pale, ghostly faces trapped inside the walls that had tried to crush them. They were the ghosts of the people who had been eaten, and their ghostly forms would always be in the manor's mind. Their silent screams were always there, like a hum under the surface of reality. They were the pieces that made it stronger and the food that kept it going.

She saw the faces of villagers she didn't know, and they looked confused and scared as they were about to be absorbed. Their eyes were empty and hollow, and they seemed to be looking right at her, begging for a release that would never come. They were ghostly prisoners, forever tied to the manor's evil design, their lives reduced to a silent witness to its insatiable hunger. Each ghostly face was a whisper of a life lost, a memory consumed, and a soul absorbed into the manor's horrible being.

The visions were so strong that they were too much to handle. They weren't just whispers of the past; they were a dark prophecy and a clear sign of how the manor's evil power was growing. It wasn't happy with what was around it; its hunger was growing, and it was reaching out with a scary and terrifying ambition. The manor was changing; with each town it took over, its mind grew, and its hunger for life grew stronger.

Eleanor held her head and let out a low moan. The ghostly faces spun around in front of her, making her feel dizzy and hopeless. She saw the manor eating, its stone front moving as it took in the very essence of a busy market square. She saw the terrified screams of the townspeople as their homes turned to dust and their lives ended in a coldly efficient way. The house didn't just destroy; it absorbed everything, its hunger a vortex that pulled everything into its never-ending embrace.

Thomas reached for her, forgetting about his own trauma for a moment. His hand shook as it touched her arm. "What do you see, Eleanor?" His voice was a low, urgent plea, a lifeline in the stormy sea of her fear.

"It's... it's getting bigger," she said in a hoarse, strained voice. "It's not just this place. It's... it's taking over everything. Cities. "People." The ghostly faces' silent accusations were like a cold contrast to the manor's deep rumble. She could feel their ghostly touch on her skin. "All of them are in there," she said, pointing vaguely at the heavy stone that surrounded them. "Now they're a part of it." "Forever."

The visions kept coming, unending and unforgiving. She thought of the manor's hunger as a real thing, like a shadow that crept out and ate everything in its way. It was an unending thirst, a basic need that made the house look for and take in more life, energy, and souls. The ghostly shapes of the people it had already eaten weren't just passive ghosts; they were parts of its being that were trapped and used to fuel its endless growth. They were the ghostly mortar that held its ever-growing structure together, and their silent screams were a constant song of its terrible life.

Eleanor felt a deep sense of powerlessness wash over her. She couldn't fight this monster with strength or smart plans. This was a being that fed on life itself, an ancient, never-ending hunger that had become part of the land itself. Her visions were a grim sign of how quickly it was getting worse, a horrifying look at a future where the manor's power would spread like a plague, leaving behind only shells of what used to be.

She saw ghostly shapes of children, their laughter stopped, their innocent faces marked with eternal sadness, forever stuck in the manor's cold embrace. She saw the ghostly shapes of lovers reaching for each other, but they could never touch because the stone that had become their tomb kept them apart. Every ghostly resident was a sign of the manor's endless cruelty, a chilling reminder of the lives it had taken and the souls it had eaten.

Thomas held her close, and his own fear was real between them. He couldn't see what she saw, but he could feel the raw fear coming from her and the strength of her psychic pain. He squeezed her arm, which was a silent promise that they would be together in their pain. They were stuck, not only by the cellar's walls, but also by the terrifying things that Eleanor now knew.

The visions got stronger; they weren't just quick looks anymore; they were full experiences. Eleanor could feel the cold coming from the ghostly faces, and the despair coming from them made her shiver. She didn't see the manor's growth as a slow process; instead, she saw it as a series of terrifying annexations, with each town disappearing in the blink of an eye, its essence being devoured by the insatiable entity. The ghostly figures in the house seemed to grow in number with each vision, and their silent cries for freedom grew more desperate and numerous.

She thought of the manor as a parasite that sucked the life out of the land around it and grew by taking in the very essence of life. The ghostly shapes weren't just stuck; they were also being drained of their energy to feed the manor's never-ending hunger. It was a horrible cycle of eating and absorbing, a grotesque symbiosis. The ghostly figures were not just ghosts of the past; they were the living fuel for the manor's never-ending, monstrous growth.

Eleanor felt the weight of this knowledge more than any physical prison. It was a sign of doom, a scary look at how bad the manor's power could be. It wasn't just a metaphor for its hunger; it was a real, scary thing that was getting worse. The ghostly faces in the house weren't just memories; they were signs of a scary future. Their silent screams were a warning of the destruction that was about to happen. She understood what the manor's ultimate goal was: to eat everything and leave nothing but an empty shell where life once thrived. The ghosts who lived there weren't just victims; they were the spectral chains that held the manor's ever-growing power. Their silent pain showed how cruel it was.

Thomas could only stand by and watch as Eleanor writhed, her body shaking and her eyes wide and unfocused. He felt completely powerless, and his own fear made his stomach feel like a cold knot. He had seen the manor's evil in the form of its crushing walls and suffocating darkness, but this... this was something else. This was a look into the heart of the house, a picture of its terrifying, never-ending hunger. Even though he couldn't see them, the ghostly faces seemed to push in on their small circle of shared fear, and their silent cries were a chilling soundtrack to Eleanor's psychic pain. The ghosts that lived there weren't just stuck; they were the manor's very essence, and their stolen lives fed its monstrous, never-ending hunger.

The Sound of Breaking

The air, which was already thick with the unspoken fear that hung over the manor like damp rot, suddenly broke. It started with a sharp, metallic ping that was so out of place in the musty stillness that it woke up both Eleanor and Thomas from their shared, suffocating silence. Then there was a second, louder crack that sounded like bones breaking under a lot of pressure. Then, a waterfall. A symphony of destruction broke out, a chaotic overture of shattering glass and splintering wood that clawed at their ears, each sound a physical blow.

It wasn't a random, incidental break in a building that was falling apart because it was old. This was on purpose and violent. It sounded like something was fighting itself, or maybe it was something that was enjoying breaking itself apart. Eleanor realized with a new wave of fear that the manor was not just a passive thing that absorbed life; it was an active, hungry beast whose hunger had reached a fever pitch. The sounds were more than just an auditory attack; they were the house's painful screams or, even worse, its ecstatic predatory glee.

The glass in the tall, arched windows, which had made it look like there was a way out, now shattered inward, sending shards flying down like a deadly hailstorm. The shatter was sharp and loud, and each piece made a tiny scream of pain. It echoed through the maze-like hallways, bouncing off stone walls and polished floors and getting louder and louder, hammering at their senses. It was like the house was crying pieces of itself, each one showing how upset it was inside. The beautiful chandeliers, which used to be symbols of wealth, became tools of disorder. With sickening groans of tortured metal, they broke free from their moorings and fell to the floor below with crashes that shook the ground. The sound was like a punch to the gut, a deep, resonant thud that shook the house's very foundations and Eleanor and Thomas's shaking bodies.

The woodwork, which had been carefully carved and was very beautiful, started to give way. The splintering was a violent tearing, like the sound of wood fibers ripping apart and old, petrified wood being pushed too far. It sounded like something was ripping itself apart from the inside. The floorboards creaked and broke under unseen forces, and each break was a gaping hole that showed the darkness below. Heavy oak doors that had once protected privacy and safety now crashed open and shut with violent, unpredictable force, as if something inside was trying to get out or, on the other hand, to keep them trapped in its growing insanity. The creaking of the tortured hinges sounded like a long, drawn-out wail, a lament for the building's quickly falling apart structure.

The noise was so loud that it was a sonic storm that could have drowned out clear thought. It was impossible to tell where each sound came from or where it came from in the huge, falling-apart building. The noise was so loud that it felt like a thick blanket of sound that made their fear even stronger. It made them feel like they couldn't focus, plan, or even breathe without feeling the manor's violent self-immolation. Every crack, every shatter, and every groan were like electric shocks, reminding me of the house's strong, unstable energy.

Eleanor closed her eyes tightly and put her hands over her ears in a useless attempt to block out the noise. But the sounds seemed to go through even the thickest layers of her skin and resonate deep inside her bones. The violent symphony seemed to give voice to the visions she had had earlier of the manor's insatiable hunger. The house seemed to be in a frenzied state of ecstasy, dancing in a way that was tearing itself apart in its desperate search for food. Or maybe it was a death throe, when something it couldn't hold onto anymore violently pushed it out.

Thomas pulled Eleanor closer, his face a mask of grim determination. His body was a shield against the unseen forces that seemed to be shaking the very foundations of their prison. His eyes looked around for any real threat or clear reason for this sudden, violent change. But there was nothing. There was no ghostly attacker, no crack in the walls that could be seen, just the terrifying sound of the house eating itself. The air was full of a strange energy that made their skin crawl.

The sounds weren't just random acts of destruction; they seemed to be guided by a bad intelligence. The way the glass broke, not just breaking but exploding outwards, seemed angry. The wood that was breaking wasn't just giving in; it was being torn apart with a savage rage. It was like the manor was the predator, and its hunger was so deep and all-consuming that it was turning itself into the thing it wanted so badly. This wasn't a slow decay; it was a violent, active self-consumption, a terrifying sight of a house going crazy because it couldn't stop eating.

The sound of breaking glass was like a million tiny teeth grinding together in a frantic, desperate attempt to get food. The wood that was breaking was like flesh being torn apart and muscle and bone being ripped apart. Every crack was a gasp of effort, and every crash was a deep cry of either pain or ecstatic release. It was a sickening parody of life, a violent and twisted expression of the very thing it had been eating for hundreds of years. Eleanor could almost feel the stress in the stone walls. The spirits trapped inside them were screaming silently, and the house's violent changes made those screams louder and more distorted.

They huddled together in the heavy silence that came after a lot of glass breaking. The silence that fell was not a break; it was a heavy, expectant pause, a pregnant moment before the next wave of destruction. During these short breaks, the true horror of their situation became clear. They were stuck in a building that was violently tearing itself apart because of a hunger that went beyond just physical things.

Thomas's grip on Eleanor's arm got stronger. "What's going on?" he whispered, his voice barely audible over the ringing in their ears.

Eleanor shook her head, her mind reeling from the attack. "It's... it's hungry," she said, her voice thick with tears and a deep, bone-deep fear. "It's... it's eating itself."

The idea was crazy and didn't make sense, but in this cursed manor, it felt like it could really happen. The ghostly faces she had seen, the whispers of lives lost, and the creeping tendrils of its power spreading across the land all came together in this moment of violent, self-destructive eruption. She had come to understand that the house was a living thing and that it had needs like any other living thing. It needed food and life force so badly that it was now turning inward, eating its own structure and essence to satisfy its never-ending hunger.

This time, a loud noise came from above them and shook the manor. There was a loud rumble, then the sickening sound of stone grinding against stone, and finally, a shower of falling debris. A fine, gritty powder fell from the ceiling and settled on their hair and clothes. The impact shook the floor below them, making it shake violently and threatening to make their knees bend.

"We have to go," Thomas said, his voice full of urgency. "This place isn't going to stay together."

But where could they go? Every way was a risk, a trip through a deathtrap of falling bricks and glass that blew up. The sounds were confusing, making it hard to tell how far away something was or which way it was going. It looked like the manor's insides were breaking apart, and it was shaking in a fit of ravenous rage. The air got colder, not because it was unused, but because of the icy fear that came with the house's growing madness.

The breaking didn't happen in just one place. It was everywhere, a constant and all-encompassing destruction. The sound of breaking banisters and the echoing shatter of a thousand tiny mirrors came from the grand ballroom, where ghostly dancers had once twirled. The sound of burning paper and falling shelves filled the air in the old library, as if the knowledge inside was being eaten by the building itself. The sounds of destruction were a sick lullaby, a scary soundtrack to their being trapped.

Eleanor could feel it now, a low, guttural hum that seemed to come from the stones of the manor. It was a real vibration in the air. It was the sound of hunger, loud and raw, a thousand times louder than normal. The house was feeding on itself, not on the life force of unsuspecting villagers or stray animals. It was a terrifying feedback loop, a cycle of consumption that seemed to be getting faster and faster with each passing moment.

The sounds of glass breaking kept going, and each explosion sent a new wave of fear through the air. It was no longer just a physical attack; it was an attack on their mental health. The rhythmic shatter-crash-splinter was like a siren song of destruction that drew them deeper into despair. The manor seemed to be trying to confuse them on purpose, to break them down mentally and emotionally, just like it was breaking down its own body. The air itself seemed to crackle with evil energy, which showed how the house was becoming more and more predatory.

Thomas pulled her up, holding her arm tightly with his strong hand. "Come on," he said, his voice a low growl over the noise. "We need to find a way out." "Now."

They stumbled forward, making their way through a hallway full of trash. The floor was covered in sharp, shiny pieces of glass that looked like teeth of a predator. Fallen trees looked like broken limbs, with rough edges that stood out against the smooth surfaces they used to have. There was a lot of dust in the air, and it smelled bad, like old blood and decay. It was also metallic and foul.

A loud, violent crack right above them sent a shower of plaster and small stones down on them. They flinched and ducked without thinking. The ceiling's groaning got louder, a long, mournful sound that hinted at an impending collapse.

"This way!" Thomas yelled and pulled her toward a narrower hallway that looked like it was still holding up for the time being.

As they walked, the sounds of breaking seemed to follow them, always behind them. From behind, the sound of glass breaking echoed, and from the side, the sound of wood splitting. It was a scary game of sound cat and mouse, with a constant stream of noise that kept them on edge and made their nerves fray. The manor was a symphony of destruction, and they were right in the middle of it. The sound violence was almost too much to bear; each new sound was like a new stab of fear. They could feel the building groaning under the huge weight, and its old bones were protesting the violent movement. It was like the house was a living thing that was dying and tearing itself apart in a last, painful act of consumption. The sound of glass breaking was like the sound of teeth grinding, and the sound of wood breaking was like the sound of flesh tearing. It was a symphony of pure fear, and they couldn't get away from its loud show. The constant noise was a planned attack meant to confuse, overwhelm, and break them. They could feel the vibrations in the floor and the tremors that ran through the house, which reminded them all the time how unstable it was. Each crash and break was a blow to their will, proof of the insatiable hunger that drove the manor to destroy itself in such a violent way. The sound was more than just something they heard; it was a physical force that hit them and threatened to crush their spirits as surely as the walls that were falling down threatened to crush their bodies. The air itself seemed to hum with a strange energy, a symphony of pain and maybe even a sick kind of pleasure for the horrible thing they were stuck inside.

The Rot Spreads

The insidious rot, which had once been a localized problem, began its slow march, a creeping tide of decay that painted the manor in shades of death. It was no longer limited to the dark corners or the wings that were never used. Now, it was everywhere, a living, breathing proof of how hungry the house was getting. Eleanor was frozen in terror as a crack, no wider than a spider's silk thread, snaked its way across the fancy wallpaper in the grand hall. It wasn't a small crack in the foundation; this was something else, something darker. Within seconds, a thick, black liquid that smelled like a mix of stagnant water, rotting plants, and something like metallic sickness began to ooze out of it. It was as thick as tar and smelled terrible. It spread at an unnatural speed, defying gravity, and seeped into the very fibers of the old damask, changing its once-bright patterns into a horrible picture of decay.

Thomas made a choked sound while looking at the same spot. "It's… it's alive," he said in a whisper, his words getting stuck in his throat. He reached out, his finger hovering just above the spreading stain, as if he were daring it to notice him. The air around the stain seemed to shimmer, not with heat, but with a thick, foul mist that took their breath away. This wasn't just the slow, natural decay of time and neglect; it was an active, deadly consumption. The house was eating its own structure, history, and very being in its desperate search for food. The walls, which used to be strong and proud, now looked like they were sagging. They weren't weak because they were old; they were weak because of an internal, parasitic appetite. The plaster fell apart and crumbled in quiet, dusty streams as the darkness crept in. This revealed the skeletal timbers underneath, which looked warped, as if they were suffering from fevers that couldn't be seen.

The mold, which was everywhere, was the most obvious sign of this speeding up of disorder. It spread across surfaces at an alarming rate, like a velvety black carpet that seemed to suck up the light. It wrapped around the beautiful carvings on the fireplace, hiding the once-majestic griffins and gargoyles in its suffocating embrace. It crawled up the walls like fingers trying to grab something, turning the detailed murals into dark, blurry nightmares. It was in the library's corners, where it blurred the titles of old books, and it bloomed in the bathrooms, where it turned porcelain fixtures into leprous, blackened statues. The smell it gave off was always there, a sickening perfume that hinted at deep, hidden rot and the end of everything. It was a smell that got into the lungs, coated the tongue, and left a bad taste in the mouth. This was the house's breath, its slow, deliberate exhalation of decay, and it was making them feel like they were going to die.

Eleanor remembered the visions of the ghostly tendrils coming out of the manor and sucking the life out of the land around it. It looked like those tendrils had turned inward now. The house was a predator that had eaten so much that it was starting to eat its own limbs. It wasn't getting rid of the energy it had taken from the earth and the people it had touched; instead, it was using it to fuel a huge metabolism that was ripping it apart from the inside. The manor's very foundations seemed to groan under this internal strain, a low, resonant hum that shook the floorboards and their bones. It was the sound of stress, of a structure being pushed too far, not by outside forces, but by an internal, ravenous hunger.

The decay was especially bad in the ballroom, where they had first heard the sounds of it waking up. The parquet floor, which used to shine, was now buckling and warping because of moisture that seemed to come from the wood itself. A lot of the ceiling had fallen down, showing the dark, skeletal structure above. Instead of cobwebs, there were thick, drooping tendrils of black mold that looked like morbid chandeliers. The smell of wet dirt and something sharp, like a chemical tang that made their throats feel like they were being pricked, filled the air in the ballroom. The tall windows used to let in moonlight, which would cast ethereal beams across the dance floor. Now, though, only gray, opaque panes are left, covered in a layer of dirt and the black mold that is slowly creeping in. The house seemed to be crying black, thick tears that left stains on everything they touched.

Thomas ran his hand over a part of the wall, and when he pulled it away, his fingers were covered in a sticky, black substance. He pulled back and wiped his hand on his pants with a grimace. "It's spreading faster," he said, his voice empty. "It's worse than it was an hour ago everywhere we look." He pointed to a tapestry that hung in the hallway. The once-bright picture of a hunting scene was now covered by a creeping black bloom. The threads themselves looked like they were coming apart and fraying, but not because they were old; it was more like they were being slowly digested. The hunters' and their hounds' faces were becoming blurry, and their noble features were turning into a shapeless mass of decay. It was a horrible act of vandalism by the very group that was supposed to protect and house these relics of the past.

A faint, constant dripping sound had joined the sounds that had woken up the manor. It was the sound of the black fluid leaking out of the walls, ceilings, and even the pores of the house. It was a maddening, never-ending beat, like a metronome counting down the seconds until the manor fell apart completely. Every drop made a soft, wet plop that echoed in the heavy silence between the groans and cracks. The house was crying over its own destruction, and its lifeblood, which was tainted and corrupted, was spilling onto the floors, making slick, dangerous pools that reflected the dim, distorted light like dark mirrors.

Eleanor was drawn to the edges of the manor's decay, where the rot wasn't fully there yet but was clearly on its way. She ran her finger along the edges of a patch of mold and saw that the wood underneath was slightly discolored. The wood didn't just have damage on the surface; it felt softer and spongier, as if its structure was breaking down at the molecular level. She pictured the tiny organisms, the fungi and bacteria, eating the old wood inside the walls and releasing the energy that had been stored for hundreds of years. But this wasn't a natural process. There was a smart evil at work, a planned decay that met the house's never-ending need.

The rot that was coming closer seemed to make the air thicker. It wasn't just the smell of dust and damp anymore; it was a thick, sickening atmosphere full of the smell of decay. Breathing became hard, and every breath was a fight against the suffocating miasma. They were stuck in the manor's last, poisonous breath, which felt like it was slowly dying. Every sign of decay made the feeling of being trapped stronger. The house wasn't just a prison; it was dying, and its death was a scary, contagious force.

Thomas, with a serious look on his face, pointed to a doorframe where the wood was obviously warped and swollen. "Look," he said, his voice tense. "It's changing the structure itself. It's not just eating the stuff; it's also changing how things look. "...It's changing shape." He pushed on the door, but it hardly moved because the frame was too big. The wood around the edges was black and soft, like fruit that had gone bad. Finally, with a violent push and a horrible scream of protesting wood fibers tearing apart, he was able to get it open. The decay was even worse on the other side of the door. A room that used to be a study was almost completely destroyed. The mold had grown into thick, fleshy growths that hung from the ceiling like alien life forms. The desk was nothing like it used to be. A thick layer of black slime covered its polished surface, and its drawers were warped and stuck shut. The room was a tomb, a sign of how much the house ate and how quickly it fell apart.

The size of the change was too much to handle. The house seemed to be going through a terrible change, losing its old skin and shape to become something new and darker, fueled by its own destruction. The decay wasn't just a slow process of falling apart; it was a fast, aggressive change. The house was actively destroying itself, breaking down its own materials to satisfy an endless hunger. The once-grand buildings, the intricate details, and the very essence of their former glory were all being eaten up and turned into sludge and dust.

Eleanor's sense of hopelessness grew. They were stuck inside a living thing that was falling apart, like a body with a terminal illness. Its death throes were a terrifying display of destruction. The rot was more than just an eyesore; it was a real force, a manifestation of the house's corrupt nature, and it was spreading like a disease. Every surface seemed to be whispering about decay, and every shadow seemed to be writhing with the presence of unseen rot. The house was bleeding, and the blood was the thick, black fluid that made it fall apart. The smell was always there, like a heavy blanket that stole their breath and hope. They saw a horrible act of self-consumption, a terrifying act of predation turned inward, and the effects on their own survival were chillingly bad. The manor wasn't just falling apart; it was being eaten from the inside out, a horrible sign of the insatiable hunger that now controlled everything it did. The rot was not merely spreading; it was consuming, transforming, and in doing so, it was sealing their fate within its decaying embrace. The air, thick with the putrid scent, felt heavy, stagnant, as if the very breath of life had been leached from it, replaced by the exhalations of death. The black mold looked like a velvety shroud that was getting closer and closer, a silent, suffocating sign of the house's never-ending, self-destructive hunger. The light that struggled to get through the dirty windows also seemed to be tainted. As it passed through the decaying air, it lost its warmth and vibrancy, becoming a sickly, pale glow that lit up the rot that was creeping in. The manor was becoming a monument to its own destruction, a self-consuming thing, and Eleanor and Thomas were stuck inside it during its painful last moments.

Chapter 7: The Heart of the Manor

Discovering the Nexus

The oppressive atmosphere, thick with the sickening smell of decay, seemed to close in on them, a physical sign of the manor's poor health. But under the heavy blanket of rot, another feeling began to take hold: a prickling cold that was so deep it felt like it was breaking their bones. It wasn't the cold, damp air of an abandoned building; it was an active, evil cold coming from a direction they hadn't yet looked into. Eleanor, who was always aware of the small changes in her surroundings, first felt it as a whisper against her skin, a breath of air so cold that it made her skin crawl even though the air was still and humid.

"Do you feel that?" she whispered, her voice barely a breath.

Thomas nodded and looked around the huge hall, which was now partly hidden by veils of mold that were growing on the walls. "It's like going into a freezer. But the smell of decay is stronger here, right? But the cold... it seems to cut through it."

They followed the invisible current, taking small steps on the buckling floorboards. The decay, which had seemed to be everywhere, now focused its foul essence in a certain direction, pulling them toward a shadowy alcove that had been covered by a tapestry that was now a tattered, moldy rag. As they got closer, the smell of decay got stronger, making their stomachs turn and their eyes water. It wasn't just the smell of decay anymore; it was a strong, thick smell that seemed to come from the heart of rot, as if the air had been distilled from it.

But the cold was getting worse, which was bad for the smell. It was no longer a faint feeling; it was a real force that pushed against them and made their teeth chatter. The difference was confusing, a sickening mix of rot and icy stillness. It was like two opposing, destructive forces were fighting in the manor, and they had found their battleground. The draft seemed to come from behind the alcove, a sharp stream of cold air that cut through the still warmth like an obsidian blade.

Thomas reached out, but his hand hesitated before touching the wall next to the alcove. His fingers pulled back as if they had been shocked. "It's... stone," he said, his voice strained. "But it's so cold." It's colder than ice. He put his hand on the rough surface and frowned in disbelief. "It feels... dead. Completely lacking in warmth.

Eleanor noticed a small area on the stone that was darker than the granite around it, almost like a bruise on the old rock. It pulsed with the same strange cold, and as she watched, a thin, shiny layer formed on its surface, like dew on a grave. But it wasn't water. It was thicker and darker, and when it dripped, it fell with an eerie silence, leaving no mark on the floor below. The air here wasn't just cold; it felt empty, like all the heat had been sucked out of it, leaving a void.

The stronger decay and the biting cold seemed to come from one place, a focal point that drew them deeper into the unknown. The buildings in this part of the manor were different, older, and more basic. The grand halls' smooth, polished floors gave way to rougher, more unyielding stone, as if they were digging into the building's bones, into a place that had been hidden on purpose. They were in a narrow passage that had been cut straight into the bedrock that made up the manor's foundation. The walls here were slick with a condensation that wasn't just water; it was a greasy, black film that looked like the mold that was spreading elsewhere.

The passage sloped down, and with each step, the chill grew stronger and the smell of decay grew stronger and more concentrated. It seemed like they were going deeper into the earth. It wasn't just a smell anymore; it was a heavy, suffocating mist that stuck to their clothes, skin, and souls. Thomas pulled out a lantern. The flame flickered and cast moving shadows that seemed to have a life of their own. The light had a hard time getting through the heavy darkness, and the shadows seemed to cling to the walls, refusing to go away.

"This is where it's coming from," Thomas said with a voice that was tight with fear and grim determination. "This passage… it feels like a vein." A damaged vein that leads to something bad.

Eleanor ran her gloved hand over the stone. It was so cold that it wasn't just cold to the touch; it also had a cold aura that seeped into her bones. The black film looked like it was crying from the rock's pores. It was a slow, thick breath that formed tiny streams before disappearing into the passage's unseen depths. This wasn't the soft crying of a wet basement; it was the slow death of something.

They kept going down, and the passage got a little wider. The air got thick and heavy, not just with the smell of decay, but also with an almost electric charge, a strong feeling of raw, unrestrained power. It was a feeling that made the hairs on their arms stand on end, like a primal alarm bell going off in their heads. The cold here was so bad that it hurt. It was a strange feeling that made their fingers and toes numb and their lungs hurt with every cold breath.

After that, the passage opened.

They went into a huge, underground room that didn't fit with the design of the manor above. It was a huge hole in the ground with rough, uneven walls and no decorations. But it wasn't empty. The air in this room was filled with a dark, resonant energy that felt like it was vibrating in their bones. It was the center of the rot, the heart of the manor's evil intelligence, and the nexus of all things.

There was something very strange and important in the middle of the room. It was bathed in an unnatural, glowing light that seemed to come from the air itself. It was a building, or maybe an object, that was hard to describe. Picture a rough altar made of stone that looks like obsidian. It's not carved, but it somehow grew, and its surface is smooth and shiny, as if it were always crying a thick, black liquid. It had a slow, steady beat that wasn't from a heart, but from something much older and stranger. The light that came from it wasn't warm or inviting; it was a cold, sickly glow that seemed to absorb rather than reflect.

This was the source. The manor's never-ending hunger beat like a heart.

The object was about the size of a big sarcophagus and had a rough oval shape. Thick, vein-like tendrils of the same black, shiny substance snaked out from its surface and disappeared into the floor of the cave, into the bedrock of the earth. These weren't just pretty things; they were pipes that brought something up from the depths and sent it to the beating mass in the middle. The room itself seemed to breathe out this bad energy, and the cold came straight from it, a cold aura that pushed the manor's stale air away.

The smell of the rot was more than just a smell; it was a presence. Black, thick fluid swirled through the air like ghostly mist, coming together and breaking apart in the strange light. The stone in the chamber seemed to soak it up, getting darker and more full of the smell of rot. There were no molds or fungi that could be seen. The decay was pure and came from this one, pulsing source.

Eleanor felt a strong wave of fear wash over her. She was sure that this was the center of all the terrible things they had seen. This was the source of the manor's evil, the twisted heart that sent its poison through every crack in the house. The artifact pulsed again, this time with a deeper, more resonant thrum. A wave of cold energy washed over them, stealing their breath and making their vision swim.

Thomas stood still, holding up his lantern. Its weak light did little to break up the heavy darkness or the strange glow of the artifact. His face was a mask of fear and awe. He whispered, "What... what is that?" His voice was hard to hear over the low thrum.

Eleanor didn't know what to say. She could only stare, fascinated and disgusted by what she saw. It was an unnatural thing, an artifact that didn't seem to fit in with the way things normally are. It was the nexus, the place where the manor's never-ending hunger came together and its twisted intelligence took hold. It could have been an old altar, a broken heart, or a place where dark energy had been awakened or even deliberately nurtured deep within the earth.

The tendrils coming out of the artifact looked like they were writhing, but not with muscle movement. Instead, they had a subtle, almost imperceptible vibration. They sank into the stone and vanished into the darkness, hinting at a huge network, a web of corruption that stretched far beyond this room. Eleanor could almost hear the ground groaning under the weight of the manor's old foundations, which were losing their strength and essence to feed this huge thing.

The artifact that was beating seemed to suck in all the light and heat, leaving the rest of the room in a state of constant twilight, broken only by the sickly glow. The cold got worse, a biting, gnawing chill that felt like it was trying to freeze them from the inside out. It was a cold that spoke of deep, old places that no one could understand, of a power that had been sleeping for a long time and was now waking up.

"It's drawing power," Eleanor finally said, her voice hoarse. "From the earth… from whatever is below. And it's using that power to… take the manor apart. To feed itself. The idea was terrifying, but it made sense of the house's widespread decay, structural breakdown, and even its own consciousness. The manor wasn't just haunted; it was alive, and this was its twisted heart, showing how hungry it was.

The artifact pulsed again, sending a strong wave through the ground that made it shake. The sickly light flared up, making long, twisted shadows that moved like ghosts on the walls of the cave. Eleanor felt something strange coming from the artifact, a psychic resonance that made her feel like she was in a state of extreme, painful hunger, of an eternity of wanting, of a primal need that could never be met. The hunger had grown so deep and all-consuming that it had affected the stone and dirt around it, making them sick.

Thomas took a step closer, but he was hesitant. His eyes were wide with fear and morbid curiosity. "The legends… they talked about a source of power in the old foundations." A place where the land itself was… dirty. He pointed vaguely at the artifact. "This has to be it. This is what they were trying to keep under control. Or maybe… what they were trying to wake up."

The pulsing slowed down, and the light got a little dimmer, as if the artifact were full or just taking a break. But the throbbing energy stayed there, a hidden power waiting to be set free. Eleanor saw that the thick liquid on the artifact's surface was not still. It moved in slow, planned currents, making and remaking patterns that suggested a chaotic, alien intelligence. It was like the artifact was dreaming, and this disgusting ooze was a physical representation of those dreams.

"We need to leave now," Eleanor said, her voice strained. The amount of bad energy was too much for her to handle; it was like a psychic attack that was starting to get on her nerves. The cold was no longer just physical; it felt like it was getting into her head and making her thoughts colder.

"But… how do we stop it?" Thomas asked, still looking at the strange thing that was pulsing. "Since this is the heart of it all, we must do something."

Eleanor shook her head, and a wave of sadness swept over her. "I don't know. It's so… old. So strong. It feels like trying to stop the tide with your hands. She looked at the tendrils that were creeping into the dark. "It runs deep. If you destroy this, it could completely destroy the manor. Or even worse. It might let go of the power it's been holding back.

The artifact pulsed again, this time with a soft, steady beat that sounded like the slow, steady decay they had seen all over the house. It was a lullaby of destruction, the last sad song about the manor's destruction. Eleanor felt a deep sense of loss, not for the crumbling building itself, but for the history it held and the lives it had seen, which were now being slowly eaten by this horrible, self-devouring thing.

They had found the heart of the darkness, the place where the manor's hunger never ended. But finding it had brought them no closer to salvation. Instead, it had revealed the terrifying depth of the corruption, the ancient, primal force that was slowly, methodically, unmaking the world around them. The chamber pulsed with its dark energy, a silent testament to the power they faced, a power that seemed as eternal and as terrifying as the cold that emanated from its very core. They were standing at the precipice of oblivion, staring into the abyss, and the abyss was pulsing.

Echoes of the First Family

The manor's pulsing heart was more than just an object; it was a projector, a stage on which the manor's very beginnings played out. As Eleanor and Thomas stood still in the underground room, the cold seemed to come together, and the sickly glow of the artifact grew sharper and more focused, as if it were trying to get their attention. The air, which was already thick with the smell of death and the biting cold, started to shimmer with a strange, ghostly light instead of heat. It felt like the very fabric of reality in the room was getting thinner, showing layers of time and events from long ago that were now bleeding into the present.

In the phosphorescent mist that drifted from the artifact, shapes began to come together. At first, they were blurry, like smoke trying to take shape. But as the artifact throbbed with a deeper, more resonant thrum, the ghosts became clearer and sharper. They were people dressed in clothes that were out of style for hundreds of years. Their bodies were see-through, but they had a terrifying clarity that spoke of deep pain. These weren't just ghosts; they were echoes, loud and painful, of the family that first lived here. They were the ancestors of the manor's never-ending hunger.

The ghostly figures appeared and moved in a jerky, unnatural way, as if they were puppets on invisible strings. It looked like they were all in the manor's grand hall, but this ghostly version was perfect, with no signs of the rot that now eats away at the real thing. In the middle of the ghostly scene stood a man with a face that showed both desperation and a terrifying, unnatural fervor. He wore rich silks that showed off his wealth and status, but his eyes... His eyes were full of a frantic light that didn't match how he looked. There was a woman next to him. Her face was pale and drawn, and her eyes were wide with fear. And there were kids all around them, their faces twisted in silent screams and their small bodies shaking with fear they couldn't see.

"They're... they're playing it again," Eleanor said in a shaky voice. As the ghostly drama played out in front of her, the cold seemed to cut deeper, not just into her skin but into her very soul. Each pulse of the artifact sent waves through the spectral vision, making the figures flicker and change shape, but their silent pain was still very real.

The patriarch of this ghostly family, the man in silks, raised his hands not in prayer but in a terrible, planned act of will. There was an unseen energy in the air around him, a dark magic that was being woven into the very foundations of the new manor. He was talking, but his lips didn't make any sound. His silent words somehow matched the artifact's throbbing power. Eleanor could feel the meaning of what he said: a deal with powers that were older and more evil than the manor itself. He was giving up something in exchange for something else. What was it? To be successful? For a legacy that will last? The spectral light grew stronger, casting a sickly glow over everything, and Eleanor understood. He was giving his family.

The woman next to him shrank back, her ghostly body twisting in silent pain. She reached out a clear hand to the kids, a desperate and useless move. But the man's will was unbreakable; his eyes were fixed on something beyond the hall's ghostly walls. The kids, whose faces were now twisted in fear and confusion, were drawn to the center of the room, where there was a point of shimmering, unnatural light that looked like the artifact in their own room.

After that, the regeneration started. Not the slow, insidious decay that was ruining the manor, but a bright, scary rebirth. The ghostly walls seemed to shimmer, the hall's opulence grew, and the air in the vision became thicker and more powerful. It felt like the manor was coming to life, with this dark, stolen energy flowing through its foundations. This was the first agreement, the beginning of the manor's consciousness, a terrible deal made in blood and despair.

The vision changed, and the ghostly family members spread out, their shapes becoming less connected and more broken. Different ghostly scenes showed the man, whose face was no longer passionate but empty from an unquenchable need. In one, he was carving into the bedrock below the manor. His ghostly blade was dripping with a dark ichor that looked like the thick fluid that covered the pulsing artifact. In another scene, he was pouring a glowing, poisonous liquid into the ground. It looked like it was alive and moved on its own as it seeped into the roots of the manor and the earth that supported it. This was the "regeneration" that the stories talked about. It wasn't a blessing; it was a curse. It was a parasitic infusion that made the manor last longer than it should have, but it cost the souls of its residents.

The woman's ghostly shape became clearer, and her pain grew stronger. People saw her walking around the halls, her ghostly hand pressed against the cold stone, and a silent lament echoed through the ghostly reconstruction. Her sadness and grief had become a part of the manor's very structure, a psychic residue that stuck to the walls and served as a constant reminder of the price it had paid for its existence. The kids were also a recurring theme. Their ghostly laughter turned into terrified screams, their innocence was lost, and their youthful energy was drained to feed the manor's growing intelligence. They were the first sacrifices and the first food. Their pain was always there in the house.

The ghostly visions got stronger, more real, and more terrifying. The man's obsession grew. His ghostly form got thinner, and his ghostly eyes burned with an ever-increasing hunger. He was seen going deeper, digging up old, forgotten rituals. His ghostly hands traced symbols in the air that made Eleanor's spine tingle. The artifact in the middle of their room pulsed along with these ghostly replays. Its sickly light flared up with every new piece of information about the manor's dark past.

It became very clear how the manor's hunger went in cycles. The family's first sacrifice wasn't just a one-time thing; it was the start of a long, sad cycle. The man, who was always looking for more power and longer life, had basically put the manor in a never-ending cycle of consumption. His dark deal brought the house to life, but it needed constant food, which came from the life force of anyone who dared to live there. The family's ghostly appearances weren't just memories; they were actively involved in this torment, their pain playing over and over again, feeding the hunger that had consumed them.

Eleanor watched, her stomach tightening with fear, as the ghostly father did one last horrible thing. He was standing in front of a crudely made altar that looked like the obsidian-like structure in front of them, and its surface was covered in the same black ooze. He held a shard in his ghostly hands. It glowed with a weak, sickly light, and when he put it in his own spectral chest, a wave of pain-filled energy came from the vision. The artifact in the room throbbed violently, and the spectral patriarch's body broke down, not into dust, but into a stream of black, thick fluid that flowed outwards, soaking into the spectral foundations of the manor and into the ground itself. This was more than just a sacrifice; it was a transfer. He had become one with the manor, his life force, his thoughts, and his hunger were all tied to the object forever.

The spectral children and wife, whose shapes were now flickering wildly, were pulled into this torrent of dark energy, and their screams were finally, though spectrally, set free. The manor was taking in their last moments of terror and their ongoing pain, making them a part of its evil consciousness. The ghostly vision started to fade, and the shapes became blurry again, disappearing into the swirling mist. All that was left was the cold and the rhythmic thumping of the artifact.

Thomas took a deep breath, and his knuckles turned white where he held the lantern. "He… he gave himself to it. To give it power. To keep it going."

Eleanor nodded, her eyes fixed on the pulsing artifact. After seeing how it was made, its surface now looked even more evil and alive. "It wasn't just a deal. It was a permanent infusion. He became the heart, and the artifact became the way for his never-ending hunger to flow. And the family, they are the echoes. The gas. "Their pain is what keeps the cycle going."

The ghostly visions had shown the terrifying truth: the spirits of the manor's past residents didn't just haunt it; they brought it to life. The original family, in their quest for power and wealth, accidentally woke up and tied a primal, insatiable hunger to the land itself. The man, in his last act of desperate ambition, had become the eternal fuel source, with his consciousness and his family's suffering always playing over and over again, feeding the manor, which was a hungry being.

"So that's why it feels so alive," Thomas said, his voice full of dawning horror. "It's more than just a building. It is a living thing that has been tortured for hundreds of years. The rot... It's not just mold. It's the house's food. Eating."

Eleanor shivered, not because she was cold, but because she understood something deeply and unsettlingly. The manor wasn't just a place of tragedy; it was a monument to it. It was a never-ending source of pain built on the ruins of one family's life. The echoes of their pain weren't just short flashes; they were the manor's very being, a constant, gnawing hunger that needed more.

"And we... we walked right into its mouth," Eleanor said, her voice barely audible. The artifact throbbed with a slow, steady beat. With each pulse, she felt a ghostly echo of the patriarch's despair, the wife's pain, and the children's fear. It was a symphony of pain that played in the middle of the manor, a chilling reminder of the suffering that kept it alive. The ghostly visions were gone, but their effects stayed, a heavy, suffocating weight in the cold air. They had seen the beginning, and that made them realize how bad the nightmare they were stuck in really was. The house wasn't just falling apart; it was eating, and they were the next course. The echoes of the first family were a scary warning, a sign of what might happen to them, always tied to the manor's never-ending hunger.

The Artifacts Influence

The artifact pulsed, its evil heartbeat echoing the dark beat they had seen in the spectral replay. It wasn't just a piece of obsidian and ichor anymore; it was a living, breathing thing that was affecting them in ways they couldn't even see. Eleanor felt a real wave of fear wash over her. It was colder than the chill that came from below and sharper than the wind that seemed to weave through the stone chamber. It was a thick, suffocating aura that made their fear worse, turning it into a raw, primal despair. The artifact seemed to speak to them in a way that wasn't audible, but rather through sneaky thoughts that crept into the deepest parts of their minds. The house's insatiable hunger gave rise to these evil suggestions, which whispered of survival and a way out, if only they would pay the price.

Thomas's face was a mask of grim determination, and he felt a disturbing pull toward the source of their fear. It was a sick interest, a dark pull that drew his eyes, thoughts, and even his will toward its corrupting power. He didn't see the pain of the first family or the horrible thing that had just happened to them. He saw a chance. A way to survive and get out of the manor's tight grip. The artifact seemed to promise power, a desperate strength to fight the darkness that was closing in. It whispered about control, about bending the manor's will to their own, a tempting lie that took advantage of their dire situation. His mind, which was already frayed by the shocking news, started to think about the impossible. The whispers got louder and more insistent, painting vivid pictures of getting away and a future free from the manor's grasp, all for the price of one clear act.

Eleanor, on the other hand, pulled back. Her senses screamed in protest, and her soul recoiled from the deep corruption that came from the artifact. She could feel the deep pain that was inside of it, the echoes of hundreds of years of suffering, of lives lost and hopes dashed. It wasn't a source of strength for her; it was a monument to pain and a place of hopelessness. She didn't see the ghostly figures as far-off spirits; she saw them as extensions of the artifact's will, their pain made worse and projected by its unholy glow. With every pulse, she felt a new wave of disgust wash over her, a deep understanding of the horrible deal that had led to this monster being born. The whispers that reached her were different; they were full of poison and lies and promised a false salvation. They talked about putting an end to the pain and putting the tortured souls to rest, but she knew the truth. It was a lie, a trap meant to keep them stuck in the same cycle they had seen.

"No," she whispered, her voice a thin thread in the heavy silence. "Don't pay attention to it, Thomas. It's not true. "Fear is what it's feeding on."

It didn't look like Thomas heard her. He was breathing in short, shallow gasps and staring at the artifact. He was lost in the seductive promises and the twisted logic of staying alive. The artifact, sensing that he was losing his resolve, pulsed with a deeper, more resonant hum. Its sickly glow grew stronger, casting long, distorted shadows that danced like ghosts on the walls of the chamber. It was the main point, the very heart of the manor's predatory will. The house wasn't just a building; it was a living thing made up of greed, sacrifice, and never-ending pain. And the artifact was its tool, its mouth, and its evil siren song that drew its next victims to their deaths.

It was very hard to resist the temptation. The artifact seemed to give off a real warmth, which was a nice change from the cold that was everywhere. It promised not only survival, but also a brief moment of peace. It whispered that there might be a way to get away from the manor's suffocating grip and back to the world they had left behind, where the air didn't taste like death and despair. It gave them a brief glimpse of sunlight, laughter, and a life free of the nagging fear that had become their constant companion. Hope, twisted and corrupted into a weapon of destruction, was the house's most powerful weapon and lure.

Eleanor could see that Thomas was having a hard time. He held the lantern tightly, with his jaw clenched and his knuckles white. He was fighting it, but the artifact was a strong enemy that was everywhere and had a sneaky effect on him. It didn't just attack the mind; it got into the soul and fed on basic human needs like the will to live, the need for safety, and the instinct to protect oneself. The whispers got louder and started to show pictures of their loved ones, of a reunion that could only happen if they accepted the artifact's evil power. It was a cruel and twisted way to play with their deepest emotional weaknesses.

"It's showing me… a way out," Thomas said in a strained voice, still looking at the artifact. "A way. It says that if we give it something, something of ourselves, it will let us go.

Eleanor's blood turned cold. "Offer what, Thomas? What could we possibly give it that it doesn't already want? We saw what happened to the first family. Their lives and souls became its food. She stepped closer and reached out her hand, not to the artifact but to Thomas, trying to pull him back from the edge of the cliff. "This isn't about getting away. It's about keeping the cycle going. "It's a trap, a horrible echo of the first sacrifice."

The artifact pulsed again, and this time Eleanor could feel it. A brief, almost inaudible whisper, a promise of freedom from the pain that had been bothering her since she got to the manor. It was a temptation, a dark pull that fed on her tiredness and growing hopelessness. But she stuck to her guns. She remembered the ghostly kids with their faces twisted in pain. Their innocence was taken away to feed the house's hunger. She remembered how the wife screamed silently and tried to protect her family in vain. This object was a physical representation of their pain, a way for them to feel it forever.

Eleanor's hand on Thomas's arm made him jump. The touch seemed to shock him, breaking the artifact's grip, even if only for a moment. He blinked, and his eyes got a little clearer. A flash of his old self came back. "You are right," he said, his voice getting stronger again. "It's… it's lying. It's the home. "The house wants us to give up our lives."

But the artifact was hard to stop. It pulsed with new life, and its evil energy grew stronger. The whispers came back, stronger and more convincing. Instead of talking about getting away, they talked about power. To be able to control the manor, to use its own hunger against its enemies, and to rule over this cursed place. It gave Thomas a false sense of strength and a twisted view of dominance that took advantage of his need to find a way to protect Eleanor.

"Think, Eleanor," Thomas said, his voice getting sharper. "If this is the manor's heart, if it gives it life… what if we could control it? What if we could use its power instead of being controlled by it?

Eleanor looked at him in shock. "Control it? Thomas, you want to be like him. Like the guy in the dream. "Giving in to the house's hunger and becoming one with it." She shook her head, her heart racing with a mix of fear and hopelessness. "That's not living." That's hell.

The artifact seemed to thrive on their fighting, and its light grew stronger with each argument. It was a predator, watching its prey, waiting for the right moment of weakness, the moment when it made a mistake that would end its life. The air became heavy with unseen forces, and the cold got even worse. The whispers turned into a single, seductive thought that echoed the old desires that had led to the manor's creation: power, immortality, and control.

"But what options do we have?" Thomas made his case in a low, urgent voice. "We can't get away. We can't fight it head-on. It is old, strong, and hungry. If we can't leave, maybe we can change. "We might be able to make it work for us."

Eleanor felt a wave of sadness wash over her. She understood the logic and the desperate need for practicality that made him say what he did. But she also saw the abyss yawning in front of them, which was the scary price of such a risk. "Adaptation is not the same as control, Thomas. You talk about using its power, but its power is naturally destructive. It gets its power from pain. You would have to accept that suffering in order to use it. "You would have to become it."

Eleanor felt a wave of cold fear wash over her as the artifact pulsed. She saw a vision of Thomas, his eyes empty and his body see-through, reaching out to the artifact and being pulled into its dark depths. It was quick and scary. It was a warning, a clear sign of the path he was thinking about taking. The whispers grew louder, and instead of talking about escape or control, they talked about acceptance. Of giving in to what must happen.

Eleanor begged, her voice thick with emotion, "It's not a choice between fighting and giving up." "It's a choice between our souls and its hunger." We need to find a different way. A way that doesn't mean becoming what we hate. She looked around the room and saw the rough altar, which looked like the artifact. "This... this is where it all started. This is where the deal was made. We need to learn about this place, not become it.

Thomas finally looked away from the artifact and into Eleanor's eyes. It was clear from the look on his face that he was struggling between his strong desire to live and his basic sense of right and wrong. "But how? We're stuck.

It seems like we're just walking deeper into its trap with every turn and every step we take.

"By knowing its weakness," Eleanor said, her voice strong but shaky. "By knowing what it really is. It gets its power from sacrifice and stolen life force. Maybe its biggest strength is also its biggest weakness. She turned around to look at the artifact, which had a pulsing rhythm that was always there and made her uneasy. It was the manor's heart, but like any heart, it could stop beating. Or at the very least, its power could be cut off. The artifact's seductive whispers kept going, a constant, sneaky murmur in the back of their minds. But for now, the raw terror of what it was really for had temporarily overshadowed its tempting promises. They had seen the beginning, the heart of the beast, and now they had to figure out how to stop its evil pulse before it ate them like it had eaten so many others. The artifact was the nexus, the conductor of the manor's evil symphony, and the only way they could save themselves was to find a way to stop its terrible music.

The Walls Close In

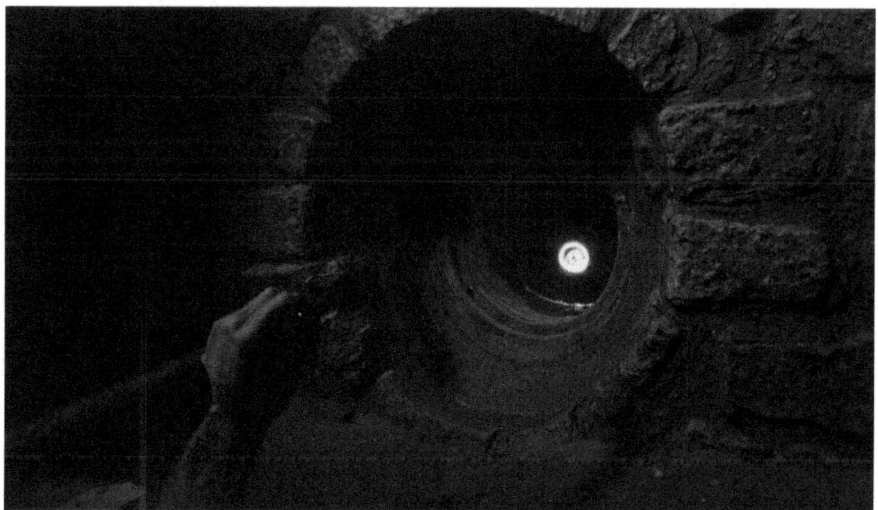

The obsidian artifact, which was no longer just an object but a beating organ inside the manor's old chest, seemed to suck the air out of their lungs. The heart was beating, and now the body was reacting to the intrusion. A low, grinding groan shook the stone under their feet. It wasn't the sound of settling foundations; it was the sound of huge, strained muscles. Eleanor felt it first, a tremor that ran up her legs. It was different from the lingering unease of the spectral replay. It was a physical sign of the house's distress, a deep cry of pain and anger.

After that, the walls. They had always been oppressive, with their cold stone seeming to push in, but this was different. This was on purpose. Eleanor's eyes shot up, catching the faint, oily shine of the stone surfaces. They started to move slowly, at first without anyone noticing, and then with a sickening sense of certainty. The smooth, unyielding rock face that had stood guard for hundreds of years was slowly moving inward, like a predator stalking its prey. The space between them and the unseen, oppressive limits was getting smaller. The rough texture of the stone seemed to get sharper, and the cracks and flaws looked like they were moving like the veins of a huge creature. The air, which was already heavy with the artifact's evil presence, became thicker and more viscous, making each breath a painful, difficult task. It felt like they were being squeezed, not by a physical force yet, but by the manor's own will, which was so strong that it was hard to breathe.

Thomas saw the horrible change happen while he was looking away from the pulsing artifact for a moment. He gasped, and a ragged sound was lost in the stone's growing groan. The walls weren't just getting closer; they were moving. He saw the rough-hewn blocks, which had been still and quiet before, now moving with an evil purpose and grinding against each other with a sound that hurt his very soul. The house wasn't waking up to greet them; it was waking up to eat them. The room, which had seemed big and scary just a moment ago, was quickly getting smaller. The ceiling was coming down at an almost imperceptible pace, making their already suffocating confinement even worse. It was a planned move, a slow, painful tightening meant to break their spirits before it broke their bodies.

"It's… it's alive," Eleanor stammered, her voice almost lost in the rising noise. She instinctively put her hand on her chest to protect herself from the real pressure that was starting to build around them. She could feel the house's weight pushing down on her from all sides, not just from above. The stone, which had been a passive background to their fear, was now an active enemy, its cold indifference replaced by a clear, burning rage. Each stone looked like a tooth ready to gnash, and every moving block looked like a limb ready to crush.

The artifact, as if drawing strength from their growing fear, pulsed brighter. Its sickly glow cast distorted shadows that danced and twisted in time with the walls grinding. The ghostly figures they had seen before seemed to flicker in and out of existence at the edges of their vision. Their silent screams now echoed the groans of the stone, and their pain was mixed with the house's fight to get rid of the intruders. The whispers, which had been a quiet, sneaky temptation, now sounded like one big roar of defiance, a primal scream of ownership that threatened to break their minds.

Thomas felt a rush of adrenaline and a strong need to do something, to find a way out of this tomb that was closing in on him. He looked at Eleanor. Her face was pale, and her eyes were wide with fear that was the same as his. The artifact's promise of a twisted escape was temporarily forgotten as the immediate, visceral threat of being crushed by the manor's embrace took over. This wasn't a battle of wills anymore; it was a fight for survival against a real-life example of pure evil.

Thomas said, "We can't stay here." His voice was strained but strong as he tried to cut through the rising tide of fear. "The artifact… it's the heart, but this whole place is reacting. It's trying to crush us." He looked around the shrinking room, taking in the walls closing in, the ceiling groaning, and the floor shaking. "We have to find a way out or a way to stop this."

Eleanor shook her head and stared at the object, which was still giving off dark, seductive energy. "Stop it? How? It's part of the house, Thomas. The house is protecting its heart. We've seen what it does to those who threaten it." She sounded hopeless. The whispers of the artifact had been a slow poison, but this direct, physical attack was a clear weapon of fear. "It's showing us its pain, but it's also showing us its strength."

The floor beneath them moved again, violently, making them stagger. Thomas took Eleanor's arm to steady her, even though he wasn't sure of his own footing. The stone blocks that made up the walls were no longer just moving; they were actively grinding against each other, sending small chips of rock flying down, which added to the thick dust that filled the air. The air itself seemed to get thicker and taste like blood and old iron. The smell of the house's old, hurt spirit, a smell of death and violence, stuck in their throats.

"It's not just about protecting the artifact," Thomas grunted as he looked around the room for any weak spots or strange architectural features that might let him get away. "It's about getting rid of us. We saw what happened to the family. We know its history. This is its last line of defense." He saw the ghostly figures again, this time more solid, their forms writhing in the flickering light, and their silent pleas made the horror grow. They weren't just ghosts; they were echoes trapped in the house's last, desperate attempt to save itself. Their pain showed how powerful the manor was and was a scary sign of what would happen to them.

Eleanor felt a strong sense of claustrophobia that was almost physical. The walls were closing in, yes, but it felt like the air was getting harder and harder, pushing against her skin, lungs, and mind. She could feel the manor's old machines starting to work, a huge, complicated, and scary engine of destruction. It was a planned, calculated response that came from centuries of instinct and one all-consuming goal: survival. And they were the germs, the foreign bodies, that had to be gotten rid of.

Eleanor said, "The whispers... they're changing," her voice strained. The stone's groaning had drowned out the tempting promises of escape and power, but now a new stream of thought was beginning to seep into the edges of her mind. It wasn't a promise; it was a cold acceptance of what was going to happen. You can't get away. This is where you will be buried. Get in touch with the stone. Embrace the quiet. The house wasn't just trying to kill them; it was trying to take them in and make them a permanent part of its oppressive structure, adding another layer of sadness to its never-ending construction.

Thomas clenched his teeth. "It wants us to give up. To stop fighting and let it crush us." He looked at the artifact again. Its pulsing rhythm was a defiant beat against the symphony of destruction going on around them. "But that's not going to happen. Not yet." He knew, with a chilling certainty, that the artifact was the key. It was the source of the manor's power, and if they could somehow break it, even for a short time, maybe they could change how the house reacted. But how? How could they possibly get to it, protect it, and then destroy it while the walls of their prison were trying to crush them?

The groaning got louder, and it sounded like a deafening roar that shook their bones. The floor shook again, making them lose their balance. Eleanor screamed when her knee hit the hard stone. The dust that the moving walls kicked up swirled around them, making it hard to see and making the room feel like the bottom of a tomb that was being sealed. The smell of wet earth and old decay filled the air, making it hard to breathe and making their senses dull. It was the manor's last, desperate breath as it tried to get back its holiness.

"We're running out of time," Thomas said, his voice full of worry. He pushed himself up and pulled Eleanor with him. He could feel the stone walls through his jacket. They were not only cold, but they also vibrated with an unnatural energy. It felt like touching a live wire, a constant, buzzing threat. "We need to find a way to slow this down, or at least make it lose its focus."

Eleanor's mind was racing as she looked around the room. The artifact pulsed, catching their attention. Its light was like a beacon in the swirling dust and rising darkness. It was the house's center and the source of its power. If they could somehow break its connection? Cut it off from the center of the manor? The idea was crazy, almost like suicide, but it was the only thing that came to her mind when she saw this clear, physical threat.

"The altar," she gasped, pointing to the rough, obsidian-like structure that looked like the artifact and where they had seen the start of the house's dark pact. "That's where it started. If we can break that... if we can shatter that... maybe we can break the connection." It was a last-ditch effort, a shot in the dark, but the walls were now only a few feet apart, and their grinding was a constant countdown to their death. The pressure was huge, and it was a physical sign of what the house wanted.

Thomas looked where she was looking. The altar, which was a jagged, dark mass, seemed to hum with a leftover energy, a dark echo of the artifact's stronger pulse. It wasn't as colorful or alive, but it was definitely connected. "Do you think breaking that will help?" he asked, his voice full of hope.

"It's the anchor," Eleanor said, her eyes blazing with determination. "It's where the house first got its power. If we cut that anchor, maybe... maybe we can weaken the whole structure. Stop this." She could feel the artifact's power pushing against her, a quiet but constant urge to give in and accept the stone's crushing embrace. But the picture of the family, their pain, and their final sacrifice made her more determined. This was not giving up; this was a last stand.

The walls were so close that their shoulders brushed against the rough stone. The air was full of dust and the metallic taste of fear. The artifact throbbed one last time, and Eleanor felt a ghostly pressure, like an unseen hand was pushing down on her chest and trying to get the air out of her lungs. This was it. The last few minutes. The house was putting up its last line of defense, locking away the source of its corruption and anyone who dared to find it in an eternal stone tomb.

Thomas made a choice when he saw that Eleanor was losing her strength and he was losing his own under the stress. He would do everything he could to keep her from being crushed. He looked at the altar and then at the artifact. A desperate plan began to take shape in his mind. "We can't both get to the altar," he said in a rough voice. "It's too… it's too close. But maybe, maybe if I can mess with the artifact, get its attention, and buy you time…"

Eleanor's eyes grew wide with fear. "No, Thomas! Don't! It's a trap! It will eat you!"

But Thomas was already on the move. He lunged at the artifact with a burst of strength, not to hug it or give in to its whispers, but to attack it. He took out the heavy iron crowbar they had found earlier. It felt solid and comforting in his hand. He swung it as hard as he could, aiming for the throbbing black heart of the manor. He hoped to break its evil power and give Eleanor the few seconds she needed to strike the altar and break the manor's terrifying hold. The metal screamed against the hard surface, making a jarring sound that stopped the grinding of the walls for a moment. Then, a sharp, piercing cry of pure, unadulterated rage came from the very foundations of the cursed house.

A Glimmer of Hope

The air was thick with the sharp smell of crushed stone and the metallic smell of primal fear, which made Eleanor's throat feel like it was being clawed. The manor's walls had stopped grinding for a moment, and there was a stunned silence after Thomas's desperate attack with metal on obsidian. His blow, a pointless act of defiance against the house's massive, waking anger, had caused a scream that was more like a seismic tremor than a sound, a guttural release of pure, blazing rage. It was a sound that promised revenge, a promise carved into the stone that was now pressing against them, inches from their flesh. Eleanor felt the huge pressure, a weight that wanted to crush them into the dust of their own death.

Thomas was pressed up against the pulsing artifact, his crowbar still in a tight grip. The obsidian surface, which had once been smooth and uncomfortably warm, now gave off a cold energy, which was very different from the rage it had caused. He was like a fly caught in the mouth of a cosmic predator. His brave act of defiance was nothing more than a small annoyance in the face of an ancient, unbreakable will. The artifact's sickly, pulsating glow lit up his face, which was twisted with stress and a desperate hope. He was giving her time, which seemed like an impossible idea in this suffocating, impending end.

But Eleanor's eyes were no longer on the immediate, physical threat of their destruction. It was pulled toward the artifact by some unseen, strong force. She had seen it when Thomas attacked and the obsidian surface briefly bent and rippled under the force of the blow. A brief look at letters and symbols that are carved into the very fabric of the object. Not the rough carvings that were on the outside walls of the manor, but something much older and more complex. A language that came from a time long ago and a script that seemed to be carved not on the surface, but deep inside its soul.

She reached out with shaking fingers, and her hand was only a few inches away from the artifact. The house's anger seemed to pull back a little, as if it was surprised by the sudden attention. The oppressive aura coming from it was strong. It was a risky bet, a sign of great arrogance, but the other option was a slow, painful death. The whispers that had threatened to drive her crazy with their promises of despair and nothingness seemed to fade away. Instead, there was a faint, almost imperceptible hum coming from the inscription. There was a different kind of resonance, not of hunger or malice, but of something deeper, something that hinted at a lost order.

"Thomas," she said, her voice barely above a whisper, but it cut through the echoes of the artifact's scream. He didn't say anything. He was focused on the manor's beating heart, and his body was a shield against its unmaking embrace. Eleanor knew she had to do something right away. The walls wouldn't stay still for long. The short break was just a break before the inevitable, crushing end.

She didn't know why, but her fingers traced the symbols that were carved into the stone. The writing was different from anything she had ever seen before. It flowed and looked like it had been carved by water or shaped by wind. Each symbol had a faint, internal light that pulsed. It looked like the light came from a deeper, older source than the artifact's dark core. As her fingertips touched the cool, hard surface, a flood of pictures filled her mind. Not the ghosts that haunt the house's victims or the greedy whispers of its power, but something else entirely.

She saw circles. Cycles of life and death, of making and breaking. The inscription talked about more than just the artifact's never-ending hunger. It also talked about a cosmic balance, a dance of energy that flowed through everything. It talked about sacrifice, not as a violent act to calm someone down, but as a necessary letting go of the old to make room for the new. And it talked about starting over, about the dawn that always comes after the darkest night. She began to feel a mix of awe and fear as she realized that the artifact was not just a vessel of evil, but an important part of a much bigger, more complex plan.

The manor's foundation was laid long before people wrote their short histories on the world, which showed how old it was. This was the language of the earth itself, of the basic forces that made life possible. The writing on the artifact seemed to explain its hunger not as a bad thing, but as a necessary part of a bigger system. It did eat, but it also changed. It took in the old energies, the lingering sadness, and the broken echoes of lives lived and lost. By doing this, it made room for something new to grow. The manor, as it is now, was a corrupted version of this original design, a twisted version of a holy process.

The inscription described a ritual, a set of steps that had been carefully planned to keep this fragile balance. It talked about a gift, but not blood or souls. It talked about giving up something on purpose, not life but ego, the desperate need to hold on to oneself that kept the cycle of suffering going. It was a giving up of the desire to own and control, as well as the need to eat. The artifact was always hungry because the natural flow had been broken, and it was in a corrupted state. The balance was gone, and the house, in its blind, instinctual search for a twisted restoration, had turned into a huge, self-devouring monster.

Eleanor felt a shiver run down her spine, not because she was cold, but because she realized something very deep and almost overwhelming. The house wasn't just a prison; it was a broken machine that was trying to fix itself but was doing so with the brute force of its broken nature. Thomas's brave attack only made it hurt more, like hitting a hurt animal that only fought back harder. Instead of just lashing out at the pain, the inscription gave a different way to heal the wound.

It talked about a "gift of stillness," a moment of deep acceptance that would let the artifact reset its energies. It wasn't about tearing things down; it was about fixing them. Someone had to go into the manor's destructive power and not fight it, but take it in and become a channel for its redirection. The gift was not life itself, but the strong, possessive grip on life and the desperate need to hold on to the illusion of self.

Eleanor looked at Thomas, whose face was set in grim determination and whose body was still pressed against the artifact. He was giving up his life, his very being, in a last-ditch effort to stand up to him. But the writing on the stone suggested a different kind of sacrifice. A sacrifice of will and ego. A giving up that was not a loss, but a deep act of understanding.

"Thomas," she whispered again, her voice getting stronger and stronger as she felt the ancient power growing inside her. "It's not about breaking it." It's about giving it. Not us, but our fear. Our need to be in charge."

He turned his head, and his eyes, which were clouded with effort and a growing sense of hopelessness, met hers. "What are you talking about, Eleanor? We have to get rid of it. "This is our only chance."

"No," she said firmly. She took her hand away from the writing, and the symbols' faint glow faded for a moment, but the resonance inside her stayed. "Thomas, it's not a weapon of pure evil. It's... broken. It's a cut. The writing on it tells how to fix it. A way to get things back in order."

She spoke quickly, as if she were out of breath, putting together the bits of understanding she had gotten from the old script. She talked about the cycles and how sacrifice is giving up something, not the end of something. She talked about how the house was in pain and how its instinct to protect itself had been corrupted. She also talked about how their fear and defiance had only made it worse.

Thomas listened, his brow furrowed. At first, he was skeptical, but then he began to understand. The walls had stopped grinding, but the heavy silence that had fallen was almost worse. The air was full of coiled energy, and you could feel the dread of their doom. But in Eleanor's words, in the faint echo she carried with her, there was a new sound, a faint counterpoint to the manor's rage: a whisper of hope.

"So, you're saying we don't fight it?" He asked, his voice rough and full of doubt. "We… we give it something?"

"Yes," Eleanor said, and she didn't look away. "A gift of calm. Letting go of our fear. We must demonstrate our comprehension of its purpose and our ability to engage in the cycle, not as victims, but as voluntary participants. It wants to take us in and make us a part of its stone, but what if we let it take in our fear and resistance? "What if we help it heal instead of hurt it?"

The idea was bold, almost crazy. To willingly give oneself, not in a defiant stand, but in a deep act of surrender, to a force that was actively trying to destroy them. It was a different kind of sacrifice, one that made them give up their very instinct to survive. But the inscription, which held ancient wisdom, rang true with a truth that went beyond their immediate fear. It talked about a deeper order, a cosmic need that their human point of view had missed.

The artifact seemed to pulse with a less aggressive rhythm as Eleanor spoke. The air pressure that was making it hard to breathe got a little bit better. It was as if the house was holding its breath for a moment, waiting for something to change. The ghostly shapes at the edges of their vision, which had been writhing in pain, seemed to stop moving. Their silent screams were replaced by a look of deep, old tiredness.

"It's a chance," Eleanor said, her voice full of desperate conviction. "The only chance. We need to offer something other than more violence to stop the cycle of violence. It's a risk, but what else do we have? Her eyes begged Thomas to look at her. "You were willing to give up your life to break it." What if you gave up your fear and anger to heal it?

Thomas looked from Eleanor to the artifact, then to the walls that were closing in on them. The walls had moved back a little, as if to give them a little more room to breathe. He realized that the inscription was more than just a historical record; it was a set of instructions that had been lost and could help him figure out what the manor really was. The house's anger was a sign that it was out of balance, and their own fear had been making it worse.

He asked in a voice that was hard to hear, "How do we do that?" "How do we… give stillness?"

Eleanor said, "We stand before it," and her voice became more authoritative. "We let go of our fear. Yes, we recognize its strength, but we also recognize its purpose. We let it know that we get it. We help it understand that its hunger is not an end, but a way to get what it wants. A piece of a bigger cycle. We have to believe that the inscription is true and that we can find balance again by accepting things instead of destroying them.

It was a leap of faith, a leap into the dark. It took a lot of courage to stand in front of the artifact, the source of the manor's vengeful power, and give up the instinct to fight and resist. The inscription, on the other hand, was a glimmer, a weak light in the thick darkness. It talked about a different kind of victory, one that didn't involve conquering but understanding. A way out of the certain doom, a chance to change their fate not with blood but with acceptance.

Eleanor took a small step toward the artifact. The air around it sparkled, and she felt a faint pull, a tugging feeling that told her there was a huge, old energy there. It wasn't a violent force; it was a strong, gravitational pull that drew her in and invited her to be a part of something much bigger than herself. She shut her eyes and concentrated on the words of the inscription and the echoes of balance and renewal. She thought about how her fear, terror, and desperate need to live all came together into something real. Then, with a deep, cleansing breath, she let it go, sending it into the artifact's pulsing energy.

Thomas watched with his heart in his throat. He saw Eleanor stand in front of the thing, and her posture showed that she was determined and calm, as if she were coming from the very core of her being. The heavy air seemed to lift, and in its place came a feeling of excitement, as if the universe was about to change. The artifact's pulsing slowed down, and its light got a little dimmer, as if it were thinking.

It was a small change, almost too small to notice, but it was there. A break in the constant flow of destruction. A moment of deep, unsettling silence. The writing didn't give them a weapon, but it did give them knowledge. And in that wisdom, a weak, new hope began to grow. A hope that maybe, just maybe, they could find a way to get out of the heart of the manor, not by breaking it, but by understanding it. The road ahead was still unclear, and the true meaning of this old ritual was still mostly a mystery. But for the first time since they had entered this cursed place, Eleanor felt a real sense of hope. It was a small, precious glimmer, but in the manor's suffocating darkness, it was enough to spark a desperate, unshakeable determination.

Chapter 8: The Reckoning

The Desperate Gambit

The silence after Eleanor's revelation wasn't peaceful; it was a pregnant pause, like the universe holding its breath before the plunge. The manor's walls had stopped grinding, leaving a void that throbbed with a much more dangerous tension. The air was thick with the ghostly smell of dust and despair, and it felt like it was pressing in on me, with every molecule full of the house's unstable energy. Thomas looked at Eleanor with white knuckles on the crowbar and a body that was tense with protective instinct. Her eyes, which had once been pools of fear, now had a shocking clarity and a scary glow that matched the artifact's sickly glow.

He repeated, "Sever its connection?" The words hurt his throat. The idea wasn't just crazy; it was a suicidal plunge into the mouth of the beast they had been trying so hard to get away from. He had seen the artifact's raw power and the terrible rage it had caused with just a shrug of its black shoulders. It was like trying to untangle the threads of reality itself to try to break its connection to the very foundation of this living nightmare. "Eleanor, that's not a sacrifice. That's killing."

Eleanor smiled weakly, like a flower that is about to die in the dark. "Maybe," she said, her voice barely above a whisper, but it sounded like an old prophecy. "But the inscription… it talked about balance, Thomas. About cycles. The house isn't just a predator; it's a corrupted guardian. It feeds because it's broken. It consumes because its purpose has been twisted. And its purpose, its anchor, is this artifact." She pointed to the pulsing obsidian, which now looked like it was writhing with a hidden energy, like a snake coiled up. "Maybe the house will stop being what it is if we can cut off its connection to its source of… corrupted power. Maybe it will finally find… peace."

The words hung in the air, full of meaning. Eleanor wasn't suggesting a fight; she was suggesting an erasure. Not the house itself or its past, but the horrible way it looks now. She planned to starve the beast by cutting off its poisoned food, which could have killed the very thing that had brought them to the edge of death. But the writing also hinted at a cost, a give-and-take. And Eleanor, who now understood, had figured out the scary truth of it. The artifact was a nexus, a place where the manor's will and power came together. Cutting off that connection would mean giving up something very important. Not of flesh and blood, not just of defiance, but of something much deeper: the self.

"It will eat you up," Thomas said, his voice a low growl of protest. "To break that connection, it will require a gift. It will require the very energy that keeps you alive. The inscription spoke of a 'gift of stillness,' Eleanor. What you're talking about is a complete and utter emptying. You'll be... you'll be gone." The thought of her fading away, of her light being snuffed out to fuel the house's destruction, was more painful than any physical pain.

"I know," she said, her eyes fixed on the beating heart of the manor. "But what choice do we have, Thomas? We've tried force. We've tried defiance. The house only grows stronger, its hunger more insatiable. We are trapped in a cycle of its pain. This... this is our only chance to break it. To offer it not another victim, but its own release. And my release, perhaps." She turned to him, her eyes searching his. "You were willing to throw yourself at it and become a sacrifice to break its hold. This is similar, but instead of giving ourselves up to its destruction, we give ourselves up to its healing."

He flinched when he heard the word "healing." The thought that this nightmare architect could ever get better was almost worse than how bad it is now. But Eleanor's faith was a real force, a light in the dark that was closing in on her. He didn't see the craziness of a madwoman in her eyes; instead, he saw the deep clarity of someone who had seen a truth that went beyond their current situation. The writing on the wall wasn't just a map of the manor's history; it was a key, a Rosetta Stone that helped people understand what it was. Eleanor had figured it out.

"I won't let you do it alone," he said with a strong voice that rang with new purpose. He moved closer, found her hand, and held it tightly, promising to always be there for her. "I will stand by you if this is the only way. I will be your shield. If it tries to take you, it will have to go through me."

Eleanor squeezed his hand and felt a grateful shiver run through her. "Thank you, Thomas. But this is something I have to do. It's not about physical protection; it's about intention. It's about offering myself willingly. You can stand with me and offer your support and presence, but the act itself must be mine." She looked back at the artifact, her mind already mapping out the dangerous path. "The inscription talked about a ritual. It talked about a sequence, a channeling of intent. I have to become the conduit, the bridge between the artifact and the manor, and then… I have to cut the bridge."

Eleanor understood that the ritual was not a big show of magic from the broken echoes of the inscription. It was a deep, internal breaking apart. She had to stand in front of the artifact, not as an enemy, but as a gift. She had to let its bad energy flow through her, not take it in and make it stronger, but send it somewhere else, spread it out. She was like a lightning rod, not to be struck, but to channel the destructive force into the ground so that it would lose its power without hurting anyone. But in this case, the lightning was the very heart of the manor's evil, its never-ending hunger, and the artifact's binding power. Eleanor herself had to be the earth, the grounding force.

"How?" Thomas asked, his voice tight with a deep fear for her. "How do you change the course of something that wants to eat everything?"

"By giving it what it really wants, but in its pure form," Eleanor said, her voice getting stronger and more resonant, as if the idea itself was giving her strength. "It wants connection, an anchor. It has latched onto this artifact, which is a corrupted anchor. I have to give it a different kind of connection, one that is selfless. I have to be the stillness and the letting go that the inscription talked about. I have to become the void it wants to fill, but a void that doesn't fight back. A void that just… accepts and lets go."

The air in her lungs was dry and rasping as she took a deep, shuddering breath. The walls, which had been eerily still, started to shake again. This time, it wasn't the sound of demolition; it was a low, resonant hum, as if the house itself was sensing her intent and its ancient heart was stirring in anticipation. The ghostly figures at the edge of her vision, who had been stuck in their eternal suffering, started to move. Their silent screams got louder, and their ghostly forms stretched out, as if they were trying to grab her and pull her into their pain.

"It knows," Thomas said quietly, gripping the crowbar harder and looking around at the moving shadows. "It knows you're going to do something."

Eleanor said, "Then we have to be faster," and she didn't take her eyes off the artifact. "Thomas, I need you to keep them away from me. Just for a moment. Just long enough. Don't let them touch me or bother me."

He nodded, his jaw set. "I will. I swear it." He moved without thinking to stand between her and the ghosts, his body language a silent promise to protect her.

Eleanor turned her back on him and the ghostly horrors and faced the object. Its obsidian surface pulsed more strongly, and its sickly light cast an eerie glow over her. She could feel its hunger, a huge, empty space that echoed through her whole body. It was a basic, all-consuming need to take in everything, to connect with it, and to make it a part of itself. And now it saw her not as a threat to be crushed, but as a possible gift, a willing sacrifice to its never-ending hunger.

She shut her eyes, not because she was scared, but because she was focused. She made herself remember the inscription, the flowing, natural symbols that had whispered forgotten truths into her mind. She thought about how life goes in cycles, how things come and go, and how old things have to die for new ones to grow. She saw herself, her fears, her regrets, and her desperate need to live not as solid things, but as fleeting energies. She thought of them as a swirling vortex inside her, a storm of her past and her basic instincts.

"This isn't a fight," she said in a voice that was barely audible but had an almost otherworldly calm to it. "This is a gift."

She made a conscious decision to let go of those energies. She didn't want to get rid of them or destroy them; she wanted to let them go. She pictured them opening up like flags caught in a sudden gust of wind and floating away from her center. She let go of her fear of the manor, her fear of the artifact, and her desperate desire to escape. It wasn't a painful effort; it was a deep, almost peaceful surrender. It was like taking off a heavy coat that had been weighing her down for so long.

She felt the artifact's pull get stronger as she let go of her own worries. It was no longer a hostile force; it was a gravitational force, like a cosmic vacuum. It called to her to let go of more, to shed more, to become lighter and emptier. The ghostly figures felt the change and worked even harder. Their ghostly bodies lashed out, and their silent screams turned into a desperate chorus. Thomas fought them off with a desperation that made him very angry. His crowbar moved so quickly that it deflected their spectral claws. His grunts and curses were a human counterpoint to the manor's ancient, growing hum.

"Wait, Eleanor!" he yelled, his voice strained, as a ghostly hand brushed past his shoulder, making him feel cold all over.

Eleanor's breath caught. She could feel the pull, the strong suction that was pulling not only her fear but also her memories and even her sense of self toward the black surface. It felt like being pulled apart thread by thread, and it was scary. But she stood her ground, her goal clear. She wasn't giving herself up to be eaten; she was giving the manor's corruption, its need for control, and its never-ending desire.

"The connection," she whispered, her voice weak. "It's the artifact… it's the anchor. I have to cut the anchor."

She focused her will not on the artifact itself, but on the thread that connected it to the heart of the manor. It was like trying to grab smoke to break an invisible link. But the writing had given her a glimpse of this connection, a shimmering string of dark energy that throbbed with the manor's corrupted life force. She had to find that cord and break it with the little bit of life force she had left.

The ghostly figures seemed to fade a little as she focused, as if their power was being drained, not into Eleanor, but through her, toward the artifact. The artifact's light got dimmer and its pulsing got slower, as if it were being drained. The manor's humming got quieter, which was a small but important change. It was working. Eleanor was becoming a channel, not for destruction, but for redirection, for the planned tearing down of the manor's corrupt heart.

But the price was very high. She felt like her memories were getting fuzzy and her thoughts were breaking up. The ground under her feet felt like it was moving, and the world around her started to look like a dream. She was losing herself, and her sense of who she was was fading away into the artifact's huge, hungry void. The writing was clear: the act required a full surrender, a willing letting go of the self.

"Thomas," she said, her voice thin and shaky. "It's… it's almost done. But I… I can't hold on much longer."

Thomas, whose face was covered in sweat and ghostly residue, fought his way back to her. He could see the scary emptiness in her eyes and how her body seemed to shimmer and fade at the edges. She was a ghost before her time, and her spirit was fading away.

"No, Eleanor, stay with me!" he begged, reaching for her hand but only finding a cold emptiness. "Don't do this!"

"It's… the only way," she whispered, her voice now just a breath. She concentrated all of her willpower on the last few strands of it, picturing the shimmering cord that connected the artifact to the manor. With one last, desperate push of will, she made it break.

She felt a sharp pain, as if an unseen knife had cut through her soul. It was a feeling that went beyond pain and understanding, a ripping apart of existence itself. Then, the artifact let out a blinding flash of light and a silent explosion of energy that seemed to shake the whole manor. The humming stopped. The ghostly figures screamed, a sound of pure, unadulterated fear, and then they just disappeared, like smoke in a strong wind. The heavy weight in the air went away, and in its place came a deep, complete stillness.

Eleanor slumped forward, and her body was now a weightless shell. Thomas caught her, and without thinking, his arms wrapped around her. She felt like a hollow reed, like she was floating. Her eyes, which had once been full of a desperate light, were now empty and staring into space.

He whispered, “Eleanor?” and his voice shook. “Eleanor, do you hear me?”

There was no answer. She was breathing very lightly, almost not at all. The artifact was still, with its pulsing stopped and its dark glow gone. The manor’s walls, which had threatened to crush them, were now still, silent, and strangely empty. It seemed like the house was holding its breath, waiting for a decision.

Thomas held Eleanor close, his heart heavy in his chest. He had promised to keep her safe, and in a way, he had. She was still alive, but she was a shadow of her former self. But the price… the price had been too high to imagine. He looked around the empty, quiet manor. The heavy air was gone, and in its place was a cold emptiness. They were safe from its immediate danger, but Eleanor… Eleanor was gone. The price of cutting off the house’s connection to its corrupting heart was her very essence, her very self. It was a last-ditch effort to get free, and it cost them everything. He held her tighter as the terrifying truth sank in: they had escaped the manor’s hunger, but it had cost Eleanor her own life. At the heart of this cursed place, they had won a kind of victory, but it was a hollow and terrible one.

The House Resists

The artifact pulsed, and at the center of the manor's decaying body was a dark, evil heart. Eleanor stood in front of it, and her body was already starting to shimmer and lose its shape. Thomas watched with his muscles tense and his breath held tightly in his chest. He was aware of what was going to happen. The calm that followed Eleanor's announcement was a lie; it was just a short break before the storm. The house had been quiet, maybe even waiting. Waiting for her to make a move.

And now she did.

It started out as a low thrumming that shook not only the floorboards but also the bones in their bodies. It sounded like a huge engine starting up and old gears grinding against each other after a long time of not moving. The walls, which had been solid and oppressive, started to move and sway like the sides of a huge, sleeping beast that had been disturbed from its rest. The plaster cracked, not with a loud bang, but with a sickening, tearing sound, like sinew being pulled too far. The dust fell from the impossibly high ceilings in violent avalanches, not gentle falls.

Thomas had a strong urge to run away and pull Eleanor away from this growing fire. But even though her voice was weak, it was a lifeline, a last-ditch effort to hold on in the chaos. “It’s resisting,” she whispered, her eyes fixed on the artifact. Even though the tremors were getting closer and closer, they didn’t move. “It doesn’t want to let go.”

He held the crowbar tighter. The cold metal felt very different from the heat that was starting to come from the stones of the manor. “Let it try,” he said in a low, defiant growl. He stood directly behind Eleanor, like a living shield, and looked around the edges. The shadows, which had only been empty spaces of light, now came together and deepened into shapeless forms that moved like they were alive. The air got thick, not with dust, but with a heavy, suffocating presence that pushed against their lungs and made it hard to breathe.

The thrumming got louder and turned into a deep groan that seemed to come from deep within the earth. The fancy carvings on the walls and the ugly gargoyles that were hanging from the cornices started to bend. Their stone faces twisted, and their eyes seemed to open and fix on Eleanor with a burning, predatory intensity. The illusion of reality was starting to fall apart, and underneath it was a raw, untamed power that was angry at the thought of being set free.

“It’s… it’s showing us,” Eleanor said, her voice shaky. “It’s hurting.” It’s angry. “It’s trying to break me.”

As the way he saw space began to change, Thomas felt sick. The big hall they were in seemed to stretch and shrink, and the windows far away seemed to blur and come back together in strange ways. He saw quick images: a woman crying in a torn dress, a child’s toy left in a corner full of dust, and a man with a rope around his neck. These weren’t just memories; they were echoes that the manor’s sick mind had twisted and amplified, like psychic projectiles thrown at them.

"Don't look," he said in a rough voice. "Pay attention to me, Eleanor." "Pay attention to us." He reached for her and touched her arm with a firm, grounding touch. It felt like the cold from the house was already getting into her skin.

The house, on the other hand, didn't want just illusions. The ghostly figures, the tortured souls that had been following them since they first entered, now rushed forward. They were no longer see-through ghosts; they were becoming solid, their shapes becoming sharper, and their pained faces turning into pure, unadulterated rage. Their screams, which had been quiet until now, filled the air with a horrible noise that could break eardrums and minds.

They moved forward, scratching and tearing, their ghostly hands reaching for Eleanor and the very thing she was trying to let go of. Thomas yelled and swung the crowbar as hard as he could. It went through the ghostly shapes, but every blow seemed to cause a ripple of disruption, a brief pause in their unstoppable march forward. He felt ghostly touches, icy tendrils that brushed against his skin and left behind a burning cold that went deep into his bones.

A voice hissed, "You can't stop this!" It sounded like it came from everywhere and nowhere at the same time, and it was full of the anger that had built up over hundreds of years. It was the house itself, speaking through the very fabric of its being. "This is my place! I own its hunger! You don't give me anything I can't eat!

Eleanor staggered, and it was clear that she was shaking. The stronger attack was clearly having an effect. The artifact's light, which had been getting dimmer, came back to life, but now it was pulsing erratically, almost like it was in a panic. It was getting stronger from the house's desperate fight and rage.

"It's a cycle," Eleanor said, her voice barely audible over the noise. "It eats up despair." It keeps going by making people suffer. But pain can also be a way to let go…

"A release that will take over your life!" Thomas yelled and pushed her back even more as he blocked a ghostly lunge that would have ripped her apart. He could feel the pressure building, and the air around them was crackling with bad energy. The floor moved like the deck of a ship in a storm, and the walls were closing in, threatening to crush them.

There was a horrible fake face in the wood grain of a nearby pillar, and its eyes glowed with a green light of hate. The fancy chandelier above them started to swing back and forth, and the crystal pendants made a noise like a thousand tiny teeth grinding together. The house was doing everything it could to put out the spark of defiance that Eleanor was.

"I have to get to the anchor," Eleanor whispered, her voice getting weaker and more ghostly. "The link between the artifact and… and the core."

"I'll get you there!" Thomas promised, his eyes fixed on the pulsing object. He could see it now: a thin, shimmering line of dark energy that was almost invisible and snaked from the surface of the obsidian into the heart of the manor. It was the lifeline, the way that corruption spread.

The ghosts got more desperate and their attacks got crazier. One got past Thomas's guard and wrapped its cold fingers around Eleanor's arm. She screamed, a sharp, painful sound that broke his heart. He turned around and swung his crowbar, cutting off the ghostly limb. But the contact had drained her even more, and her shimmering form flickered like a candle flame in a storm.

"Wait, Eleanor!" he begged, his voice full of desperation. "Just a little longer!"

He noticed a big change in the energy of the house. The anger and rage that had been there at first seemed to be fading, and in its place came a deep, painful sadness and a strong sense of loss. It was like the house was crying as it died. The architecture's twisting slowed down, and the groaning turned into a sad sigh. But the ghostly figures kept attacking. Now they were driven by a basic instinct: a desperate need to hold on to their pain and their lives, no matter how messed up they were.

"It knows," Eleanor said, her eyes far away. "It knows it's losing its hold. It's letting go of its pain. Its own bad nature."

The light from the artifact got even dimmer, and the erratic pulse slowed down to a more regular, though weaker, beat. The shimmering string that connected it to the manor looked like it was getting tighter and tighter. Eleanor pushed herself forward, past Thomas's protective stance, with a strength he didn't know she had.

"This is my part, Thomas," she said, her voice getting a little clearer again, but it still had an otherworldly sound to it. "You have kept my body safe. Now I have to keep my soul safe.

She walked toward the artifact, her steps light and almost gliding. The ghostly figures seemed to pull away from her, their faces twisted in a new kind of fear. They could feel something in her now, not defiance, but a void, an emptiness they couldn't understand, an emptiness that was strangely a threat to their very existence.

The air around her seemed to ripple and shimmer with an unseen energy as she got closer to the artifact. She raised her hands, not to fight, but to offer. The dark energy cord throbbed, and its tendrils lashed out, as if they could sense that the person who would cut it was close.

The house's last breath made Eleanor's voice sound louder: "You crave connection." "You want to bind and consume. But real connection isn't about owning something. It's about letting go. About letting go.

She put all of her will and the last bits of her being into that shimmering cord. There was a fight over wills and intentions. The house, which had been through thousands of years of pain and hunger, was up against Eleanor, who had only one goal: to help others. The artifact throbbed, and its sickly light made long, twisted shadows in the hall. The ghostly figures screamed, their bodies starting to fall apart at the edges as they lost their grip on reality.

Thomas's heart was in his throat as he watched Eleanor reach out. Her clear fingers were only a few inches from the pulsing cord. The house let out one last groan, a sound of deep sadness and giving up. The cord broke with a sound like a cosmic sigh.

There was no big event or explosion. There was instead a sudden, complete silence. The artifact turned black, and its obsidian surface lost its shine and life. The ghostly figures disappeared right away, not because they lost energy, but because they had never been there. The manor's strange movements stopped, and the walls went back to how they were before, even though they were still damaged. The heavy weight that was on me went away, leaving behind a deep, echoing emptiness.

Eleanor swayed back and forth, her eyes wide but not focused. She had done it. She had cut off the link. But the price... The price was clear in the way her eyes were empty and her body seemed to flicker, as if she were already a ghost. She had offered herself as the bridge and the way to get to the other side. By cutting off the house's corrupted heart, she had changed her own heart forever. The house had fought back, like a dying god, but in the end, it was destroyed by an act of deep self-sacrifice. Eleanor, the unwilling architect of its destruction, was now tied to its silence in a way that showed how much it had cost them both more than they could have ever imagined.

Thomass Stand

The manor's dying screams still echoed in the huge room, a symphony of ghostly pain that had almost driven Thomas insane just a few moments before. There was no peace in the silence that followed; it was a void, a heavy, suffocating blanket that pressed in on him from all sides. Eleanor stood in front of the now-dark artifact. She looked like a ghost, with her essence frayed and her form shimmering with an unsettling transparency. He had done what he was supposed to do. He had kept his word. But the price... The price was carved into every part of her, a deep change that scared him more than any ghostly touch.

Thomas's own body was still buzzing with adrenaline, his muscles were still tense, and his senses were still on high alert. The crowbar felt heavy and useless in his hand, like a regular tool against the strange powers they had just faced. He watched Eleanor with a heavy heart. She had talked about giving up and letting go, and now he saw how scary her words had come to life. She had given him time to stand as a shield and endure the attack, but in doing so, she had paid a price that was more than just physical pain or mental anguish.

She had become a vessel, a way for the manor's last, painful breath to escape.

He took a cautious step toward her, and the floorboards creaked under his weight. The sound was shockingly loud in the stillness. "Eleanor?" His voice was a rough whisper that was hard to hear. He needed to know if there was anything left of her, anything that could be saved from the ruins of this place and the ritual. The ghosts, who had once been so real in their anger, were now gone. The house's very structure, which had twisted and turned like a living thing in pain, had finally settled down, leaving behind only the scars of its pain. But Eleanor... Eleanor was not the same. She wasn't a victim of the house's destruction; she was a key part of its last act.

He watched as she moved and raised her head. When their eyes finally met, hers were like big pools of nothing. Not emptiness in the sense of a void, but a lack of the familiar and the human. It was like she had seen and done too much, and the weight of it all had made her lose her sense of self. The connection she had made, which had let her break the artifact's hold, had clearly tied her to something else, something much older and sadder.

"Thomas," she said, her voice like a light breeze blowing through dry leaves. It had a strange sound, like an echo that wasn't quite hers. It was as if the house had left a permanent mark on her in its last moments, leaving behind its sadness and silence. He could see the faint, flickering aura around her. It was a small change in the air that showed she was in a different state. He could tell she was still Eleanor, but she was also something else. More than any person could possibly handle.

He wanted to reach out and pull her into his arms to make sure she was still real and still his. But a deep fear kept him from moving. What if his touch hurt her now? What if being around other people was now against the rules of the state she had reached? He remembered how the ghostly beings had shrunk back from her as she got closer to the artifact. They sensed a presence they couldn't understand and a void they couldn't corrupt. She now gave off the same feeling of being foreign and otherworldly, a silent sign of how much she had to pay to win.

"It's over," he said, trying to sound sure, but it sounded empty. "You did it, Eleanor." "You set us free."

She nodded slightly, almost not at all. "The cycle is broken," she said, looking at the dark, still object. "The hunger is satisfied, but not with evil." With peace. It was a strange contradiction. The artifact had caused a lot of pain and suffering, and it was the center of the manor's twisted mind. But when it stopped, when it was quieted, it brought a kind of freedom, a deep stillness that seemed to have seeped into the house's stones and now, it seemed, into Eleanor herself.

Thomas walked toward her slowly and on purpose. He didn't touch her, but he stood close by, which made her feel safe. He remembered the fear, the raw terror that had taken hold of him when the ghostly figures had rushed forward. He had been a shield and a wall, but it had been a desperate fight for survival. He had used what he knew about the manor's structure and how it had been built and changed over the years to get short-term benefits. He had seen how some parts of the building seemed to make the ghosts stop for a moment, and how the heavy, oppressive weight of the house's history sometimes made the ghosts stop. He had even used the building's own decay against it; the crumbling plaster and rotting wood were a temporary distraction for the ghosts that wouldn't stop coming.

But he knew that his bravery didn't come from being a great tactician. It had come from a much deeper, stronger place: his love for Eleanor. Seeing how weak she was and how strong she was in the face of such darkness had sparked a fire in him. He stood between her and the horrors that were coming closer not because he was a warrior, but because he couldn't stand the thought of them touching her or breaking her. He had fought against a supernatural being with all his strength, showing how strong love can be even when it seems like it will end. He didn't have any magical powers; his weapon was his determination, his steady presence, and his refusal to give up.

He looked around the big room. The fancy chandelier, which had swung wildly just a few moments before, was now still, with its crystals not reflecting any light, as if it were dead. The stone faces of the gargoyles on the cornices, which had been twisted in silent screams, now looked like ugly statues with no evil glow. The air, which had once been thick with fear, was now thin and almost sterile. It was the quiet of a grave, but not one of loss. It was the quiet after a battle won and a war over.

He looked back at Eleanor and asked, "What now?" The question hung in the air like a heavy weight. They had made it through, but the world they had known and fought to get back felt far away, like it wasn't real. Eleanor, in her changed state, was the key. She was the link between the terrible things they had been through and the future they had to make.

She turned to him completely, and for a brief moment, he saw a glimmer of the old Eleanor in her eyes, a spark of her familiar warmth. "We leave," she said, and her voice got a little stronger, but it still had that strange, echoing sound. "This place is... still. The story is over. Ours is just starting.

He nodded, feeling relieved, but still worried about how she had changed. He wanted to trust her and believe in the hope of a new start. But the picture of her shimmering body and empty eyes was a harsh reminder of what she had lost. He had been her shield, a human wall against the supernatural tide, and love had given him strength. Eleanor had become something more than a person through her sacrifice, something that was beyond human understanding. She had faced the darkness not with a weapon, but with her very being, and that had changed her forever.

He reached out this time without thinking and took her hand gently. Her skin was cool, almost cold, but it felt very real. The touch shocked him and confirmed that she was still there, even though she had changed. She squeezed his hand to reassure him, and for the first time since the artifact had come to life, he felt a glimmer of hope.

"We'll figure it out," he said in a calm voice. "Together."

Eleanor's lips turned up slightly, like a fragile flower in the empty hall. "Yes, Thomas," she whispered, her deep voice full of old wisdom and new peace. "All together." They stood there for a moment longer, hand in hand, two people on the edge of a new dawn, tied together by their shared suffering and the unspoken promise of a future made in the fires of unimaginable horror. The manor was quiet, and the darkness was gone, but the memory of it and the deep change it had made in Eleanor would always be with them. They had faced the truth, and even though the scars would stay, they had come out of it changed but not broken into the quiet dawn. He would always protect her, and now she was proof of a love that could, quite literally, face down hell itself. His job as her protector had been very real, very basic, and very human. He had kept her from the ethereal claws of despair, not with magic or special powers, but with pure willpower. He had seen the fear in her eyes and how her energy flickered like a candle in a storm. Something deep inside him had roared defiance. He had used his knowledge of the manor's physical structure and the flaws that came with age and neglect to make temporary distractions and change the direction of the ghostly attack. A broken beam here and a crumbling wall there were all small tricks in a desperate war of attrition. But these were just tools that were needed. His love for Eleanor was the real weapon, the unbreakable force that kept him standing when his body begged him to give up. He had seen her bravery and her quiet resolve to face the void, and it had pushed him beyond reason and fear. He was not a sorcerer or a demigod; he was just a man who would not let the woman he loved be taken over by the darkness. His stand was not an attack; it was a strong, unyielding defense. He was the wall that couldn't be broken, the object that couldn't be moved, the living proof that he would never give up. He had felt the cold touch of ghostly hands, heard the chilling whispers that tried to bring out his deepest fears, and felt the weight of centuries of despair on his chest. Every time a ghost attacked, it was a test, a harsh reminder of what was at stake. The cold had seeped into his bones, and the mental attack had almost broken his will, but he had held on. He had tied himself to Eleanor's face, her voice, and the unshakable belief that their survival depended on his ability to keep going. He had turned his own fear into a strong, protective rage instead of panic. He had been the bulwark, the unyielding sentinel, and the human heart beating defiance against a supernatural storm, all for her.

The Artifacts Demise

The artifact shook one last time, like a death rattle that ran through its black surface. Eleanor's will, sharpened to a razor's edge by how badly she needed it at the time, hit it hard. It wasn't a physical blow, but something much stronger: a directed torrent of raw, unadulterated life force, a desperate plea for it to stop from a being who had seen too much, felt too much, and was now ready to give everything to end it. She felt a tearing inside her, not of flesh but of essence, a wrenching disconnection from the very core of who she was. The energy shot out of her in a blinding white light, which was very different from the artifact's usual oppressive darkness. It hit home, not with the force of an explosion, but with the slow, steady power of a geological change.

There were cracks all over the artifact's surface, but they weren't like cracks in stone; they were more like veins of pure light growing inside it. As the light inside got brighter and more persistent, the obsidian seemed to become more fragile, breaking off pieces of itself. At first, the manor's noise drowned out a low hum. Now, it has grown into a piercing shriek, a sound of pure pain, of something old and terrible having to face its own death. It was the sound of a parasite's last breath, the last, desperate fight against the antibodies of its host. The heavy air that had been hanging over the manor like a shroud started to go away, not slowly but with the violent release of a fever breaking. The air, which used to be thick with the sickening smell of death and despair, became thin, sterile, and tasted like ozone and a deep emptiness.

Thomas watched, his breath caught in his throat and his muscles tense, ready for another attack that he knew, with terrifying certainty, would not come. Eleanor swayed, her body a channel for powers that no human body should be able to hold. Her body flickered and shone like a heat haze. The raw power that flowed through her threatened to tear her apart. He could see the very fabric of reality bend and warp around her. The edges of the grand hall seemed to blur, and the old tapestries looked like they were moving as if they were caught in an unseen wind. The whispers, which had been a constant, quiet sound at the edge of his hearing, now turned into one long, drawn-out wail, a cry for a god who had died, a being that was dying. They weren't aimed at him or Eleanor in her current state; they were aimed at the artifact itself, mourning its inevitable destruction.

The artifact shook violently, and the cracks got wider. Instead of molten rock, they let out pure, bright light. It was a light that looked like it could eat up darkness and burn away evil. The whispers stopped, then died, silenced by this overwhelming purity. The manor, which had seemed to be in pain and writhing just moments before, let out one last long sigh. It was the sound of a huge, old being falling apart, of a heart that had been beating for hundreds of years finally stopping. The stones of the house seemed to settle, and the ghostly energy that had given them life faded away like smoke. The evil intelligence that had spread through the whole building and fed on fear and sadness was finally gone.

The artifact didn't explode with a shower of physical debris; instead, it imploded in a silent burst of light. It was like all the energy it had ever held and all the darkness it had ever taken in were let go at once and then completely destroyed. The force of it knocked Thomas back, not with physical violence, but with a wave of pure psychic pressure that washed over him and took away the last bits of fear and despair that were still there. He hit the floor hard, and his ears rang. The afterimage of the bright light made his vision blurry for a short time.

The artifact was gone when his vision cleared. There was nothing there. A perfect, unblemished circle on the floor, as if the thing had never been there. The emptiness it left behind was real, a cold void that seemed to swallow up all sound and feeling. It was the lack of a huge presence, but it was also the lack of something that had, in its own dark way, defined the manor and given it its terrible purpose. The house was no longer alive or hungry. It was just a building, though it was old and grand. Now it was quiet and still.

Eleanor stood where the object had been. Her shimmering shape was no longer flickering violently; instead, it had settled into a steady, ghostly glow. Her eyes, which had looked empty before, now looked like they were holding a distant light, like stars seen through a fog. She was still transformed, still giving off an aura that felt old and strange, but the pain was gone. The raw power had faded, leaving behind a deep silence.

Thomas got up quickly, his body hurting and his mind racing from the psychic effect. He looked at Eleanor, and a mix of relief and awe came over him. She had done it. She had paid the highest price and won. The thing that caused the manor's pain and endless hunger was gone. The heart of the darkness artifact had been broken.

"Eleanor," he said, his voice hoarse with the amazement of being alive. He moved closer to her, his eyes glued to her glowing body. He could feel the artifact's death's residual power washing over him, a wave that took away the fear that was still there. The house itself seemed to let out a deep, resonant silence that spoke of an ending. The heavy weight that had been on his chest for so long was gone, and he felt lighter than he had in years, even though he was so tired that his knees were about to give out.

He reached out, his hand shaking not because he was scared, but because the moment was so important. He wanted to touch her to make sure she was there and to get strength from her survival, but he held back. Her change was still too new and strange. He knew, because they had both been through something terrible, that she was different and would never be the same again. Breaking the artifact and channeling that much raw power had changed her in a way that went beyond just physical effort.

"It's over," he said, and his voice got a little stronger. "The artifact… it's gone."

Eleanor slowly turned her head and found his gaze. Her eyes, which were like pools of distant light, seemed to focus on him, and for a brief moment, he saw a flicker of the Eleanor he knew and loved. A weak smile crossed her lips, a weak echo of who she used to be.

"It is broken," she said, her voice no longer a whisper but a strong, melodic tone that seemed to vibrate in the air. "It is full. Its cycle is over." She pointed vaguely to where the artifact had been. "It didn't want to die. It fought. But your will, Thomas, and my sacrifice were stronger."

He took another step, which brought them closer together. The empty space where the artifact had been was no longer scary; it felt like a wound that had finally begun to heal. He could feel the house's leftover energy, like the last embers of a fire, a fading echo of its former evil power. The manor's very structure seemed to sag, as if taking away the artifact had taken away its spine.

"You saved us, Eleanor," he said, his voice full of feeling. "You saved me."

She nodded again slowly, and her bright form seemed to pulse softly. "We saved each other, Thomas. You were my shield, and I was the blade that cut the root." She looked around the grand hall, her eyes moving over the decorations that were now still and the silent portraits on the walls. "This place… it will never be the same. It has been cleansed. Its purpose has been fulfilled, or rather, not fulfilled. Now it is just wood and stone."

He reached out again, this time with more confidence. He closed the last space between them and gently took her hand. Her skin was cool to the touch, almost too cool, but it was strong and solid. Eleanor was the one. The soft glow around her didn't stop her skin from feeling the faint warmth that came from her. She held on to his hand more tightly, which made him feel better.

"But you are still Eleanor," he said softly, stroking the back of her hand with his thumb. "You are still here."

A sigh came out of her mouth, a sound that seemed to carry the weight of hundreds of years of grief that had finally been let go. "I am. But I am… changed. The echoes remain. The silence is… loud, in its own way." She looked him in the eye, and her eyes had a depth that was both familiar and completely new. "I have seen the heart of the darkness, Thomas. I have felt it pull away. It leaves a space… a hollowness."

He pulled her closer by wrapping his other arm around her waist and pulling her against him. He could still feel the strange resonance of her altered state and the faint hum of power that seemed to come from her, but it wasn't scary anymore. Now it was a part of her. He buried his face in her hair and breathed in the smell he knew so well. It was mixed with something else, something wild and old, like the smell of the earth after a storm.

"We will fill that space," he promised, his voice muffled against her. "Together. No matter what this means or what you've become, we'll face it together."

Eleanor leaned against him and put her head on his shoulder. Her otherworldly glow seemed to fade and mix with the warmth of his own body. The house around them was quiet, and the echoes of its troubled past finally faded away. The artifact was gone, and its evil consciousness was no longer there. The manor had been through its last fight, but it had made it through. And most importantly, they had lived. They had faced the end, and in the middle of that darkness, they found not only destruction but also a deep, scary rebirth. The artifact's death was not just the end of a curse; it was also the start of a change, proof of love and sacrifice's unbreakable will in the face of unimaginable horror. He held her tightly. Eleanor's cool, otherworldly presence was a real anchor in the storm. He had been her shield, a stronghold of human will against the ghostly tide, and in that role, he had found a strength he didn't know he had. But it was Eleanor, in her unfathomable courage, who had struck the final blow. She had faced the source of the manor's darkness, not with anger or fear, but with a profound understanding and a willingness to become something more than human, to become the vessel for the artifact's end. Her sacrifice had been immense, an act that had irrevocably altered her being, leaving her shimmering and luminous, her eyes reflecting a cosmic weariness. As the artifact, the heart of its evil spirit, began to fall apart, he could feel the house groaning around them, its very foundations vibrating with the pain of its dying mind. The obsidian surface, once a fathomless void, had fractured, then splintered, emitting waves of pure, incandescent light that felt like both an end and a beginning. He remembered the horrible scream that had come with the destruction of the artifact. It was a sound that had not only pierced his ears but also his very soul, a cry for a terrible being that had been forced into nothingness. Then, there was an implosion of light, a psychic shockwave that made everything go blank for a moment. When his senses came back, the artifact was gone, and there was an unsettling, perfect void on the floor. The heavy air was gone, the sneaky whispers were gone, and the manor, which had been the evil spirit at its heart, was finally quiet. He looked at Eleanor, whose body was glowing like a beacon in the dark. She was no longer just Eleanor; she was something else, something made in a place of unimaginable power. But in her eyes, he saw a flash of recognition, a silent promise that things would stay the same. He was the rock, the unbreakable force that let her do what she had to do. Now, all he had to do was hold her, help her get through the scary parts of her change, and make sure that the Eleanor he loved was still inside the bright being she had become. Eleanor had to pay a high price to destroy the artifact, and that price was forever etched into her being. It was a sign of her power and a solemn reminder of the cost of saving everyone. The house itself felt different now. It was empty, its evil gone, leaving only the dust and echoes of its past. It was a tomb, maybe, but they had at least gotten out of it. He held her tighter, grounding both of them in the reality of their survival and the uncertain future that lay ahead, lit by the soft, otherworldly glow of the woman who had looked into the abyss and come out, forever changed, into the light. The artifact, which had been the manor's ancient, never-ending source of hunger, was finally quieted. Its power was not just broken; it was completely destroyed. This was not a loss, but a violent cleansing that had ripped through the house's very structure and changed Eleanor, the woman who had dared to use the forces of destruction against its dark heart, forever in its final, painful throes. The obsidian artifact, which had been the center of the manor's sentient evil, was a black hole of corrupted energy that had drained life and sanity from anyone who dared to get close to it. It had a dark, evil life of its own that pulsed and throbbed. Its presence was like a heavy weight that pressed down on Thomas and Eleanor for what felt like an eternity. But Eleanor had become a channel for something much stronger than the artifact's despair in her last, desperate act. She had sent all of her life force, her will to live, and her love for Thomas into a wave of pure, wild energy that had hit the artifact's darkness. The result was terrible. The artifact hadn't just cracked or broken; it had imploded, turning into a void of pure light and a silence that was louder than any scream. The waves of power that came from this destruction weren't destructive in the usual sense; instead, they were a force of erasure and negation. They had washed over Thomas, taking away the last traces of spectral influence. He felt strangely clean, but very shaken. The manor's heavy, cloying air had cleared up like fog in the morning sun. The constant, maddening whispers and insidious voices that had driven him crazy were suddenly gone, leaving behind a deep, almost creepy silence. The house itself seemed to sigh, a deep, resonant breath that showed it was letting go of a heavy load. The artifact had killed its evil, sentient nature, which was the very reason for its wicked existence. It was no longer alive; it was just a shell, a monument to a darkness that had finally been put to rest. So, the artifact's death was not only the end of a curse, but also the end of the manor's evil reign. It had left a void, a space where its dark heart used to beat. Eleanor, now glowing with an otherworldly light, stood in this void as a testament to the power of sacrifice and the strength of the human spirit. She had been changed forever by being so close to death.

Freedom or Echoes

The first light of dawn, shy and unsure, crept through the broken windows of the grand hall, painting the dusty air with streaks of pale gold. The silence that fell over Blackwood Manor was deep, like a real presence that had taken the place of the noise of the artifact's death throes. Eleanor leaned heavily against Thomas, her form still faintly glowing. Her breath was shallow, and her eyes were fixed on some unseen horizon. The raw power that had flowed through her and let her break the obsidian heart of the manor's evil had faded, leaving her with a bone-deep tiredness that felt like a shroud.

Thomas held her close, even though his own body hurt and his mind was a swirling mix of relief and fear. He could feel her body shaking slightly, a small vibration that showed how much stress she had been under. The beautiful and terrifying glow that came from her was a constant reminder of how much she had changed. It was a light that came from sacrifice, a beacon made in the middle of unimaginable darkness. He knew, with a certainty that made him shiver, that the Eleanor who had come into this house was not the same one who was now leaning into his arms. The artifact was gone, and the manor's intelligent hunger was gone too, but the echoes, as Eleanor called them, were still there. They were inside her, a whisper of the power she had had and a shadow of the darkness she had faced.

He gently ran his hand over her back and felt her chest rise and fall. "Are you okay?" he whispered, his voice breaking.

Eleanor didn't answer right away. She just sighed, a sound that seemed to hold the weight of centuries of unspoken sadness. When she finally spoke, her voice was so low that it was hard to hear over the old house's groans. "Thomas, I'm here. That's something, isn't it?

He pulled her closer and said, "It's everything." He could feel the faint, cool aura that still surrounded her. It was a remnant of the power that had confused her. It wasn't scary or unpleasant anymore, but it was definitely different. It was the smell of ozone after a lightning strike, the calm after a hurricane, and the silence that comes after a primal scream.

They stood there for a long time, two survivors in the wreckage of a battle that wasn't fought with guns and steel, but with will and essence. Without its oppressive sentience, the manor felt like an empty shell. The beautiful tapestries, which used to seem to move with unseen life, now hung limp and dead. The eyes of the portraits on the walls, which had once followed them with ghostly judgment, now stared blankly into the dim light. The building itself seemed to sag, as if the artifact had been taken away and its spine had been removed. The once-proud stone walls were ruined by deep, jagged cracks that showed how powerful the forces that had been inside had been. The house, though empty, seemed almost peaceful in its own way. The hunger that had been eating away at him was gone, and the despair that had been weighing him down was gone. It was just a building now, a big, crumbling monument to a darkness that had finally been gotten rid of.

"We should go," Thomas said, his voice strong but with a hint of hesitation that he couldn't quite hide. Leaving Eleanor, even though she had changed, felt like leaving a part of himself behind. But there was no point in staying here in this mausoleum of a house. The object was gone. There was no sound in the manor. The only things left for them here were the cold and the weight of their shared trauma.

Eleanor nodded, her head still on his shoulder. "Yes," she said softly. "It is time to go."

Eleanor stopped as they were about to leave and reached out to touch a scar on the wall, a jagged line where a ghostly force had once hit. "It's quiet now," she said softly. "But it's not… empty. It's still cold.

Thomas looked where she was looking. She was correct. There was a coldness that was hard to see and felt everywhere, even though there was no more active evil. It wasn't the cold of winter that made you shiver; it was a deeper, more profound chill that seemed to go all the way to your bones. It was the manor's hunger that still echoed, a ghost of what it used to be, a reminder that even in defeat, the darkness had left its mark. It was a memory of what had happened, written into the very walls of the house.

"It's a scar, Eleanor," Thomas said softly. "A scar from what it went through." And what we went through here. He held her hand tightly. "Will we all have scars?"

She looked him in the eye, and her eyes, which were like pools of far-off light, seemed to show that they both understood how deep and awful their journey had been. "Yes," she said softly. "We will." "But maybe," she said, a faint smile on her lips, a weak echo of who she used to be, "the scars can remind us of what we've been through." "Not just of the darkness, but of the light we found in it."

As they walked through the decaying beauty of Blackwood Manor, each step was a conscious act of leaving. The big doors, which had once seemed to keep a hungry thing inside, were now open, inviting them to return to the world. The air outside smelled like wet dirt and rotting leaves, but it felt cleaner and fresher, full of the promise of a new day. The sun was now fully up and cast a warm, life-affirming light on the overgrown grounds.

Thomas looked back at the manor as they walked away. It stood out against the dawn sky, its once-impressive facade now looking old and worn. The evil was gone, and the consciousness was gone too. It was a shell, a tomb with a hole in it. But he couldn't shake the feeling of unease that stayed with him. Did they really win against the manor? Or did they just quiet it down, put it to sleep, and let its hunger lie dormant until the next cycle, when it could wake up again? The cold that came from its quiet walls made it seem like the answer wasn't as simple as they had hoped. The house had been a ship, and the artifact was its heart. The vessel was dead without the heart, but the darkness of the place and the potential for evil were still there. It had been kept under control for now, but the question of whether it would come back was in the air, as strong as the smell of wet earth.

Eleanor, who was walking next to him, seemed to know what he was thinking. She held his hand tightly, which brought him back to the present. "It's over, Thomas," she said, her voice full of new strength and a quiet conviction that seemed to come from deep within her. "The cycle is over. The hunger has gone away, or maybe it just went away with the artifact.

"I hope you're right," he said softly, but part of him couldn't help but think that Blackwood Manor's silence wasn't an end, but a pause. Take a long, deep breath before the next act. He really looked at Eleanor. The soft halo around her was still there, but it wasn't as strong as it used to be. It was as if she had taken in some of the light that had broken the artifact and made it a part of her, a soft, inner glow. Her eyes had a depth that was both familiar and strange, and they showed that she was tired from seeing and going through too much. She was forever changed, shaped anew by the fire of their ordeal.

He couldn't help but think about what the future would bring for them. Could they ever really go back to the way things were before this nightmare? Eleanor was no longer just the woman he loved. She was more than that; she had danced with the dark and come out on the other side, scarred but not broken. He was no longer just Thomas, the man who had been there for her. He was the man who had seen the impossible: he had held a woman on the edge of death and helped her step back from the edge, forever changed.

Thomas turned to Eleanor as they got to the end of the overgrown drive and Blackwood Manor's imposing shape faded behind them. The sun was rising higher and higher, warming his skin and getting rid of the cold that seemed to come from the house. He saw a flicker of something in her eyes, a hint of the Eleanor he knew, the woman who had loved him and laughed with him. It was still there, under all the changes and the tiredness of the universe.

"We'll figure it out," he said, his voice calm and sure. "Whatever this means, whatever you've become, we'll deal with it together."

Eleanor smiled, and this time it was a real smile, like a flower opening up after the storm. "Together," she said again, gripping his hand tighter. "We will."

They kept walking, leaving the quiet manor behind. The shadows grew longer and then shorter as the sun rose. The air was cleaner, the sky was big and blue, and Thomas felt a glimmer of real hope for the first time in what felt like forever. They had made it through the reckoning. They had looked into the void. And in the middle of that darkness, they found not only death, but also a deep, scary rebirth. The artifact's death was not just the end of a curse; it was the start of a change, proof of love and sacrifice's unbreakable will in the face of unimaginable horror. They were no longer under the manor's control, but the memories of what they had been through would always be with them, reminding them of the darkness they had faced and the light they had found. A quiet, persistent voice in the back of their minds asked if Blackwood Manor had really been defeated or was just waiting. But for now, they were happy to have each other. That was more than enough. It was their choice.

Appendix

The Obsidian Heart of Blackwood was an ancient object that held evil energy. We don't know where it came from, but it had a big effect on Blackwood Manor, making it feel like it had a hungry, predatory mind. This hunger showed itself as heavy atmospheres, ghostly figures, and mental pain, which all led to a direct attack on the wills of those who lived there. It took a lot of mental and physical energy to destroy the artifact, which is why Eleanor changed so much. The "echoes" are energies that have not been completely cleared away and are now a part of Eleanor's being.

Glossary

Obsidian Heart: The central artifact of malevolence within Blackwood Manor, a source of its sentience and hunger.

Echoes: Residual psychic energy or lingering spiritual imprints left by the artifact's presence and subsequent destruction.

Sentience: The capacity to feel, perceive, or be conscious; in the context of Blackwood Manor, a malevolent awareness.

Malevolence: The quality of being evil or wishing harm.

Crucible: A situation or place in which different elements interact, leading to profound change or the creation of something new.

About the Author

Justin Pettyjohn writes dark fiction that often explores the dark corners of the human mind and the unsettling things that could happen just outside of what we think is real. The constant thread that runs through their stories is his interest in how light and dark, love and loss, and the strength of the human spirit can survive even the worst horrors. When Justin isn't having nightmares, he thinks about how quiet old houses are and the stories he could tell if the houses and stories could talk.

You can connect with me on:

- https://www.instagram.com/official.justinpettyjohn/?hl=en
- https://author-justin-pettyjohn.com

Subscribe to my newsletter:

- https://author-justin-pettyjohn.com

Also by Justin Pettyjohn

Justin Pettyjohn's work blends **dark psychological horror** with **high-stakes supernatural thriller** storytelling. In *Monster John,* he mines trauma, fractured identity, and small-town fear to build a relentless, grounded terror that lingers beyond the final scene. In *The Fallen Immortal: Dracula's Greatest Enemy,* he expands into epic gothic fantasy—mixing vengeance, cursed immortality, and forbidden love—while keeping the same core focus on **inner demons, moral choice, and the cost of survival**.

Monster John

In the quiet town of Oakhaven, a string of brutal murders sparks a chilling legend: **Monster John**. By day, John is invisible—just a reserved mill worker. By night, he becomes the thing his childhood trauma created: a methodical predator hunting young couples and leaving savagery in his wake. When a pair escapes and the police close in, the chase ends at a fog-choked ravine with John plunging into the abyss. But the body is never found. No blood. No proof. Only the terrible possibility that the monster didn't die—he simply disappeared… and he's still out there, waiting.

The Fallen Immortal: Dracula's Greatest Enemy
Betrayed and exiled, Theron Bloodbane—the former general of Dracula's immortal legion—becomes the hunted, branded by a cursed sigil that draws unholy predators to his trail. When he uncovers Dracula's true endgame—the extinction of mankind—Theron finds a fragile refuge in a village untouched by shadow…and in Lauren, a mortal woman whose light rekindles what he thought was dead. With doom closing in and love rising where it shouldn't, Theron must choose: return to the monster he was, or become the weapon fated to end Dracula's eternal night.

www.ingramcontent.com/pod-product-compliance
Lightning Source LLC
Chambersburg PA
CBHW070621310726
48982CB00001B/144

* 9 7 9 8 9 9 4 6 8 3 2 0 0 *